"So, what's your foreman's story?"
Steve asked his aunt.

She shot him an arch look. "What do you want to know?"

"Just the basics. Where she's from. How you found her. Why *she's* raising Daniel, instead of his parents."

"Why don't you ask Kelly if you're so interested in her?"

"I'm not—"

"Well, it sounds like you are to me. I wouldn't blame you, either. Kelly's a real pretty woman and a smart one, too."

Steve scowled at his aunt. "Tell me I don't smell the scent of matchmaking. In case you didn't notice, your Miss Kelly can't stand me."

Peg waved one hand as if Kelly's opinion of him wasn't important. "She just doesn't know you yet, hon. If you want to find out about her background, you'll have to convince her to tell you herself."

"I tried that all the way from Missoula," Steve said. "I couldn't get zip out of her."

"Well, then, you'll have to earn her trust, won't you?"

Dear Reader,

Happy New Year! I hope this year brings you all your heart desires...and I hope you enjoy the many books coming your way this year from Silhouette Special Edition!

January features an extraspecial THAT SPECIAL WOMAN!—Myrna Temte's *A Lawman for Kelly*. Deputy U.S. Marshal Steve Anderson is back (remember him in Myrna's *Room for Annie?*), and he's looking for love in Montana. Don't miss this warm, wonderful story!

Then travel to England this month with *Mistaken Bride,* by Brittany Young—a compelling Gothic story featuring two identical twins with very different personalities.... Or stay at home with *Live-In Mom* by Laurie Paige, a tender story about a little matchmaker determined to bring his stubborn dad to the altar with the right woman! And don't miss *Mr. Fix-It* by Jo Ann Algermissen. A man who is good around the house is great to find anytime during the year!

This month also brings you *The Lone Ranger,* the initial story in Sharon De Vita's winsome new series, SILVER CREEK COUNTY. Falling in love is all in a day's work in this charming Texas town. And watch for the first book by a wonderful writer who is new to Silhouette Special Edition—Neesa Hart. Her book, *Almost to the Altar,* is sure to win many new fans.

I hope this New Year shapes up to be the best year ever! Enjoy this book, and all the books to come!

Sincerely

Tara Gavin
Senior Editor

Please address questions and book requests to:
Silhouette Reader Service
U.S.: 3010 Walden Ave., P.O. Box 1325, Buffalo, NY 14269
Canadian: P.O. Box 609, Fort Erie, Ont. L2A 5X3

MYRNA TEMTE
A LAWMAN FOR KELLY

Published by Silhouette Books
America's Publisher of Contemporary Romance

This book is dedicated to Kathie Hayes, Terry Kanago
and Mary Pat Kanaley. Thanks for picking me up and
dusting me off every time I stumbled.
You're all absolutely fabulous.
My thanks for help with research go to
Dr. Chris Schneider at the Fairwood Animal Hospital,
Spokane, Washington, and to Bill Licatovich,
U.S. Marshals Service, Washington, D.C.

 SILHOUETTE BOOKS

ISBN 0-373-24075-9

A LAWMAN FOR KELLY

Copyright © 1997 by Myrna Temte

Printed in U.S.A.

Books by Myrna Temte

Silhouette Special Edition

Wendy Wyoming #483
Powder River Reunion #572
The Last Good Man Alive #643
*For Pete's Sake #739
*Silent Sam's Salvation #745
*Heartbreak Hank #751
The Forever Night #816
Room for Annie #861
A Lawman for Kelly #1075

Silhouette Books

Montana Mavericks
Sleeping with the Enemy

*Cowboy Country Series

MYRNA TEMTE

grew up in Montana and attended college in Wyoming, where she met and married her husband. Marriage didn't necessarily mean settling down for the Temtes—they have lived in six different states, including Washington, where they currently reside. Moving so much is difficult, the author says, but it is also wonderful stimulation for a writer.

Though always a "readaholic," Ms. Temte never dreamed of becoming an author. But while spending time at home to care for her first child, she began to seek an escape from the never-ending duties of housekeeping and child-rearing. She started reading romances and soon became hooked, both as a reader and a writer.

Now Myrna Temte appreciates the best of all possible worlds—a loving family and a challenging career that lets her set her own hours and turn her imagination loose.

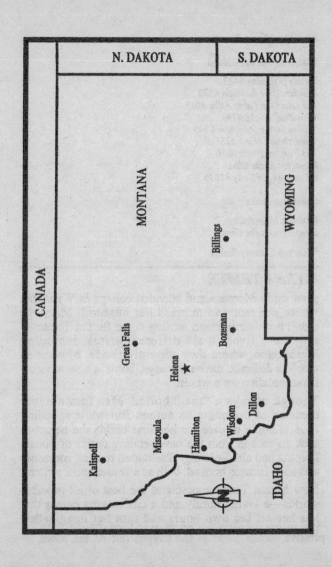

Prologue

"In my office, Anderson. *Now.*"

Deputy U.S. Marshal Steve Anderson returned Noah Solomon's fierce scowl with a defiant one of his own. Ignoring the surreptitious glances of his fellow deputies, he brushed past his boss and entered the room, bracing himself for the crash of the door slamming behind him. It didn't slam.

Uh-oh. Standing at six foot eight, the warrant supervisor dwarfed everyone else in the Chicago office. There wasn't a deputy on the staff who wouldn't rather face a bellowing Noah than one who was too furious to bellow. Well, tough. Noah could be as angry as he damn well pleased, but even if Steve could go back and live the afternoon over, he wouldn't change his actions.

Shoving his hands into his jacket pockets, he sat in the battered, brown vinyl chair across from Noah's desk, crossed one leg over the other and slouched down as if he didn't give a damn what his boss might say. Noah parked himself on the edge of his massive, gunmetal gray desk and let a dark, oppressive silence suck all the oxygen out of the room. Steve opened his mouth to tell him what he could do with his lecture, but the warrant supervisor shut him down with a look.

"What the hell did you think you were doing out there, cowboy?" Noah asked, his voice deceptively calm. "Trying to commit suicide?"

"Aw, Noah, it wasn't that bad."

Noah leaned forward, looming over Steve like a wrathful god. "I was *there* this time, Anderson, so save that load of bull for somebody who'll believe it."

"Oh, yeah?" Steve shot back. "Well, I suppose I could've let that murdering son of a bitch get away so he could kill some more people, but—"

"You should have waited for backup, and you know it."

Lunging to his feet, Steve jabbed his index finger at Noah's chest. "No, I *don't* know it. And you don't, either."

Noah looked at Steve's shaking finger, then studied his face with a thoughtful expression that made Steve feel as exposed as if he'd dropped his pants in the middle of Wrigley Field. Shoving his hands back into his pockets, he turned away, paced over to the window and propped one shoulder against the casing.

He gazed down at the traffic as if the roofs of the cabs, trucks and minivans held the answers to life's most important questions. For all he knew, they probably did.

Damn. His strongest asset had always been his ability to maintain absolute control over his emotions and physical reactions, no matter how bad a situation got. At the moment, however, his throat and chest felt tight and his hands trembled so much when he took them out of his pockets, he doubted he could hold a cup of coffee without slopping it all over himself.

Finally, Noah sighed, then walked around the desk to his swivel chair. "You want a vacation or disability leave?"

Steve shot a quelling glance over his shoulder. "Neither. I'm fine."

"Right. We'll start with all that vacation time you haven't used before you start losing it. I'll put you down for a month, and you can decide if you want to take the other one you've got coming later."

"Dammit, Noah, I said I don't *want* any time off."

"And I don't *care* what you want, cowboy. It's my job to make sure everybody's nice and safe, and you're screwing that up. You haven't had your mind where it's supposed to be since Anne Miller remarried her ex."

"Baloney."

"Hah! Look, Steve, it's not that I don't sympathize. Anne's a dynamite lady, Chad's a great kid and you were with them a long time. But it's been almost two years. Anne and John have a new baby now, and it's time you found something to live for besides tracking down fugitives. Get on with your own life, man."

"It's none of your business."

"When you pull stunts like you did today, I have to make it my business. Everybody's getting twitchy about working with you. I'd hate it if you got yourself killed, Anderson, but I'd really be upset if I let you get somebody else killed. You're officially off duty for the next thirty days."

"I'll go nuts if I can't work," Steve protested. "C'mon, Noah, give me a break."

Noah shook his head. "No can do. Go home to Montana. Get drunk, raise hell and howl at the moon with the coyotes or whatever you hicks do out there for fun. I don't want to see your face again until you get over losing that woman. You read me?"

"Yeah, I read you." Steve straightened away from the window casing and turned to face the other man. "But it won't work."

"How do you know it won't?"

Uttering a laugh that sounded bleak even to his own ears, Steve met Noah's worried gaze head-on. "Hell, boss, thirty days won't even touch it. I'd be lucky to get over losing Anne and Chad in thirty years."

Chapter One

"Look, Billy, there's Daddy's airplane!"

Kelly Jaynes looked up from the newspaper she'd found on an empty seat in the passenger lounge, smiling with sympathy for the young mother who'd been wrangling a fussy toddler since the ticket agent had announced a delay for the flight from Billings. She remembered when her nine-year-old nephew, Daniel, had been Billy's age. He'd been nothing but grabby little hands and churning little legs, insatiable curiosity and ferocious energy.

Trying to keep track of that kid had been like trying to control the calves when you were moving cattle—as soon as you got one of them following the herd, three more took off in different directions.

A silver plane swooped out of the low-slung clouds that usually clung to the mountains surrounding Missoula. Kelly's gut clenched and sweat broke out on her palms. She rose with a practiced casualness as phony as one of Dolly Parton's hairdos, stuck her hands into her jeans pockets and ambled back to the gate entrance.

Propping one hip against the railing, she crossed her arms over her chest and settled in to wait for the arrival of the Nephew. Bud Ryan, her sneaky old boss who was about as subtle as a truck when it came to matchmaking, might have manipulated her into picking up his sister's ''boy'' at the airport, but she'd be dam—no, *danged*—if she'd act like she was happy about it. The Nephew was a cop, for God's sake. Well, according to Bud, Steve Anderson was really a deputy U.S. marshal, which, in her book, was even worse than being a cop. Her one experience with those guys had left a real nasty taste in her mouth that hadn't faded in eight years. If he knew about her family, he wouldn't like her much. Not that she gave a rabbit's bu—no, *behind*—what he thought of her.

If he was as nosey and suspicious as every other cop she'd ever met, she wouldn't much care for *him*, either. It was stupid to feel so threatened by his visit to the Haystack Ranch. After all, *she* hadn't done anything wrong. Neither had Daniel. But old habits died hard, and she suspected she would never feel at ease around a cop, no matter what kind of a badge he carried.

The trickle of disembarking passengers grew into a stream and then a river. It shouldn't be hard to spot Anderson, though. For one thing, Montana airports weren't all that big. For another, Bud's wife, Peggy, had at least a thousand photographs of ''Stevie-boy,'' from the naked-baby-in-the-bathtub variety, right up to, through and beyond his college graduation. The memory of one particularly unflattering photo brought a wicked smile to Kelly's lips.

Peg wasn't a whole lot more subtle than Bud. To hear her rave about the Nephew, a person would think he was one gorgeous hunk of man. In Kelly's humble opinion, however, he wasn't anything to get in a sweat over. To put it kindly, the poor guy just wasn't what you'd call photogenic. He'd probably want to strangle his sweet old aunt if he knew she'd been showing those god-awful pictures to the hired help.

Well, my, my, my, Kelly thought, raising an eyebrow in surprise when the Nephew finally stepped off the jetway. Pictures really didn't do the man justice. In fact, he was at least half as handsome in person as Peg had claimed he'd be.

Tall and broad-shouldered, he had thick blond hair and even features set in a pleasantly rugged face. His slacks, sweater and loafers made him stand out from all the other guys in their jeans, boots and Stetsons. He carried himself with an air of confidence that drew female attention without any obvious effort on his part.

Not too shabby, if you were interested in a man's looks. Which, of course, Kelly was not. She'd tried to tell Bud and Peg that at least fifty times, with zero success.

Hel—no, *heck*—aw, nuts, giving up cussing was gonna drive her batty one of these days. She could hardly even think straight without cussing, much less talk. Now, where the he—ck was she?

Smiling to herself at that small, but significant victory, she shifted her weight to her other leg. Oh, yeah. Men. Well, on top of having Daniel to raise, she always had too much work to do to waste time thinking about 'em. With her luck, not to mention her substandard genetic makeup, she'd probably fall for some jerk who was as useless as her dad, or worse yet, one who was as mean and rotten as her brother, Johnny.

She stuck her hands back into her pockets and cleared her throat as the Nephew approached. "Excuse me. Mr. Anderson?"

He paused, gazing down at her from his superior height, his gray eyes suddenly focused on her with unnerving intensity.

"You *are* Steve Anderson, aren't you?" Kelly said when it became obvious that he didn't intend to speak until . . . well, he—ck, maybe the Second Coming.

"Who are you?" he asked.

"Kelly Jaynes. Foreman at the Haystack Ranch. Bud asked me to pick you up."

Any polite human being would have at least smiled at that point. Stevie-boy didn't. But then, outside of Andy Johnson back in Pinedale, since when had cops ever bothered to be polite to somebody like her? As far as she was concerned, Sheriff Johnson was just the odd one who was the exception to the rule.

Anderson's eyes narrowed. "He didn't say anything about it to me."

Kelly resisted the urge to roll her eyes in exasperation at his automatic suspicion, but just barely. Honestly, did he think she was trying to kidnap him? Hah! She was five foot eight and strong for a woman, but he topped her by at least six inches, outweighed her by sixty pounds and looked as if he was no stranger to a weight bench. Probably had all kinds of martial arts training, too. Well, she'd be da—nged if she'd let him push her around or think he could grill her whenever he wanted.

"Mister," she drawled, looking him square in the eye, "I came here as a favor to your uncle, but I don't have all day. I've already waited over three hours for you to get here, and I'm gettin' a might short on patience. Now, you can either put a move on it and ride out to the ranch with me, or find your own transport."

Turning on the heel of one battered boot, Kelly walked away. Hearing the Nephew mutter under his breath and then hurry after her was almost enough to make her snicker. Almost, but not quite. She owed Bud and Peg so much, she really shouldn't offend their beloved Stevie-boy. But, dang it, she still had a ton of stuff to do today and he was acting like a darn jerk.

It only took a couple of seconds for him to catch up with her. She declined to acknowledge him with so much as a glance, but she couldn't avoid feeling intensely aware of his aggravating presence pacing beside her.

"Look, Ms. Uh... What did you say your name was?" he asked, his voice laced with irritation.

"Jaynes. And it's *Miss* not *Miz.*"

"Fine. *Miss* Jaynes, would you mind telling me why my uncle didn't meet me himself?"

Kelly walked faster, forcing him to hustle to keep up with her, even with his longer stride. "Bud lost his glasses. Extra pair was so old, one of the bows fell off when he put 'em on. Wouldn't pay to go to a one-hour place, and his new pair won't be in until next week."

"What about my aunt?"

"Peg's got her hands full ridin' herd on Bud and cookin' your favorite supper. Been in a twitter ever since you called and said you were comin'."

The Nephew chuckled, a low, rich sound that drew Kelly's gaze to his face. The laugh lines around his gray eyes crinkled, and the expression in his eyes warmed with affection. "Yeah, she always does that."

He gave Kelly an amazingly boyish grin for a man who must be pushing forty. Damn, I hope he doesn't do that very often, she thought, feeling an irrational urge to like the guy.

His grin turned into a friendly smile. His gaze roamed over her face with a new interest, as if he'd just realized there was a woman underneath her jeans, boots and work shirt. His voice took on a softer tone. "If the offer of a ride's still open, I accept."

Ignoring the charm of that smile, Kelly shrugged. "Suit yourself."

"Can you spare a minute for me to grab my bags?"

"I'll get the pickup and meet you out front."

Kelly's spine prickled with the sensation of being watched while she crossed the baggage claim area, but she refused to turn her head and see if Anderson was doing the watching. She just couldn't risk the chance, however slight, that he might interpret that as a sign she was interested in him. Well, she wasn't interested, no way, no how.

She'd admit he was more attractive than she'd expected. She'd even admit that, since she might be a tad prejudiced about cops in general and U.S. marshals in particular, he might not be a complete jerk. After all, Bud and Peggy looked on him as if he were a son instead of a nephew, and she trusted their judgment more than she'd ever trusted anyone else's, bar none.

But for her own sake and Daniel's, she had to keep her distance from this guy. If he found out about Jay and Johnny, he might expose them to the community. He might even convince Bud to get a new foreman, and she needed this job.

Ranching was her only marketable skill. There weren't all that many ranchers around who could afford to hire help anymore; fewer still who would hire a woman, much less a woman with shady relatives and a boy to raise. Bud paid her a fair wage, didn't hit on her and both he and Peg doted on Daniel like adoring grandparents. Other than having her own spread again, Kelly couldn't have dreamed up a better situation.

She wasn't about to put it at risk for a man, not even one who could leap tall buildings and all that other good stuff. One way or another, most men were nothing but trouble. Steve Anderson was no exception. Oh, he wouldn't bring her the kind of grief her dad and brother always had, but he was trouble all the same. With a capital *T.* She could feel it in her bones.

Catching sight of the Haystack Ranch sign arching over the lane leading to his uncle's house, Steve Anderson exhaled a quiet sigh of relief. He'd made the trip from Missoula down to the Big Hole more times than he could count, but never with such a grumpy, taciturn companion as *Miss* Jaynes. He'd love to know what he'd done to put such a twist in her tail, but at the moment, he was too eager to see Uncle Bud and Aunt Peg to worry about it much.

Damn, but it was good to be back. The Big Hole Valley still looked as if time slowed down when you crossed Chief Joseph Pass on the road to Wisdom. Forget about fancy technology. The ranchers here still used the old log beaverslides to make haystacks that looked like giant loaves of bread.

Forget about freeways and cities. This high, flat, wide valley, sheltered by mountains on all sides, was prime hay and cattle country. Other than summer tourists and avid fishermen, it was too isolated and shy on urban amenities to attract the swarms of newcomers who'd been pouring into other parts of the state for the past couple of years. Thank God.

Noah had been right to make him take a vacation, Steve thought, feeling the tension and burdens of his job sliding away with each familiar curve in the gravel road. The snow-capped mountains, the broad vistas, the narrow, empty highways, the clean air and that bright blue sky had always replenished him. It had been too long since he'd reconnected with the part of himself that never left Montana, wherever his job happened to take him.

A lump formed in his throat when the white, two-story ranch house came into view. The old house could use a fresh coat of paint, and the porch railing needed some work. Well, Uncle Bud wasn't getting any younger. What was he now? Sixty-eight or sixty-nine? A wisp of smoke rose from the stovepipe, and Steve's mouth watered at the thought that Aunt Peg had probably fired up the old black range to bake him an apple pie.

A yellow-and-white checked curtain fluttered at the kitchen window when the truck rumbled into the yard. The back door banged open and his aunt and uncle rushed down the steps, smiling wide enough to show the fillings in their back teeth, their arms open to greet him with hugs that would put a full-grown grizzly to shame. Opening the passenger door the instant they stopped rolling, Steve jumped to the ground.

Before the dust had settled, he grabbed Aunt Peg by her ample waist and whirled her around while she fiercely hugged his neck, both of them laughing their fool heads off. When it was Uncle Bud's turn, he alternately hugged Steve and pounded him on the back with his big, gnarled hands, making him feel what he'd always felt whenever he'd come to the ranch.

Welcomed.

Absolutely and completely welcomed. Enjoyed and admired for whoever he was at the moment. Loved and accepted without question or condition, simply because he existed. That he'd finally come home.

"Hey, Aunt Kelly! Guess what happened at school today."

Surprised at the sound of another voice, Steve glanced toward the barn, then froze. A dark-haired boy around nine or ten years old charged across the yard, his face flushed with excitement. For a moment he looked so much like Chad, Steve had to blink and look again to convince himself otherwise. Pain slashed into him, sharp and swift and deep as the hole losing Chad and his mother had left in his life.

Unable to look at the boy any longer, Steve turned his gaze to *Miss* Jaynes. Well, now, would wonders never cease? The woman knew how to smile. It wasn't just a polite smile, either, but a real one. He could hardly believe how much it changed her face. He'd thought she was attractive before, but that smile made her ... beautiful? Gorgeous? Stunning?

Well, not exactly. At least not physically, like an actress or a model. It was more of an attitude thing, as if the love she obviously felt for the boy racing to tell her about his day had softened her hard edges and given her a warm, maternal glow from inside. The same glow he'd always seen on Anne's face whenever she looked at Chad.

Damn it all, Steve thought, closing his eyes when the pain hit him again. It hadn't hurt this bad since the last time he'd seen Anne at the Bozeman hospital after her surgery to remove the bullet Manny Costenzo had pumped into her. She'd been so eager to see her ex-husband John, the nurses had been practically forced to tie her to the bed.

Walking away from her and Chad had been the hardest thing he'd ever done. Not that he'd had another choice. His relationship with Anne had always been platonic, and he'd always known she would go back to John if she ever had the chance. But that was over and done with, dammit, and Noah was right. It was time to let go of the dream and get on with his life.

Oh, yeah? a mocking voice inside his head demanded. *What life, Anderson? Guys your age are supposed to have a wife and kids, and you don't even have a cat. That's what you really want, isn't it? A wife and kid to replace the ones you lost when Anne and Chad went home?*

He glanced back at *Miss* Jaynes, and almost laughed out loud when he felt a faint stirring in his groin. Man, he must have banged his head one too many times. Since going to work for the U.S. Marshals Service, he'd dealt with more than enough surly characters to last him a lifetime. He sure as hell didn't want to marry one.

If—and in his mind, it was still a mighty big if—he should decide he was ready to give up law enforcement and get married, Kelly Jaynes would be the last woman he'd ever pick.

He wanted a woman who was soft and feminine. One who smelled like perfume instead of a sweaty horse. One who at least *liked* him a little bit. Which, Miss Kelly had made absolutely clear, she did not.

And that was pretty darn strange, now that he thought about it. He wasn't movie-star handsome, but he wasn't ugly, either, and he always treated women with respect. In fact, he could honestly say, without undue conceit, that most women liked him right off the bat. So why didn't Kelly Jaynes?

Uncle Bud motioned to the boy with his left hand. "Hey Daniel, c'mon over here and meet my nephew."

Daniel obediently ran to Bud's side, then turned to face Steve. Up close, the kid's resemblance to Chad evaporated. For one thing, he was bigger. His face was longer, and his hair had some curl in it, while Chad's was completely straight. His eyes were a dark brown instead of Chad's green.

But there was a deep, painful yearning in Daniel's expression that told Steve this boy didn't have a dad. He'd seen the same look in Chad's eyes before he'd met John Miller. Steve had seen it in his own eyes, too, after his dad had been killed in the line of duty. A boy needed a father to help him grow up. If his own father wasn't around, he'd look to a man around his dad's age to get the advice and approval he craved.

Bud had filled some of that need for Steve, and Steve had done his best to fill it for Chad. From the wary but blatantly wistful way Daniel was studying him, Steve guessed that, given the least bit of encouragement, the kid would latch onto him like a tick on a dog. Steve wouldn't mind spending some time with Daniel, but he had a feeling Kelly wouldn't like it.

He glanced at her after Bud had made the introductions. Yup. There was enough disapproval written on her face to make a guy think she'd swallowed a slug. But, what the hell? There was fear in her eyes, too. She was watching him as if she half expected him to attack Daniel with fangs or hit him.

The instant he made eye contact with her, Kelly looked away. He saw her chest and shoulders rise as if she'd inhaled a deep breath. Then she gazed back at him again, her eyes so cool and direct, he wondered if he'd simply imagined her fear.

No way, Steve thought. His instincts had saved his hide more times than he could count, and he wasn't about to start ignoring them now. Kelly Jaynes was afraid of him, all right. The question was, why?

Before he could come up with a plausible reason, Aunt Peg said something to Kelly. Steve didn't catch it all, but it had an interesting effect on Kelly and Daniel. A toothy grin spread across Daniel's face and he nodded enthusiastically. Kelly shook her head and held both hands in front of her as if warding off an unwanted gift.

"Don't you give me that old song and dance, Kelly," Aunt Peg scolded good-naturedly.

"It's not a song and dance, Peg," Kelly replied. "This is a family occasion. I'm sure Mr. Anderson would rather have you folks all to himself for a while. Daniel and I'll get by on our own just fine."

Daniel's eyes widened into a horrified expression. "You mean *you're* gonna cook?"

Kelly shot him a dirty look. "You got a problem with that?"

"Yeah, I'll starve to death," Daniel retorted.

"My cookin's not *that* bad."

Daniel stuck his finger into his mouth and made gagging noises. "Burnt potatoes. Lumpy gravy. Charcoal meat." He shuddered, then rolled his eyes toward heaven. "Aunt Kelly, your cookin' even smells so gross, it'd drive off a skunk."

Kelly's eyebrows swooped together in a scowling V, but a hint of a smile lurked at the corners of her mouth. "You can always cook for yourself, D.J."

Daniel shook his head hard enough to rattle his brain. "No way! I'm even worse than you are. And I want some of that pie Mrs. Ryan made."

"You'll get some, honey," Aunt Peg said, quelling further objections with a voice Steve recognized from personal experience. "You're both a part of our family now, and you're having supper with us tonight, and every other night. Seven o'clock. As usual."

Aunt Peg turned and swept into the house with the arrogance of a born despot. Kelly looked as if she wanted to tell Aunt Peg a thing or five, but, much to Steve's amusement, she settled for a disgruntled sigh. Not that he blamed her.

Except for Bud, nobody with a lick of sense argued when Peggy Ryan trotted out that voice. She rarely used it, of course.

Ninety-nine percent of the time, Aunt Peg was sweet and gentle as an old mare who'd spent her life giving rides to little kids. Steve figured she got instant obedience when she used that voice because it was always a shock to hear such a repressive tone coming out of her mouth.

Man, it was good to be home.

"Well, c'mon, son, let's haul your stuff inside," Uncle Bud said. "Then we'll have a shot or two of hootch before Peg calls us to the table."

"Sounds great." Steve turned toward the pickup and practically did a double take when he saw Kelly lift his bag out of the back with one hand and set it on the ground as if it was filled with feathers. She must have excellent upper-body strength for a woman, because that was one heavy suitcase. He'd crammed in so many books before he'd left Chicago, the burly cabbie who'd driven him to the airport had asked if he was a brick salesman.

She gave him a brief, impersonal smile when he thanked her for the ride, then told Daniel it was time to leave.

"I wanna go with Mr. Ryan and Mr. Anderson," Daniel protested. "I've got my chores all done."

"What about your homework?" Kelly asked.

"I don't have much."

"You know the rule, Daniel."

"Aw, come on," Daniel griped, with just enough whine in his voice to set almost any adult's back teeth on edge.

Without speaking, Kelly pointed a finger to the east of the barn, toward the old trailer Steve used to stay in when he'd worked at the Haystack during his college vacations. Daniel glared at her for a long moment, then slowly turned back to Steve with his shoulders slumped, his head drooping and a sad, long-suffering expression on his face.

"Well, I guess I'll see you at supper, Mr. Anderson," he said, dejection dripping from every word.

Steve smiled, silently congratulating the kid on one of the best martyred-child acts he'd ever had the privilege to witness. "I'll be here at least a month, Daniel. Maybe longer. You might as well call me Steve."

Daniel shook his head. "Oh, no, sir. I'm not allowed to call grown-ups by their first names. It ain't polite."

"It's *not* polite," Kelly said, her voice quiet but firm.

Daniel ignored her.

"Okay," Steve said. "Are you allowed to go fishing?"

Standing directly behind Daniel, Kelly couldn't see the boy's eyes brighten with excitement, but Steve sure could. He almost laughed out loud when Daniel answered, his voice retaining that poor-little-me note to perfection. "Sometimes. If my chores and homework are done."

"Maybe we can go together sometime."

"That'd be real nice, Mr. Anderson." Scuffing his feet, Daniel slowly took his leave. "I hope we can do that."

Steve grinned. This kid was *good*. Not that it appeared to help him much. With the unblinking stare of a raptor, Kelly calmly and silently regarded Daniel until he gave up dragging his feet and trotted off in the direction indicated by her pointing finger. Watching these two over the next month ought to be fun.

Turning back to face her, Steve found himself on the receiving end of her eagle-eyed gaze, and completely forgot whatever he'd been about to say. She didn't look scared of him now. She looked like she'd enjoy taking a swing at his nose. Maybe two swings.

"Is something wrong?" he asked.

"I'd appreciate it if you wouldn't encourage Daniel to hang around you, Mr. Anderson."

"I like kids, Miss Jaynes. He won't bother me."

"I know he won't," she said. "Daniel's a good kid."

"Then what's the problem?" he asked.

"Daniel misses havin' a dad. Sometimes he tries to get attention from guys like you."

The way she said that led Steve to believe she hadn't intended it as a compliment. "What do you mean, guys like me?"

"You may think you were just makin' a friendly suggestion about goin' fishin', but Daniel thinks you promised to take him. He's gonna be real disappointed when you don't."

"What makes you think I won't take him?"

"Bud's the only man Daniel's ever known who hasn't let him down."

"Lady, I've never broken a promise to a kid in my life," Steve said.

"You might be the best pal a boy could ask for," she said, eyeing him as if she doubted he'd ever be any such thing. "But for how long, Mr. Anderson? It'll be easier on Daniel when you leave, if he hasn't gotten himself attached to you."

Before Steve could think of an appropriate reply, Kelly turned and walked away, just as she'd done at the airport. He would have been seriously insulted if he hadn't suddenly noticed what a fantastic backside she had. It wasn't fat or jiggly, but it wasn't one of those skinny, little-boy butts so many of the women at the health club had, either. A man could really fill his hands—

Bud snapped his fingers in front of Steve's nose. "Whoa. Down boy," he said with a chuckle. "Kelly's quite a gal, but she wouldn't approve of what you're thinkin' about her."

Steve gave him a sheepish grin. "Does she hate all men, or is it just me?"

"Plenty of guys from Wisdom and Jackson have asked her out, but she's never given any of 'em the time of day," Bud said with a shrug. Then his expression turned sober. "Kelly's a little rough around the edges sometimes, but don't make any judgments until you get to know her better. Life hasn't been too kind to that little gal."

Life wasn't too kind to a lot of people without turning them hostile, but Steve didn't waste his breath pointing that out to his uncle. Kelly Jaynes had obviously won his aunt and uncle's respect and affection. Once a person had done that, it was impossible to find friends more loyal than Bud and Peg Ryan.

While Steve admired that quality, it also worried him. His aunt and uncle were intelligent folks, but they'd spent almost their entire lives in this safe, sheltered corner of Montana. They were so open and honest themselves, it didn't occur to them that other people might not always operate that way.

Take Kelly Jaynes, for instance. She was too wary of him and too determined to keep him away from Daniel. It was almost as if she had something to hide.

The rich aroma of fresh apple pies coming out of the oven hit him in the face when Bud opened the back door. Telling himself he'd have plenty of time to discover Kelly's deep, dark secrets if she had any, Steve followed his uncle inside. At least keeping an eye on her wouldn't be any hardship.

Focusing his binoculars on the homecoming scene in the ranch yard, the man crouched on the ridge watched with a cynical, utterly satisfied smile. He didn't know who the big blond dude was down there, but it didn't matter. At least now he knew for sure where the kid was. When the time was right to make his move, nothing and nobody was gonna stop him.

Looping the binoculars' strap around his neck, he backed into the timber, then hiked to the car he'd borrowed from his new girlfriend, who was waiting for him in Butte. Of course, what he really wanted to do was go on down there right now and grab his kid, but this time he was gonna do things right.

First he was gonna take his time instead of goin' off half-cocked. Then he'd make a real plan and set up a new network so they could live like humans were supposed to. And then...well, then he was gonna make his snotty little sister pay for what she'd done to him.

Oh, yeah. She was gonna pay, all right. She was gonna pay big time.

Chapter Two

Kelly sat at the Ryans' dining-room table an hour later, fervently wishing she was someplace—no, make that *any*place else. A person could starve waiting for Peg to quit flitting around as if the President had come for dinner. If that wasn't irritating enough, Kelly found the starched white tablecloth and fancy-schmanzy place settings intimidating as hell.

She'd never eaten in a real dining room before coming to the Haystack. She'd never had to sweat which silverware to use, because her family had never owned more than one fork, knife and spoon for everybody. She'd never had to worry about breaking a china plate or a crystal goblet, either. And why anyone would mess with a tablecloth when somebody was bound to slop gravy or jelly on it, was beyond her.

Unfortunately, Peg loved to use all this stuff, especially for special occasions, like holidays and birthdays. Kelly should have guessed Stevie-boy's visit would qualify. And, dammit, she should have checked out the book on etiquette she'd seen at the library last month and studied up on it, instead of going for that ranch journal.

She'd already learned a lot about table manners from watching Peg and Bud, and she'd been trying to improve her own and Daniel's, too. But they didn't eat in the dining room often enough for her to remember all the ins and outs from one time to the next. Well, she'd just have to do what she always did, sit here like a fool and wait for someone else to start eating so she'd know which utensil to use.

Peg carried in a platter from the kitchen and set it in front of Stevie-boy. Since Peg had ordered her to sit directly across from him, it was all Kelly could do to keep from drooling over the beef roast and the potatoes and carrots surrounding it. At least she couldn't complain about the guy's taste in food.

"Go on and help yourselves before it all gets cold," Peg said, settling onto her chair with a proud smile.

The woman had a right to be proud of her cooking, Kelly thought, surveying the spread. Besides the meat, potatoes and carrots, there were homemade rolls and apple butter, pickled beets, a salad, a relish tray with radishes, celery and olives, gravy and home-canned green beans with those little chunks of bacon Daniel loved so much. If anyone ever left Peg Ryan's table hungry, it was their own dam—no, *dang*—fault.

Praying her stomach wouldn't embarrass her with a ferocious growl, Kelly forced herself to wait patiently for the food to make the rounds. By the time all the plates were filled, she thought she just might be hungry enough to pass out. When she looked to see what fork Peg or Bud would pick up first, though, she discovered ol' Stevie-boy gaping at her plate.

"Somethin' wrong?" she asked.

His gaze rose to meet hers. To her surprise, a dull flush climbed up his neck and over his face, as if maybe he hadn't expected her to catch him looking. Then he cleared his throat and grinned at her. "No, I'm, uh, just not used to seeing a woman with such a . . ."

"Such a what?"

Steve glanced back at her plate and grinned again. "Such a healthy appetite."

Looking over at Peg's plate, Kelly felt her own face heating up. Lord, compared to Peg, she'd been a real hog. Not that she gave half a da—rn what this jerk thought of her eating habits.

Bud scowled at his nephew. "Well, for cryin' out loud, Steve. Try keepin' up with Kelly for a day, and we'll see how much *you* eat."

"I'm sorry, Kelly. I didn't mean to be rude." Steve gave a soft laugh and shook his head. "I guess I forgot what it's like to do ranch work all day. Once I'm back at it, I'll probably put away twice as much as the rest of you combined."

"Back at it?" Kelly asked. "You're plannin' to work while you're here?"

"You bet." He flashed that boyish grin at her again. "You didn't think I'd freeload for a whole month, did you?"

She shrugged. "I hadn't thought about it."

"Well, you've got yourself an extra hand for a few weeks."

Gray eyes weren't supposed to be so warm, Kelly thought, finding herself strangely unwilling to pull her gaze from Steve's. She wasn't supposed to get these weird, fluttery sensations in her belly just because a man smiled at her that way, like maybe he thought she wasn't too ugly or something. And she sure as heck wasn't supposed to like the idea of spending time with a marshal. Not even a little bit.

Confusion at her reactions to him sharpened her voice. "I don't need one, Mr. Anderson. And I don't have time to teach you how to be one. This isn't one of those ranches that caters to city folks who want to play cowboy."

The warm expression in his eyes took an arctic turn. "I'm aware of that, Miss Jaynes. But I doubt you'll have to teach me too much. There's got to be *some*thing useful I can do around here. Something you haven't been able to get to?"

Yeah, right, Kelly thought. Did he really think she was dumb enough to admit any such thing? In front of Bud? Not hardly. She forced a smile. "Gee, I can't think of any. Why don't you just relax and enjoy your vacation?"

A thoughtful, sort of sad look crossed his face. Then his jaw muscles hardened, and he met her gaze head-on, silently telling her he didn't care what she wanted, foreman or not. He had a closer relationship with Bud and Peg, and he'd do whatever he pleased. "I don't want a vacation, Miss Jaynes. If you can't put me to work, I'll do it myself."

A whole string of cuss words danced on the tip of Kelly's tongue. Why, the rotten snake was trying to make her look incompetent in front of Bud. Wouldn't surprise her a bit to find out he was after her job.

"Hold on there, you two." Bud glared at Steve, then Kelly, then Steve again. "Number one, I know we can find enough work around here to keep everybody happy. Number two, since when did either one of you get so formal, you can't call each other by your first names?"

Anderson shrugged, his face a picture of innocence. Kelly figured that look had probably gotten him out of plenty of scrapes over the years. "Just trying to be polite to your foreman, Uncle Bud."

"Well, it's about the dumbest thing I've heard in a long time, so cut it out, both of you," Bud ordered. "Peg and I thought you two would enjoy each other's company."

"I'm sure we will when we get acquainted." Anderson gave Kelly a grin that irritated her more than a long, hard ride with a chapped butt. Then he had the unbelievable gall to wink at her. "Won't we... Kelly?"

It wasn't easy to keep a snide note out of her voice when she'd really rather have shot him, but somehow, Kelly managed. "Oh, I'm sure we will... Steve," she said. Silently, she added, *Like hell we will, bucko.*

"Now that we've got that settled, let's eat," Peg said, using what Daniel called her do-it-or-else voice.

Kelly grabbed the first available fork, right one or not, stabbed her pile of green beans and poked them into her mouth. The sooner she finished eating, the sooner she could get away from that big, dumb son of a— No, uh... he—ck, the only polite substitute that came to mind was *stinker,* and it just didn't pack the same punch as the original phrase. Maybe if she just spelled out *S-O-B,* she wouldn't be breaking the rules too badly.

Ah, thank God. Food at last. She hadn't had a bite since breakfast because she'd missed lunch at the ranch and she wasn't about to spend her precious, hard-earned money on overpriced junk food in Missoula. The room was quiet for the next few minutes while everyone else started eating.

When the conversation resumed, Kelly made it a point to stay out of it. Her mother had always said a person learns more from listening than from talking. As usual, Mama had been right. In fact, about the only dumb thing Louise Winslow had ever done was marry Kelly's old man. What she wouldn't give for a dose of Mama's common sense right now.

Given a moment's thought, it wasn't hard to figure out what Mama would have said about this situation. Her conclusion made Kelly want to squirm like a kid with a guilty conscience sitting in church. Mama would undoubtedly tell her to lighten up and stop assuming the worst about ol' Stevie-boy. She'd also tell her to stop thinkin' of him in such derisive terms. And, that she ought to give him a chance before deciding she despised him.

Kelly snuck a peek across the table. Steve was leaning forward, listening to every word Daniel said, as if the kid was an absolute genius. Daniel was basking in the attention, his gaze riveted on Steve like a waterlogged plant seeking the sun after a flood. That weird, fluttery sensation hit her again, kind of up under her rib cage this time.

With a good meal under her belt, she felt a more rational frame of mind replacing the stresses and irritations of the day. Sometimes a plate of hot food could do amazing things for her outlook. At the moment, Steve Anderson was starting to look a little better to her.

Well, all right, she'd admit she liked the way he looked. A lot. She liked the rich, deep sound of his voice, and the way his eyes crinkled up at the corners when he laughed, sort of like he was inviting you to join in. She liked how patient he was with Daniel, too. Any man who could listen to one of the kid's long-winded explanations without letting his eyes roll back in his head, and then ask an intelligent question afterward, couldn't be all bad.

To be honest, he seemed like a decent enough guy whenever he talked to anyone but her. So why did he rub her the wrong way just by sitting there and breathing?

She really didn't believe he wanted her job. She loved ranching, but if she had a college education like his, she'd probably never look at the hind end of a cow again. Sh—oot, if she'd explained herself a little better at the airport, he probably wouldn't have acted like such a suspicious jerk. And if she hadn't acted like such a snot when he'd tried to talk to her on the way back to the ranch, maybe they *could* have enjoyed each other's company.

Much as she loved Bud and Peg, it would be nice to talk to someone closer to her own age. Steve had probably been to all kinds of interesting places she'd never get to see. If he could tell a story as well as Bud, he might even make some long, hard days pass faster.

If only he wasn't a marshal.

If only she didn't have such lousy relatives.

If only she could be like other women. Just once. To see what it felt like to laugh and flirt with a man and . . .

And that's enough of that, she chided herself, swallowing a snort of disgust at such useless ideas. Life dealt certain cards. If you were smart, you played them as best you could, and didn't waste energy wishing for different ones. She had Daniel, her dogs, and a good job working for folks who treated her with respect, which was more than she'd hoped for when she and Daniel had left Wyoming.

She was going to give her nephew opportunities she'd never had. She was going to buy him a computer and see him through high school and even college, if he wanted to go. She would raise him to be a decent, honorable man, and break the damn tradition or curse, or whatever it was that had plagued her family for generations, until it had finally killed her mother and cost both her and Daniel their rightful heritage. No matter how handsome Steve Anderson was, or how nice he might turn out to be, she couldn't afford to forget he wouldn't want anything to do with her if he knew the truth. He wouldn't want her anywhere near Bud and Peg, either.

Much as she might wish things were different, there wasn't room in her life for a man like Steve Anderson. There wasn't room for any man but Daniel.

After dinner, Bud went into his den to make some phone calls. Kelly dragged Daniel off to "get ready for school tomorrow." Steve suspected she just wanted to get away from him, and though it shouldn't have bothered him, it did. He lingered at the table with Aunt Peg, sipping a second cup of coffee while she caught him up on the latest family news. Not that he really cared much about what his mother and stepfather were doing, any more than they cared about him. Finally, she pushed back her chair, came around the table and ruffled his hair as if he were still twelve years old.

"More pie, Stevie-boy?"

Steve groaned inwardly at the childish nickname he'd never been able to erase from his aunt's vocabulary, though God knew he'd certainly tried. "Wish I could, Aunt Peg, but if I eat one more bite, it's liable to leak out my ears."

Aunt Peg scooped up a bunch of dirty dishes and headed for the kitchen. Gathering another load, Steve followed her.

"So, what's your foreman's story?" he asked.

"What do you want to know?"

"Just the basics. Where she's from. How you found her. Why she's raising Daniel instead of his parents."

"Why don't you ask Kelly if you're so interested in her?"

"I'm not—"

She shot him an arch look. "Well, it sounds like you are to me. I wouldn't blame you, either. Kelly's a real pretty woman and a smart one, too."

Steve scowled at his aunt. "Tell me I don't smell the stench of matchmaking."

Her expression of outraged innocence was about as genuine as Monopoly money. "Would I do a thing like that?"

"In a heartbeat," he said, chuckling. "But in case you didn't notice, your Miss Kelly can't stand me."

Peg waved one hand as if Kelly's opinion of him wasn't important. "She just doesn't know you yet, hon. It takes her a while to warm up to strangers, that's all. You'll really like her when she relaxes around you a little."

"Then tell me about her."

After studying him for a moment, Peg slowly shook her head. "Nope. Most of what I know about Kelly was told to me in confidence. If you want to find out about her background, you'll have to convince her to tell you herself."

"I tried that all the way from Missoula," Steve said. "I couldn't get zip out of her."

"Well then, you'll have to earn her trust, won't you?"

Snorting in exasperation, Steve brought in another load of dishes from the dining room. When he'd deposited them beside the sink, Peg shooed him out of the kitchen. "We'll have plenty of time for you to do your share of chores, Stevie-boy. Go on outside and have a look around before it gets dark. Fresh air'll do you good."

Grabbing his jacket, Steve followed orders, stepping out the back door into the twilight of a May evening in the Big Hole. He inhaled deeply, catching the scent of lilacs blooming around the side of the house and a hint of pine drifting on the breeze. The sun had already set, but there was still enough light coming from the far side of the mountains to bathe the valley in hues of purple and blue. Best of all, it was quiet. Really quiet.

No traffic. No boomboxes. No angry voices, gunshots or sirens. The only sounds here came from nature. The bawl of a calf who'd lost track of its mother. The gurgle of the creek winding its way across the ranch. The melancholy song of a meadowlark.

After pausing to soak it all in, Steve set off toward the barn. It needed a coat of paint as much as the house did. Planning to explore it later, he skirted around the west side and ambled down to the south pasture. The horses trotted over to the fence to check him out. When they realized he had nothing to offer but conversation and ear scratching, they lost interest and went back to their own pursuits.

Hands in his coat pockets, Steve moved on, retracing the trails of his adolescence, feeling more lonely with every step. He finally ended up in the barn's loft, his favorite place for privacy back when he'd been a kid. Opening the hay doors, he sat on the floor, dangling his feet over the edge. Then he settled in to watch the darkening sky for the first star.

He should probably go back to the house, but he really didn't want to. Maybe coming here hadn't been such a good idea, after all. A month at a nice, sunny beach with nothing to do but watch babes in bikinis would probably do more to get his mind off Anne than a sentimental trip down memory lane.

"Wild Bill, sit. Pat, sit. Wyatt, come. No, Wild Bill. You go on back over there and wait your turn."

Startled by the sound of Kelly's voice, Steve jumped, then scooted closer to the side of the doorway until the trailer came into view. The sight of her sitting on the bottom step, her face illuminated by the light shining from the open window to her right, banished all thoughts of beaches and babes.

She'd worn her dark hair pulled back from her face in a ponytail before, but now it hung past her shoulders in soft, natural waves. A big dog sat at her feet, his expression one of canine ecstasy as she tugged a metal comb through his thick fur, praising and petting him all the while.

"You're a sweet boy, aren't you, Wyatt? Yeah. You let those ol' cows know who's boss. Yeah." Kelly raised the comb, squinted at it, then, wrinkling her nose in disgust, picked something wiggly out of the comb's teeth, dropped it on the ground and smashed it with the heel of her boot. "I sure wish you'd learn to stay away from the ticks, though. I won't have you guys draggin' those nasty critters into the house."

Steve smiled at her nonsensical patter. Wyatt gazed up at her with unabashed adoration and thumped his bushy tail at appropriate moments. The other two mutts sat at attention about five feet away, their hides trembling with eagerness. Steve couldn't blame them. Damned if he wasn't getting a little hot and bothered himself from listening to Kelly's voice and watching her strong, sure hands move over the animal in caressing motions that were almost...erotic.

Finished with Wyatt, Kelly let him into the trailer, then called Pat over. Wild Bill came too, so she had to send him back to wait his turn again. Though Pat's shorter coat required less work than Wyatt's had, Kelly fussed over him in much the same way, laughing when he gave her a slurpy dog kiss on the side of her chin. She put him inside and called Wild Bill.

Wyatt was reddish brown, and looked as if at least one of his parents had been a golden retriever. Pat had the mottled coloring and conformation of a Blue Heeler. Though neither of them was what Steve would call pretty, they were downright gorgeous compared to Wild Bill.

Steve wasn't sure what combination of breeds had populated Wild Bill's family tree, but he had to be the biggest, ugliest, mangiest-looking dog alive. Rawboned and angular, he had a shaggy, brindle-colored coat and a long skinny tail that looked as if it might've been slammed in a door once or twice. On the other end he had a set of jaws and teeth that could probably sever a limb if he chose to attack.

Though Wild Bill acted as if he enjoyed Kelly's attention as much as the other dogs had, it made Steve nervous to watch her run the comb over him.

"Hey, Daniel," Kelly called a moment later. "You've got five seconds to get that shower goin', or else."

Daniel's voice came through the open window. "Or else what?"

"Or else, I'm gonna come in there and toss you in myself."

"Oh, no you won't. You can't see me naked."

"Too late. I already did."

"Aw, I was just a baby then."

"Yeah, but since I've already seen it all, one more time won't make any difference. We've still gotta read tonight, and your teacher won't like it if you fall asleep in class."

"Yeah, yeah, yeah," Daniel grumbled.

"And don't forget to brush your teeth."

A moment later the shower came on, however, and when Kelly heaved an obvious sigh of relief, Steve had to smile to himself. He could like this woman. Without her prickly defenses locked in place, she seemed warm, loving and nurturing, at least where boys and animals were concerned.

"Look, Wild Bill, there's the first star," she said, pointing up at the sky. "We'd better make a wish."

Wild Bill whined and rubbed his big head against her chest, as if demanding more combing. Gazing at the star, she ignored him for a moment, then chuckled and went back to work when he whined again. "All right, you big baby. But if I don't get my wish, you're in deep trouble."

The shower turned off. After cleaning out the comb and setting it aside, Kelly stood, brushed off the seat of her jeans and massaged her lower back with both hands. Wild Bill shook himself and pranced around, his crooked tail whipping back and forth like a hyperactive scythe. To Steve's horror, the beast suddenly reared up on his hind legs and draped his big front paws over Kelly's shoulders.

She staggered under his weight, but quickly righted herself. Wild Bill's long, pink tongue lashed the side of her face. Laughing, Kelly grabbed a handful of fur behind each of his ears and, after a minute of playful tussling, wrestled him to the ground. Wild Bill rolled onto his back, shamelessly begging to get his belly scratched. Kelly obliged, cooing at him as if he were an adorable child.

"Oh, you're just a big ol' silly sweetums, Billy. Aren'tcha? Yes, you are."

Then the bathroom light went out, and the light came on in the bedroom next door. The window was wide open there, too, and there were no curtains, allowing Steve to see inside as clearly as if he were looking at a TV screen. The sports posters on the wall and the schoolbooks on the desk suggested that this was Daniel's room. Sure enough, the boy came through the doorway wearing bright blue pajamas and the fresh-scrubbed glow of a clean kid. He yanked back the covers and jumped into bed, then shouted, "I'm ready, Aunt Kelly!"

"Be right there."

She picked up the dog comb and let Wild Bill into the trailer, then paused and looked around as if she sensed she wasn't alone. Holding his breath, Steve leaned away from the loft door. He didn't know what Kelly would do if she caught him spying on her, but he doubted it would be pretty.

Not that there was anything wrong with what he was doing. He was just trying to see what she was like on her own turf, maybe learn something about her that would help him understand her better, and in doing so, get along with her better. It wasn't as if he was doing anything sleazy, like watching her undress or take a shower.

That thought produced a mental picture, which in turn produced an uncomfortable tightness in his jeans. While there was nothing provocative about Kelly's clothes or the way she wore them, they did little to hide the strong, but delightfully feminine shape of her body. A dead man couldn't help noticing her. And he sure as hell wasn't dead. Jeez, he had to get out of here.

Before he could leave, though, Kelly carried a big book into Daniel's room. The boy made a face and shook his head. Of course, Steve had to stay to see what would happen next.

"Do we have to read *that* one?" Daniel whined, his voice coming through to Steve as clearly as a commercial for a telephone company.

Kelly pulled the desk chair over to the bed and sat on it. "Would you rather have the Bible than *The Book of Virtues*?"

"No, but why can't we read something else for a change? Like R. L. Stine or Christopher Pike? Or maybe Chris Crutcher?"

"You can read that stuff on your own time," Kelly said. "But it's my job to teach you decent values, and this is the best way I know how to do it."

"Why don't you just *tell* 'em to me? It'd be lots faster."

Kelly rubbed the back of her neck before answering. "How can I teach you what I don't know myself? I'm learnin' about this stuff right along with you, Daniel."

"Do you think I'm bad or something? I try real hard not to be, but—"

"Oh, Daniel, I know you do, and I think you're really terrific. I just hope you'll remember some of these stories and poems when you're old enough to start makin' your own decisions, and that they'll help you make better ones. Understand?"

"Yeah, I guess so." Daniel shivered, then pulled the covers up to his neck. "I'm gettin' cold, Aunt Kelly. Will you shut the window?"

After handing Daniel the book, she got up, closed the window and returned to the chair. Steve bit back a disgruntled sigh and climbed to his feet. He had more questions about Miss Kelly Jaynes than ever, but there was no sense in hanging around if he couldn't hear the rest of the conversation.

Well, as Aunt Peg had said, he'd have to work at winning Kelly's trust until she was willing to tell him what he wanted to know. Instinct told him she wasn't going to like it much. He just hoped he wouldn't tick her off enough to sic that monster dog on him. Even if he was "just a big ol' silly sweetums."

Chapter Three

"Oooh, Suzanna, now don't you..."

Gritting her teeth at Anderson's off-key bellering, Kelly kicked Babe, her quarter-horse mare, into a lope and veered off toward the west. Of course, Anderson followed, and Reload, his big Appaloosa gelding, caught up with her in two minutes flat. Well, at least she'd had two minutes of relative peace.

"What's the matter?" he asked, giving her a devilish grin. "Don't like my singing?"

"That was singing?" Kelly opened her eyes wide in feigned astonishment "I thought you were tryin' to attract a lady moose so you could have your way with her."

"Was that nice, Jaynes? I'm hurt. Really hurt." His lower lip stuck out in a pout, but the twinkle in his eyes ruined the effect. "I'll have you know I only get the hots for human females." Waggling his eyebrows, he lowered his voice and rode closer to her. "Smile at me once in a while, sweetheart, and I might even get 'em for you."

"Please, Lord, spare me," Kelly muttered.

Anderson clutched at his chest. "Oh, the pain of it. Your rejection wounds me."

Torn between laughter and a screaming fit, Kelly clamped her mouth shut and turned her head away from him, but did that stop Anderson? No such luck. As he'd done for the past three days, he simply transferred his conversation to her dogs, who trotted along beside her wherever she went. The lousy canine traitors ate up his attention, not to mention the treats he snuck out of the kitchen for them.

"How can such a beautiful woman be so mean?" he asked Wild Bill. "Don't you think she's mean, boy?"

Wild Bill barked and gave him a dopey-looking doggy grin.

"Right. Hey, tell me something. How long has she had lockjaw? You didn't know she had it? Well, why do you think she hardly ever talks?"

Desperately wanting to laugh, but refusing to give him that much satisfaction, Kelly forced the words out from between clenched teeth. "Shut up, Anderson."

Anderson raised an eyebrow at Wild Bill. "See what I mean? If she doesn't have lockjaw, that poor woman's jaws must have seized up from lack of use. Or maybe they rusted shut. You know, like the Tin Man's in *The Wizard of Oz?*"

In true Blue Heeler fashion, Pat Garret scared a jackrabbit out of the brush. Wild Bill Hickock and Wyatt Earp raced after Pat, and between the two of them, flushed three more jacks. Wild Bill chased one, then another, then another, getting so confused by so many different targets, he finally sat on his rump and howled in frustration. Kelly found it easy to sympathize. Dealing with Anderson made her feel like doing the same thing at least four times a day.

The man was nuts—absolutely, certifiably, delightfully nuts. He told terrible jokes and teased her unmercifully, but he poked as much fun at himself as he did at her, so she couldn't stay mad at him for long. He was opinionated, gabbier than three normal people and nosey enough that she enjoyed dodging his questions.

One minute, he could be extremely entertaining; the next, he could be downright infuriating. He was also a da—rn good hand, and he'd already taken Daniel fishing. Twice.

Of course, Wild Bill's performance tickled the wretched man no end, and while she struggled valiantly to keep a straight face, Kelly finally had to give in and laugh along with him. Honestly, the dog looked so silly, hopping after those rabbits with his long, gangly legs. But it wasn't really fair to laugh at him. Despite his size, Wild Bill was hardly more than a pup, and he hadn't figured out he was designed to chase bigger game than rabbits.

"What possessed you to buy that crazy mutt?" Anderson asked.

"He's not a mutt, and I didn't buy him," Kelly said. "I found him wanderin' down the road, half-starved and all banged up. Like maybe he'd been shoved out of a car, ya know?"

Anger flashed in Anderson's eyes. "You're kidding."

"Nope. His owner probably fell in love with a cute puppy and didn't stop to think about how big he was gonna get. I got Wyatt the same way."

"Damn, I hate that." Anderson shook his head in obvious disgust. "I don't understand why people think any big dog can survive out here. Most of the time they end up starving or getting run over, eaten by predators or shot by a rancher for bothering his stock."

"That's a fact," Kelly agreed, wishing he'd go back to being annoying. He was too attractive for comfort even then, but when he wasn't actively trying to irritate her... well, it was da—ng hard to remember she didn't like him. And when he looked at her mouth that way, like he might be wonderin' what it would be like to kiss her...

She jerked her gaze from his when she realized where her thoughts were heading. Men like him didn't get serious about ignorant cowgirls. He was probably just messing with her mind for the sheer hell of it. Or maybe he figured she'd be convenient for a vacation fling. Well, the devil would get frostbite first. Just because she didn't have much experience with men in a romantic sense, didn't mean she was stupid.

"What is he, then?" Anderson asked.

Kelly looked back at him and felt her toes curl up inside her boots. Geeminy Christmas, what was it about him that always got to her? He wasn't all *that* handsome, or—

He waved a hand in front of her face. "Yo, Jaynes! The lights are on upstairs, but where is everybody?"

"What?"

"I said, if Wild Bill's not a mutt, what is he?"

"Oh. An Irish wolfhound."

"He has an actual breed?"

"Uh-huh. I looked him up in a dog encyclopedia once. They used to hunt with kings."

"Right." Anderson kept a straight face, but she just knew he wanted to smirk. "I noticed what a great job he did on those vicious bunnies back there."

Kelly shot him a dirty look. "If he was trained for it, he could chase down a full-grown elk or a wolf."

"Is that why he practices on the cows all the time?"

"He's only tryin' to help, and when he sees Pat workin'—"

Anderson chuckled. "Hey, I wasn't complaining. I think he's a riot. He earns his kibble in entertainment value alone."

Since it was too disturbing to focus on the man, she watched Wild Bill run after Wyatt. He was awkward as the dickens most of the time, but when he stretched out into a full gallop, he was absolutely gorgeous. "He's quite a character, all right."

"Oh, Kelly, don't move."

His brow furrowed, Anderson rode up beside her. Leaning way out of his saddle, he studied her face at such close range, she could feel his breath strike her cheek and smell the aftershave on his skin. Wondering if she'd suddenly developed a rash or grown a tumor or something, she tolerated his silent scrutiny for as long as she could. But when he reached out and gently stroked the skin beside her mouth with the backs of his knuckles, the suspense got the better of her.

"What's wrong?" she whispered.

His gaze slowly rising to meet hers, he settled back into his saddle. Then he backed the gelding up a couple of steps and smiled at her. Uh-oh. If that wasn't fiendish delight in those gray eyes, it was a mighty close relative.

"Nothing."

"What were you lookin' at then?"

"Your face."

"Well, duh, Anderson. Why?"

"I was afraid it might crack and fall off."

She should have left right then, and she damn well knew it. Unfortunately, sometimes knowing the smart thing to do and making yourself do it were entirely different things. "Okay, I'll bite. Why did you think that?"

"Because for a second or two there, you really smiled. Do you have any idea how rare that is?"

It took incredible self-discipline to shut her mouth and ride away, but Kelly did it. When he caught up with her, she pretended she could neither see nor hear him. Not that he made it easy. With Anderson, nothing was ever easy.

"Come on, Kelly, it didn't hurt when you were talking to me before, did it? No, it didn't. And don't try to tell me you didn't enjoy a little conversation for a change, because I know you did."

He went on and on, coaxing, scolding, even whining occasionally. The guy could talk the ears off a corpse, and he'd say almost anything to get a rise out of her. It was just his tough luck she was a pro at keeping her reactions to herself. God knew she'd had enough practice while she was growing up.

"Aw, Kelly, what did I ever do to make you hate me so much?"

"I don't hate you."

"Then why won't you talk to me?"

Spotting a calf she hadn't seen for a few days, she dismounted and walked over to check it. "If you'd ever shut up for five seconds, maybe I would."

He swung his leg over the gelding's rump and crossed the ground between them in three long strides. "No, I tried that, and you were about as talkative as a tree stump."

Kelly shrugged one shoulder. "Maybe I like to hear myself think once in a while. Ya know, some of us don't talk unless we've got something intelligent to say."

"I've heard you shoot the breeze with Uncle Bud and Aunt Peg." He stepped even closer to her. The man had this thing about invading her space. "You do it with Daniel, too, sometimes. That's all I'm asking for."

Though she wanted to back up in the worst way, Kelly raised her chin and stood her ground. "Well, I like *them*. I'm not too sure about you yet."

A low, husky chuckle rumbled out of him, and his gaze roamed over her face as if everything about it pleased him. "Aw, Kelly, you like me, too. Admit it."

The sincere warmth in his eyes and his voice touched her like a physical caress. Her heart kicked into a higher gear and her lungs suddenly forgot how to function. Oh, man, this guy could charm a wolverine with one foot caught in a steel trap. And he knew it, too. Just like her dad.

"Don't push your luck, Stevie-boy."

He stepped back with such a horrified look on his face, she had to chuckle. Since the calf was obviously in great shape, she went back to her mare, grabbed the reins and led her down the fence line, watching for loose posts or drooping wire. When Anderson caught up again, though, his good humor had returned.

"Aunt Peg's been talking about me, huh?"

"Yup."

"Do I have any secrets left at all?"

"Nope." Kelly grinned at him. "None that Peg took pictures of, anyhow."

He groaned. "Not the photo albums."

"You sure took a lot of baths when you were a kid."

He was quiet for a long time. Well, it was only five minutes, but for him, that was a long time. Then he turned to her with a challenging smile. "Well, since you know so much about me, don't you think it's only fair that I should know a few things about you?"

She raised an eyebrow at him. "What kind of things?"

"Nothing kinky," he assured her. "Why don't we just start out with the usual, get-to-know-you kind of things?"

"We did that."

He shook his head. "No, *I* did that. You didn't answer your share of questions."

"Such as?"

"Such as, where are you from, Kelly?"

"I already told you. Wyoming."

"Wyoming's a big state. *Where* in Wyoming?"

"Up north." She really did enjoy tormenting him. He rolled his eyes in such a perfect imitation of Daniel, she thought maybe that was some kind of a guy thing.

"How old are you?" he asked.

"Old enough to vote."

"Cute, Jaynes. Real cute. Where do your parents live?"

"My mother's dead."

"Sorry to hear that. What about your dad?"

"He's not dead."

"Where does he live?"

"I haven't had any contact with him in years." She was especially proud of that one. It didn't answer his question, but it wasn't really a lie, either.

"What about Daniel's parents?"

"They're not around."

"Why not?"

Kelly scowled at him, and found that the teasing, good-natured man who'd been driving her nuts had been replaced by the grim-faced, frosty-eyed cop she had feared all along. She'd been right not to trust him. "Is this an interrogation, or what? Maybe I'd better call my lawyer."

"Jeez, I'm not asking for any deep dark secrets here."

"Coulda fooled me." Turning her back on him, she remounted and looked down at Anderson. "You wanna talk about the ranch or the weather, fine. But I don't happen to think all this personal stuff is any of your business."

"Can't we even be friends, Kelly?"

"I don't need any more friends. If you do, try the bars in Wisdom. You might find some there, as long as you don't sing."

He didn't smile at her feeble joke. In fact, he just stood there and looked at her with such an air of disappointment about him, Kelly actually felt a little guilty. Telling herself that was ridiculous, she rode off again.

When she realized he wasn't going to tag along after her this time, she told herself it was a good thing. She wouldn't have to listen to any more of his god-awful caterwauling, his corny jokes or his stupid conversations with animals. Now she could relax and do her job in peace.

The only problem was, instead of feeling relaxed, she suddenly felt . . . disappointed. Maybe even a little . . . lonely.

Steve watched Kelly ride away, then climbed back onto Reload and headed for the barn. He found his uncle in the storage room, counting out the ear tags they would need for branding at the end of the week. Bud turned away from the cabinet when Steve walked in.

"Thought you were ridin' fence with Kelly today," he said.

Bracing his butt on the battered desk, Steve stretched his legs out in front of him and crossed his arms over his chest. "We seem to be having a personality conflict. What's going on with her?"

Bud immediately turned back to the ear tags. To Steve's surprise, his voice took on a warning edge. "Nothin' important."

"I don't buy that. Whenever I'm around, she's twitchier than a con getting ready to testify against the mob. In fact, that's exactly what she reminds me of."

"Not everybody's gonna like you, Steve."

"It's more than that, and I think you know it. Did she have any references when you hired her?"

Bud shook his head. "Didn't need any. After talkin' to her for ten minutes, I could tell she knew cattle. She's got a real nice touch with horses, too."

"You know better than that," Steve scolded. "Maybe I should do a background check on her."

"Maybe you should mind your own damn business," Bud said, reinforcing his suggestion with a finger pointed at Steve's nose. "Kelly's honest and dependable, she's not afraid to work hard and she does a job right the first time. That's good enough for me."

"Now, wait a minute. For all you know—"

"No, *you* wait a minute, Steve. Good help's hard to find now, and I'm gettin' too damned old to handle everything by myself. Leave Kelly alone unless you're ready to stay here and take over this ranch for good."

"Take over the ranch for good?" Steve shook his head to make sure he was hearing right. "Me? What are you talking about, Uncle Bud?"

Bud snorted with impatience. "What do you *think* I'm talkin' about? Peg and I decided a long time ago that you'd inherit this place. Who else would we leave it to?"

"Well, uh...jeez, I haven't really thought about it."

"Then it's time you did. Tell you the truth, we wouldn't mind turnin' it over to ya now."

His mind reeling with the implications of his uncle's announcement, Steve raised both hands in surrender. "Hold on, man. I don't think I'm ready for that."

"Well, it doesn't have to be right this minute," Bud said with a grin. "Anytime in the next three or four years'd be fine. We'd just like to do some travelin' before we get too old and rickety to have any fun. Unless, of course, you don't want it."

"I don't know what to say, Uncle Bud." Steve laughed and shook his head. "I'm just kind of...flabbergasted. And flattered that you thought of me."

A wry smile crept across Bud's mouth. "We'll see how flattered you feel after you've taken a look at the business end of things. This ain't like havin' a regular job that pays you every two weeks, ya know. There's not a whole lot of difference anymore between ranchers and professional gamblers."

"Why didn't you ever say anything about this before?"

Bud shrugged. "Never thought you were ready to hear it before. When you'd come for a visit, you were always pretty gung ho about bein' a marshal. But this time, you seem different. Like maybe you could use another option."

Steve let out a disgruntled laugh. "I guess you could say that. My boss is about ready to fire me."

"You wanna talk about it?"

"Maybe later. Right now, I'm more concerned about your foreman. It just doesn't make sense for a young, single woman like her to isolate herself way out here. Unless she's hiding from something."

Bud's scowl returned. "You're way out of line, kid, and you're lettin' your imagination run off with you."

"I'm a cop, Uncle Bud, just like my dad was, and I'm not imagining anything. Hell, I've been trying to get to know her for three solid days, but she won't answer the simplest personal question. Do you even know where she's from?"

Bud nodded. "Kelly's real protective of her privacy, but she's always been honest and aboveboard with me."

"How do you know that?"

"I just do. You're gonna have to trust me on this one, Steve. She's got her reasons for actin' the way she does." Bud crammed the ear tags back into the cabinet and banged the door shut. "You let me worry about Kelly. I want you to think about takin' over the Haystack. It's a big decision."

Watching his uncle stomp off toward the house, Steve slowly shook his head. He'd rarely seen Bud display a temper, and he'd *never* seen him walk out in the middle of an argument. There was something fishy going on around here, all right.

Kelly was more than "protective" of her privacy. Hell, he'd known FBI and Secret Service agents who were downright chatty compared to her. Her physical strength and don't-mess-with-me attitude undoubtedly fooled most people into thinking she was tougher than old leather boots. But he wasn't most people.

His experience with witness protection had taught him to look beyond outward appearances. After spending the past few days with Kelly, he'd seen firsthand that beneath her tough exterior beat the heart of a marshmallow—at least where boys, dogs and horses were concerned. And somewhere, under all that bluster, was a sensitive woman who'd been hurt. Badly hurt.

There was also a woman who was very much afraid. Steve couldn't pinpoint exactly what she was afraid of, but he promised himself he would find out. There was a mystery here, and he never could stand to see a mystery go unsolved.

And that was probably the answer to Bud's offer right there, Steve thought. He enjoyed ranch work, but he was a cop at heart. Always had been and probably always would be. He'd really never imagined doing anything else for a living.

On the other hand, he'd sure hate to see the Haystack pass out of the family. This place had always been his refuge, and the thought of never being able to come here again hurt. The price of land had gone up so much since Hollywood had discovered Montana, an ordinary guy like him could never hope to afford a ranch at all, much less one as nice as the Haystack. How could he possibly turn down such a wonderful inheritance?

Well, he'd just have to do what he'd promised, and think about it. Surely, by the end of his visit he'd have a better idea of what he wanted to do with the rest of his life. In the meantime, he'd find out everything there was to know about Kelly Jaynes.

A week later, along with the mail, Aunt Peg delivered the first and only real clue he needed to unravel the secrets of Kelly's past. When Kelly and Daniel came in for supper, Peg handed the younger woman two envelopes, then picked up a third and examined it.

"You know anybody from Pinedale, Wyoming, hon?" she asked.

Kelly's complexion paled a couple of shades. "I used to a long time ago," she said slowly, as if reluctant to admit it. "Can't imagine who'd write to me from there, though."

"Well, I'm not sure anybody did," Peg said. She held up the envelope for Kelly's inspection. "It's addressed to a Kelly James, not Jaynes, and they just put General Delivery in Cody,

Wyoming, on it. See, it's been forwarded several times since then. Does that handwriting look familiar?''

His interest piqued, Steve saw Kelly's eyes widen, while the rest of the color drained from her face. A barely perceptible tremor shook her hand as she took the envelope. Studying it, she swallowed, then cleared her throat. "Yeah. It's for me, all right. Thanks, Peg.''

"Who's it from, Aunt Kelly?" Daniel asked.

Kelly rammed the envelope into her hip pocket and tousled Daniel's hair. "It's nothin' important. I'll tell you about it later.''

The rest of the meal went pretty much like those before it, but Steve noticed a fine tension in Kelly's posture. She didn't eat much, either, which was damned odd. They'd been working hard all day, and he felt hungry enough to eat a whole steer. When she passed up cherry cobbler for dessert and left without complimenting Peg's cooking, he knew she was upset. And he'd bet his badge that letter had something to do with it.

Pinedale, Wyoming. Pinedale, Wyoming. He'd have to look at a map to be sure, but in terms of Wyoming geography, he thought Pinedale was "up north." And if he remembered right, there'd been some federal action there a few years back. Something to do with drugs. Could Kelly have been mixed up in that?

Nah. That just didn't seem possible. He'd never even seen her drink a beer, which made her a pretty straight arrow for this part of the country. But wait a second. There was a memory tickling at the back of his mind, a story he'd heard in a bar in Denver. Another deputy had told him about a ranch somewhere in Wyoming the U.S. Marshals Service had seized because the DEA had found a big crop of marijuana growing there.

Steve couldn't remember all of the details, but the deputy had raved on and on about a young woman who'd screamed and fought like a crazed wildcat when they'd gone in to take over the property. Could that young woman have been Kelly? And if so, who had written her that letter?

He hadn't run a background check on her yet, out of respect for his uncle's wishes. And, or so he'd self-righteously told himself, because his own suspicions about her had been too nebulous and unsubstantiated to justify invading her privacy. The fact that, despite her cantankerous attitude toward him, he was more attracted to her than he'd been to any woman in recent memory had had nothing to do with his decision to back off.

Yeah, right.

But now, there was no getting around it. If she was connected to any kind of a drug-running operation, he had to know. His aunt and uncle's safety might well depend on it.

Chapter Four

"Aunt Kelly!"

Biting back an impatient snarl, Kelly inhaled a deep breath. Didn't it just figure? The one night all week she was dying for Daniel to go to sleep so she could have some privacy, was the one night he couldn't seem to settle.

He probably sensed the tension she was feeling over the letter Peg had given her. Which, of course, wasn't going to lessen one bit until she'd at least read the darn thing. Which she couldn't do, until she was sure her nephew wasn't about to pop out of his room to tell her just one more thing. Which he just might do, unless she calmed down.

Chuckling half-heartedly at her own Catch-22, she went back to his room and stuck her head through the doorway. "What is it this time, Daniel?"

"Can Wyatt Earp sleep in here tonight?"

"No."

"Come on, Aunt Kelly. Please?"

"You're drivin' me nuts, kid."

"Why not?"

"Wyatt's a big dog, and if you let him sleep on the bed once, he'll want to do it every night." At the mention of his name, the golden retriever trotted over, sat at Kelly's feet and cocked his head to one side, giving her a soulful look that seemed to say, "Yeah, why not? You know I'll be good."

"I won't let him up here," Daniel promised.

"Maybe you won't while you're awake, but the second you fall asleep, he'll jump right up there beside you."

"No, he won't."

Kelly shut her eyes and counted to ten. "Look, Daniel, I'm tired, cranky and scrapin' the bottom of the patience barrel. If you're gonna question the rules around here, give me a break and wait till tomorrow to do it."

"Was that letter from my dad, Aunt Kelly?"

Nuts. She should've known better than to hope he'd forget about it. Ordering Wyatt to stay, she entered the room and sat on the side of Daniel's bed. "No, it was from your grandpa."

"Did he say anything about my dad?"

"I haven't read it yet."

"Do it now. Maybe my dad got out early. For good behavior or something."

Her heart aching, Kelly hushed him by laying two fingers across his lips. "Honey, it should be another six to twelve months before there's any hope of that. But it doesn't matter if he's out or not. We're not gonna have anything to do with him again, or with your grandpa. Not ever."

Daniel sat up, his face turned red, his dark eyes glinted with fury and his chin jutted out in a perfect imitation of Kelly's brother Johnny whipping himself into a rage. "It's not fair!" he shouted. "You can't just decide that."

Her stomach twisted itself into a familiar knot and her pulse pounded in her temples. Grasping his chin between her thumb and forefinger, she gazed straight into his eyes and forced herself to speak calmly.

"Daniel, I want you to stop that right now. You either talk to me in a civil tone of voice, or we won't talk at all."

He took a deep breath and expelled it, then pushed her hand away and said in a more moderate tone, "Well, all that stuff happened a long time ago. Maybe they've changed. Maybe they've been reha—reha— What's that word again? The one that means they've learned their lessons?''

"Rehabilitated?"

"Yeah, that's it. Maybe that's happened."

"I know you want to believe that, and I wish I could," Kelly replied, carefully choosing her words, "but you were just a little guy when our dads went to prison. You don't remember them as well as I do. Believe me, those two are never gonna learn their lessons."

"You don't *know* that. Not for sure."

"No, I don't," she admitted, "but I'm not willing to risk your future or what's left of mine on some pie-in-the-sky hope that they *have* been rehabilitated."

"Well, I *am*," Daniel insisted. "He's my *dad*."

"And what has he done for you lately, Daniel? Huh? What has he ever done for you?"

"I still want to see him."

Kelly pushed herself to her feet. "Fine. When you're eighteen, you can track him down and see him whenever you want. Until then, I'm your legal guardian, and what I say goes. I'm warnin' you, Daniel, if you let your dad or your grandpa back into your life, they'll destroy it. That's just the way they are. Now, go to sleep, will ya?"

"Okay," he grumbled.

He flopped down onto his pillow, his glum expression making her heart turn over. He irritated her sometimes, and even acted like a polecat once in a while, but he really was a good kid at heart. In spite of his lousy parents and her bumbling attempts at mothering him, he was turning out okay. No matter what that damn letter said, she would protect him or die trying.

"I love you, Daniel," she called through the closed door.

Though there was still a grumble in his voice, he dutifully called back, "I love you, too, Aunt Kelly."

She made it to the end of the hallway before she heard his door quietly open and close, the interval in between just long enough to sneak a big dog into the room. A glance over her shoulder confirmed her suspicion, but she walked on into the living room. She just didn't have the oomph to go back and deal with Daniel again tonight.

Besides, if the kid thought he was getting away with something, he'd stay in his room for sure. She could always drag the dog out later. Wyatt's calm presence was bound to reassure Daniel, and right now, she'd do just about anything to help him get to sleep.

She waited half an hour, just to make sure, then inhaled another deep breath and fished the battered envelope out of her pocket. The postmark was hopelessly smudged, and the address had been crossed out and rewritten four times, but she would have known her dad's elegant handwriting on the original address anywhere. When had he gotten out? she wondered. And the ranch was gone, so what was he doing back in Pinedale?

More important, which persona was he using now? He had several he could slip in and out of, and God knew how many others he'd invented while he was in prison. Heaving a deep, ragged sigh, she opened the envelope, pulled out the stationery—expensive stuff by the look of it—and started to read.

Dearest Kelly,

"Dearest?" Kelly snorted in disgust. "Aw, jeez, Jay, please, not the refined gentleman."

I hope this letter finds you, and that it finds both you and Daniel in good health. It was quite rude of you to return my letters unopened, but I suppose I can understand your reluctance to communicate with me while I was away.

"Away?" Kelly swore under her breath. "Oh, right, Jay. Is that what they call going to prison now? Being away? Well, isn't that just convenient as hell?"

I'm out now, however, and there is no excuse for you to continue this farce. I find it unforgivable that you would leave Pinedale with no notification of a forwarding address to me or to your brother. Surely, you must have known I'd be worried sick when I arrived and found out you were no longer living here.

"The thought never crossed my mind, Pops," Kelly muttered. Since her dad liked to write almost as much as he liked to talk, she skimmed the next four pages, which contained exactly what she'd expected—a long list of complaints about his present situation, denials of responsibility and numerous suggestions that, if she was a good daughter, she would send him money as soon as possible. Lots of money.

"In your dreams. For once in your miserable, worthless life, try working for a living!"

Wild Bill raised his head and whined, making Kelly realize she must have spoken out loud. Jay always made her so dang mad, she could have been yelling at full volume without even realizing it. After a guilty glance toward Daniel's room, she looked back at the wolfhound. "It's all right, sweetie. I'm not mad at you." Wild Bill thumped his tail twice, sighed and laid his head back down on his front paws.

Kelly skimmed on through the letter until she came to a surprisingly honest-sounding section on the last page.

Kelly, I know that losing the ranch was devastating to you, and I don't blame you for being angry with me and Johnny. It has been over eight years, however. Too long, I should hope, to hold a grudge against your only living relatives. We are a family, and families are supposed to stick together and help each other. Let's put the past behind us, kiss and make up, bury the proverbial hatchet.

Well, it wasn't exactly an apology, Kelly thought, but it was about as close to one as she was ever likely to get from either Jay or her brother.

Johnny will be released in a few months, and he wants to see his son. Regardless of the judge's decision, you have no right to hide Daniel from your brother. After all, Johnny *is* the boy's father.

"It takes more than a sperm to be a father," Kelly whispered forcing the words past the sudden, unreasoning fear clogging her throat.

Not that she was afraid of Jay. He was a smarmy, lazy, unscrupulous son of a bitch, but deep down, he was a coward and a weakling. Her brother, Johnny, on the other hand, could be a walking nightmare.

Besides that, we have serious business we *must,* I repeat, *must* discuss with you. It could be a matter of life and death. Please, don't waste any time, Kelly. If you cooperate now, I can and will convince Johnny to forgive you for what you did. Tell me where you are, and all will be well.

Crumpling the letter in one hand, Kelly surged to her feet and paced across the room and back. Of course, the trailer wasn't big enough to burn off the excess energy rushing through her system. She had to get outside where she could move. Where she could breathe. Where she could think. She grabbed a jacket off the coatrack by the back door, rammed her hands into the sleeves and stuck the letter into a pocket. Then, leaving the dogs to guard Daniel, she stepped out into the night and set off for the horse pasture.

Before she got past the corral, however, a big, dark shape stepped out of the shadows, scaring a startled squawk out of her. Adrenaline poured into her bloodstream. Dancing back a step for more room to maneuver, she whipped both fists up in front of her, ready to use them without hesitation or mercy. She wasn't an expert fighter, but she'd be damned if she'd go down easy.

"Hey, I surrender," Anderson said with a startled laugh. "If you hate cherry cobbler that much, you don't have to eat it."

Kelly froze when her brain recognized the sound of his voice. Breathing hard, she slowly lowered her hands to her sides. "Sorry. You, uh, surprised me a little there."

"Yeah, I guess so. Is something wrong, Kelly?"

The concern in his voice brought a stinging sensation to the backs of her eyes. God, what would it be like to be able to fling herself into a man's arms and sob out her problems? Fearing she would do exactly that if she saw any kindness in his face, she turned her head away and consciously straightened her spine. This definitely was *not* the time to start falling apart. "No. I just, uh, needed some fresh air."

"Me too." He held out a small paper plate covered with plastic wrap. "And, I thought maybe you'd be ready for dessert by now."

"Oh." She took the plate, then couldn't for the life of her figure out what to do with it, other than shift it from hand to hand. "Thanks. That was, uh . . . nice of you, Anderson."

"Yeah, it was." His grin flashed briefly in the twilight. "Especially since you still refuse to be friends."

"Then why'd you do it?" she asked.

Resting one forearm along the top rail of the corral fence, he gazed at her with a thoughtful sort of expression for a long moment. "Because I don't think you really mean it. I think you're just scared of me."

"Scared of you?" Her hoot of laughter didn't quite ring true, even to her own ears. "Why would I be scared of you?"

"Beats the hell out of me." Flashing his grin again, he sidled a little closer to her. "See this white hat?" he asked, pointing at his Stetson. "It means I'm one of the good guys. Or is it my job that scares you?"

"Don't be ridiculous. I'm not scared—"

"Yes, you are." He sidled closer, crooked a finger under her chin and raised it, forcing her to meet his gaze. "The way I see it, there's only two reasons you might feel that way."

The tender skin under her chin tingled where his finger touched. The air she was trying to breathe thickened. His eyes willed her to come closer yet. "Oh, yeah?"

"Yeah. The first one is that you're in some kind of trouble with the law."

Though it wasn't true, his suggestion brought a familiar sense of shame with it. Denying an equally familiar urge to run away and hide, Kelly cracked a smile and casually stepped out of his reach. "You've got *some* imagination, Anderson."

He shrugged. "I see it happen all the time. Sometimes even good people make mistakes."

"Yeah, well, I don't. Not that kind, anyway."

"Good. I like the other reason a whole lot better."

"What's that?"

His voice took on a husky note and his mouth curved into such a sexy smile, she barely noticed he was moving in on her again. "You're scared because you really do like me, Kelly. In fact, you're even . . . attracted to me."

Her shoulder came up against a post, making her realize she'd let him chase her the full length of a section of the corral fence. Under other circumstances, the thought would have made her laugh. But here and now, she just felt . . . vulnerable. Shaky. Terrified he might be right.

"Ya know, Anderson," she drawled, snaking around the post, "if that ego of yours gets any bigger, you're liable to get a hernia from haulin' it around with you."

His laugh boomed in the quiet evening. "Yeah, well, there's no danger of that with you around. Much as I'd love to argue the point, though, there's something else we need to talk about."

Then, as if he had every right to do so, he took her arm and ushered her around the corral and across the backyard. For just a moment, Kelly allowed herself the pleasure of pretending they were like any other couple out for a walk in the moonlight. When he wasn't talking, Anderson had a nice way about him that made her feel . . . protected.

It was an illusion, of course. If Johnny decided to come after her and Daniel when he got out, nobody could protect her. Shivering at the thought, she pulled out of his grasp.

"What did you want to talk about?" she asked.

"Let's sit down, Kelly." He gestured toward an old wooden bench flanked on three sides by lilac bushes. It was a good location, far enough from the main house that they wouldn't disturb Bud and Peg, but close enough to the trailer that she would hear the dogs bark if something happened.

The bench creaked when she wearily plunked herself at one end. Anderson sat beside her, propped his elbows on his thighs and clasped his hands between his knees. He stared off into the distance, his expression bordering on somber.

Figuring he'd start talking when he was good and ready, Kelly tucked the cherry cobbler under the bench. Then she stretched out her legs and settled back, watching the bats swoop by the yard light, hunting insects. No need to panic. She'd covered her tracks well. There was no way Johnny and Jay could find her.

"I really want to thank you, Kelly."

Startled out of her reverie by the sound of her own name, she looked at Anderson, raising her eyebrows in query. "Sorry, I didn't catch what you said."

"I said, I really want to thank you."

"For what?"

"For doing such a good job here for Uncle Bud. Everywhere I look on this ranch, I see places where you've gone the extra mile for him."

Intensely uncomfortable with the direction of his conversation, Kelly shrugged, then looked down at her rough, unfeminine hands. "Bud's a good boss. I like workin' for him."

"I can see that. I just want you to know I appreciate it. Bud and Peg are really important to me."

Unable to think of a thing to say, Kelly nodded, but didn't look at him. Steve went on, his tone growing thoughtful.

"My mom didn't have a clue about raising a boy on her own when my dad died, so she used to send me out here to stay with her big brother just to get me out of her hair. Bud and Peg are really more like parents to me than an aunt and uncle."

"They've been wonderful to Daniel," Kelly said. "Just like grandparents."

"Then maybe you can understand why I'm a little... protective of them."

She looked up in surprise at the rough edge that suddenly entered his voice, and found herself facing the frosty-eyed cop again. Her stomach took a nosedive for the toes of her boots, but she faced him without flinching. "Yeah, I can understand it just fine. What's your point, Marshal?"

"My point is, if you're in some kind of trouble that could hurt Bud, Peg or this ranch, I want to know about it."

Incensed, Kelly lunged to her feet and poked her forefinger at his chest. "I would *never* do anything to hurt Bud, Peg or the Haystack."

He stood, too, glaring down at her as if he'd like to shake her. "Then why all the secrets? Why won't you even tell me where you're from?"

"I told you, it's none of your damn business."

"When my family's involved, honey, *every*thing's my business. Let's see now, that letter you got tonight was originally from Pinedale, Wyoming, right? What do you suppose the sheriff down there would say if I called him and asked if he'd ever heard of a Kelly *James?* Should I do that?"

"Aw, go right ahead." Lord, she hated hearing such bitter defeat in her own voice, but she couldn't help it. Crossing her arms over her chest, she turned her back on him. "No matter what I say, you're gonna do it anyway, aren'tcha? Well, you won't hear one blessed thing about me Bud doesn't already know."

"Then tell me." Though his tone softened, it was no less insistent. "I'd rather hear it from you, Kelly. If there's anything I can do to help you, I will."

"Uh-huh. Why would you do that?"

His hands closed around her shoulders from behind. "For one thing, you're a valuable employee of this ranch, and none of us want to lose you. For another, my aunt and uncle care a lot about you and Daniel. And for another..."

Pausing, he turned her around to face him again. When she looked up at him, he stroked her cheek with his fingertips, stirring up a swarm of ambivalent emotions inside her. Emotions that had steadily grown stronger since his arrival, despite her desperate attempts to stomp them out of existence.

"Truth is, Kelly, I'm as attracted to you as you are to me."

"You are not." The instant the words came out of her mouth, she regretted them. She should have known better than to challenge a man like that. She should have known better than to stand out here in the moonlight with him. Hell, she should have known better than to—

Before she could complete that thought, he slid his fingers across her temple and into her hair, curving them around the back of her head. Then he wrapped his other arm around her waist, pulled her against him and kissed her.

If he'd been rough, she could have fought him. *Would* have fought him. She'd fended off enough horny cowboys in her day to populate a small town. But Anderson was different. The wretched man used the one weapon she was helpless to resist. Gentleness....

Earthquakes and fireworks. Earthquakes and fireworks. Earthquakes and fireworks.

The phrase echoed through Steve's brain like an irritating line of a song he couldn't forget. Kelly still smelled more like a horse than perfume, and he wasn't planning to challenge her at arm wrestling any time soon. But even though she wasn't the soft, feminine sort of woman he wanted, damned if kissing her didn't bring on the earthquakes and fireworks he'd once expected to find with Anne.

If he hadn't been standing right here, experiencing it himself, he would have refused to believe that simply pressing his mouth against Kelly's could produce such a rush of excitement. And the weird part was, that while she wasn't pushing him away, she wasn't exactly cooperating, either.

She seemed so...shy, or maybe...hesitant—he wasn't sure what word he was looking for—but it was almost as if she'd never really been kissed before. Which couldn't be true. She might not fit his picture of ideal womanhood, but she was hardly a woman other men would ignore. And the longer he kissed her, the fuzzier his picture of ideal womanhood became.

Her lips were soft and warm, her breasts firm and full where they rested against his chest, her waist perfectly curved to fit his arm. Too long denied, his sexual needs kicked in with unexpected and brutal swiftness. Man, he hadn't gotten this hard, this fast since puberty.

Instinct told him, however, that a smart man wouldn't push his luck. Kelly was like the horses she loved so much—strong in body, but fragile in spirit. Or maybe she was more like a porcupine—prickly as hell on the outside, but deeply vulnerable underneath.

This was not the kind of woman to coax into a summer romance. She would need plenty of time, patience and wooing to get used to the idea of being close to a man. But when she did get close, Steve suspected she would give that man everything—body, heart and soul. The question was, how close to her did he really want to get?

An emotion he refused to name filled his chest, cutting off his oxygen until he had to pull back. She looked so sweet, so...stunned, so...amazed. As amazed as he felt by the earthquakes and fireworks.

Oh, damn. Kissing her had been a mistake. A huge mistake. He wasn't ready for this. It had only been a kiss, for God's sake, and he hadn't even used his tongue. But he must have been imagining things. You didn't get earthquakes and fireworks from one little kiss. Did you?

There was only one way to be sure.

Knowing she should protest, but absolutely unable to bring herself to do it, Kelly watched Steve's head descend toward her again with a terrible mix of anxiety and anticipation. She'd been kissed before, but not like this. Never like this. In fact, she'd never wanted anyone else to kiss her a second time. The first had always been more than enough, thank you very much.

Oh, wow. That warm, floaty sort of feeling came back when their lips met again. It was even better this time, because she knew he wouldn't mash her lips against her teeth or try to ram his tongue clear down her throat or grab at her breasts like he was gonna milk some old cow.

His mouth glided over hers, as if he had all night, and kissing her was all he wanted to do with it. A certain, aroused part of his anatomy pressing against her suggested that wasn't entirely true, but she never would have known about it from the way he kissed. When his tongue slowly skated across her lower lip, it only seemed natural to open her mouth and invite him in.

He groaned. His arm tightened around her waist. Tomorrow, Kelly told herself, she'd regret kissing him back with so much gusto. But for now, she was too wrapped up in the giddy sensations, too weak in the knees, too busy clinging to his broad shoulders to worry about tomorrow or anything else.

Lord, she could get addicted to his taste. To being held. To being touched with something that at least felt like affection. Daniel didn't want hugs much anymore, and she hadn't realized just how starved she was for physical contact with another human being.

Long before she was ready, Steve pulled back and stared down at her, the cadence of his ragged breathing matching hers exactly. What was he thinking? What was he feeling? Did he want to kiss her again as much as she wanted him to?

Evidently not. Looking up at the sky as if he'd never seen stars before, he released her, stepped back and cleared his throat. It didn't help much, because his voice still sounded like he'd swallowed a shovel full of gravel.

"The attraction's real, Kelly," he said.

Remembering the way she'd wanted to beg him to kiss her again, Kelly felt her cheeks grow hot. Who said regret would even wait until tomorrow? What on earth had possessed her? This guy was so far out of her league—

"Kelly."

"What?"

"Say something, dammit."

"I don't know what to say, dammit." Crossing her arms over her midriff, she turned away, gazing toward the mountains to the west, though it was way too dark to actually see them.

"You could admit you feel it, too. The attraction, I mean."

Jeez, he didn't have to sound so crabby, did he? After all, *he'd* started this. "All, right. I feel it. So what?"

"So, what are we going to do about it?"

She shot him a resentful look over her shoulder. "Nothin'."

That put his nose out of joint in a hurry. "What do you mean, nothing?"

She turned back to the mountains. "Nothin'. *Nada*. Zippo. Pretend it didn't happen."

He stomped around in front of her and moved into her personal space with a determined glint in his eyes, openly daring her to object. "No way. I can't do that."

Holding out her hands to ward him off, she backed up. "Sure ya can, Anderson. It'll be easy. Just think of me as a hired hand, ya know? One of the guys."

"I don't want to, Kelly." His voice softened, but he advanced on her again. "I've waited a long time to find a woman who could kiss me the way you just did. I'll be damned if I'll brush it off like it didn't mean anything."

"But it didn't," she insisted, backing up another step. Oh, nuts, she was right on top of the lilacs. "Dammit, will you stop crowding me? It *can't* mean anything."

He halted, then propped his hands on his hips while he studied her. "Why not? You don't have a boyfriend or a husband tucked away somewhere, do you?"

"No. But it just wouldn't be . . . proper. You're a *law*man, Anderson."

"What's that got to do with anything?"

She gulped. Squared her shoulders. Inhaled a deep breath. "My last name *is* James. Bein' a marshal, you've probably heard of my great-great-great grandpa. A fella by the name of *Jesse*."

Chapter Five

Astonished at what she'd said, Steve stared at her for a moment, then laughed and shook his head. "Yeah, right. And he had a brother named Frank—"

"And they had a gang that robbed banks and trains and killed people from 1866 until 1882."

"Uh-huh. Pull the other leg." He reached for her, but she slapped his hands away with enough force to cause pain. "For God's sake, Kelly, will you knock it off?"

"No! Not until you listen to me."

"Oh, come *on.* James is a common name. You don't really expect me to believe—"

"I don't care whether you believe it or not. Tell you the truth, I'm not even sure *I* believe it. My dad and the rest of his family are such a pack of liars, who knows if we're really related to Jesse James?"

"Then what's your point?"

"I've had enough relatives behind bars to make me believe it's probably true. Trust me, Marshal, this is not a bunch you'd want to get mixed up with."

"Who said anything about getting mixed up with your relatives? Let me get to know you first—"

Scowling, she shook her head at him. "No way. I don't do flings. And even if I did, I've got too many problems of my own right now to spare the time or energy to have one."

"What if I wanted more than a fling with you?" he asked, surprised to hear those words coming out of his mouth. It hadn't been that long ago when he'd thought Kelly would be the last woman on the planet to attract him, but she fascinated him. Really fascinated him.

She shook her head again, then none too gently pushed him aside and stalked out of the lilac bushes. "Gimme a break, Anderson." Planting her hands on her hips, she turned to face him. "All you want from me is sex. Well, I'm not interested."

Steve grinned. She looked so defiant, so...indignant, he couldn't help it. "Liar."

Her posture stiffened. Her chin rose. Her fingers curled into fists. "Is this where you tell me I'd better start gettin' interested if I want to keep my job?"

"No!" Appalled by her accusation, Steve raised his hands beside his head in surrender. "Relax, Ms. Jaynes, I don't do sexual harassment. In fact, I won't touch you again without a written invitation."

She looked at her feet. When she allowed her gaze to meet his again, he thought he saw a touch of regret in her eyes, but it was too dark to be sure. "Hey, if you want to be friends—"

Steve dropped his hands to his sides. "Thanks, but I'll pass. We'll both be better off if I just stay the hell out of your way." He would have stomped right past her and into the house if she hadn't put a hand on his forearm.

"Wait," she said, her voice low and husky. "That wasn't fair. I, uh...I know that's not what you meant."

"Then why did you say it?"

Lowering her gaze again, she shrugged one shoulder. "Well, maybe I *am* attracted to you. A little bit." She swallowed. Cleared her throat. "And, I guess, maybe I'm, uh...a little bit...scared of getting hurt."

"You think I'm not?" Steve asked.

That made her look at him in a hurry. Plastering a reassuring smile on his face, he fought down an urge to pull her into his arms and kiss that surprised expression off her face. "I got my heart broken about two years ago, and I'm still trying to get over it."

"No sh—uh, kidding?"

"Why do you do that, Kelly?"

"Do what?"

"Always try so hard not to swear."

A sheepish grin curved her lips. "Daniel was gettin' in trouble for cussin' at school, so I figured we needed to learn to talk better. I've spent so much of my life hearin' it all the time, I don't usually remember until a bad word's half out of my mouth. Believe it or not, I'm doin' better'n I used to."

"You're doing fine. Did you mean what you said about being friends?"

"Yeah."

"Why don't we try that for a while and see what happens?"

"All right," she said softly. "Let's do."

"And if something's worrying you, you'll let me help?"

She hesitated, then gave him a grudging nod. "Yeah. Maybe. Night, Anderson."

Turning away, she practically fled back to the trailer. Steve watched until she was safely inside. Tucking his fingers into his jeans pockets, he ambled halfway back to the house before it hit him. Though he thought he had a better idea of what was going on with Kelly and Daniel, he still didn't know anything for sure.

Dammit all, he didn't believe for one second that she would ever willingly ask anyone for help. She was too stubborn, independent and suspicious. Well, he didn't have any more time to waste on trying to pry every scrap of information out of her. Hey, she'd told him to go ahead and call the sheriff in Pinedale, hadn't she?

By the end of the week, Kelly decided there was something to be said for being friends with Anderson. She'd been awfully uncomfortable with him the morning after that kiss, but he'd never once mentioned it or tried anything even remotely romantic with her. In fact, if she had to describe his behavior toward her, she would have said he'd acted like the brother she'd always wanted, instead of the one she'd been cursed with.

She could hardly believe how much they'd accomplished this week. Bud still pitched in wherever he could, but he'd broken too many bones over the years and gotten too arthritic as a result, to help much when it came to hard, physical labor. Out of necessity, Kelly had learned to be inventive to do the jobs that required more brute strength than she could muster alone.

With Steve there to supply some extra muscle and a second set of hands, everything went quicker and easier. And since he'd stopped irritating her on purpose, he'd become a fairly decent companion. Not that she needed one, of course. An introvert by nature, she'd always enjoyed the company of animals more than that of her fellow human beings—with a few notable exceptions—namely Daniel, Bud and Peg.

Still, she had to admit that Anderson's warped sense of humor was kind of fun. His stories about his adolescent days at the Haystack and his career as a deputy U.S. marshal were entertaining. His keen sense of observation and thoughtful comments about human nature challenged her to think more than she had in years about life in general and her own life in particular.

With each passing day, he seemed a little less like a cop and a little more like a regular guy. More like he really belonged here at the ranch. More like a friend. When she was with him, she felt more interested in the world around her, more connected, more . . . alive.

In what was getting to be a bad habit, she looked across the pasture and felt a smile form on her lips when she spotted him expertly shifting his weight in the saddle as Reload chased a calf out of the brush. He glanced around when the calf rejoined the herd, spotted her and smiled.

"Hey, Kelly," he called, wiping the back of his wrist across his forehead. "How many more?"

"That's it. Open the gate and head 'em toward home."

He waved in acknowledgement. She signaled for Pat Garret to go after a straying calf, then trotted Babe around the back of the herd, shouting and waving a coiled rope at the stragglers. This was the last bunch they had to bring in for branding tomorrow, and she wanted to get them back to the holding pen in time to grab a shower before supper.

Mooing in protest, the cows lumbered along. The calves darted around like klutzy ballerinas, kicking up clouds of dust with their hooves. Late afternoon sun beat down with unseasonable heat for the middle of May, raising a sweat on humans and horses alike, making the dust stick to every inch of exposed skin and hide.

A bald-faced cow balked halfway to the gate, turned and trotted into a stand of willows. Of course, her calf had to go and follow her, which attracted the attention of another calf and his mama. Babe automatically lowered her head and went after the leader. The cow stood her ground as if she didn't give a damn what that stupid horse wanted. She liked this pasture, and she wasn't going to leave it.

Babe would have run right over the rebel, but Kelly reined her in, remembering a tangle she'd had with this particular cow last year. She'd been riding Reload at the time. Dang, ornery cow had charged the gelding, dumped Kelly hard enough to separate her shoulder and caused more trouble than a skunk in church.

"Why, you mangy old she-devil, get your butt movin', and I don't mean maybe," Kelly hollered, waving her rope.

The cow didn't move.

"Want me to sic Pat Garret on ya? He'll chew your scrawny tail so short the flies'll eat ya alive in July."

The cow didn't move.

"C'mon, ya dimwitted grass-guzzler. Let's go get your baby branded and doctored."

Still unimpressed, the cow didn't move.

This was exactly the kind of situation that had taught Kelly how to cuss. God's truth, it seemed like some cows just wouldn't move one inch unless you cussed 'em up one side and back down the other. Familiar words and phrases sizzled on her tongue, begging to blister that stubborn old cow's ears.

Well, Kelly decided, this time she wasn't gonna do it. She'd worked too hard and had come too far to let a dingbat Hereford throw her into a relapse. Besides, it probably wasn't the actual cuss words that put a cow in gear so much as the loud, angry tone of voice used to deliver 'em. It was worth a shot, anyhow.

The cow blew out a snort and shook her head as if she hadn't been dehorned years ago. Keeping a wary eye on her, Kelly backed Babe up five feet and shook out a couple of coils from her rope. She rode to the left. The cow turned with her. She rode to the right. The cow turned again, blew out another snort and pawed the ground.

Cracking the loose end of the rope like a whip, Kelly nudged Babe into a walk. "'Four score and seven years ago,'" she shouted, "'our fathers brought forth on this continent a new nation.'"

Riding back and forth in front of the renegade, she cracked the rope again and turned up the volume on her voice, "'Conceived in liberty, and dedicated to the proposition...'" The cow shifted direction whenever Babe did, but the mare was more agile. Eventually, she got in close enough to allow Kelly to smack the cow's rear end with the rope, "'that all men are created equal.'"

The cow trotted a few steps, then turned back to face Babe. "Aw, c'mon, ya blusterin' bag of stew meat," Kelly muttered, shaking out another coil. "Now where was I? Oh, yeah." The dance began again.

"'Now we are engaged in a great civil war...'" The rope cracked. The cow trotted a few steps. "'Testing whether that nation, or any nation...'" The rope cracked. The cow trotted. "'So conceived and so dedicated, can long endure.'"

By the time Kelly pushed the old girl through the gate, she'd darn near finished the Gettysburg Address, and Steve and Pat Garret had the rest of the bunch moving right along. Steve rode back to join her.

"So, what's next on the program?" he asked. "The Constitution? The Pledge of Allegiance? Shakespeare?"

"Whatever works, Anderson," she replied, intentionally keeping a deadpan expression on her face.

He tipped back his head and laughed, a rich, booming sound that made her grin. "Wait'll I tell Uncle Bud and Aunt Peg," he said. Flinging out his right arm like an overly dramatic stage actor, he proceeded to imitate her performance.

"Knock it off, Anderson," she grumbled after the first two lines. "It wasn't that funny."

"It was a classic, Jaynes." Slapping his thigh with his hand, he laughed some more. "You should have seen yourself out there, cracking that rope and reciting for that old cow. Talk about cowboy poetry!"

That set him off again, and the wretch laughed until he was out of breath and his eyes watered. Realizing she must have looked pretty silly, Kelly let him hoot all he wanted. When he finally wound down, she said dryly, "Well, it sure doesn't take much to entertain some people."

"Well, we haven't had much entertainment since I've been here," he said. "Hey, it's Friday night. What say we drive into Wisdom after supper, have a beer and hit the pool tables for an hour?"

She hesitated, wanting to go, but afraid of undermining their new friendship if he mistook the outing for a date. As if she'd spoken her doubts out loud, he added, "No big deal, Jaynes. Just a couple of pals washing down the dust from a day's work."

"All right," she said. "If Daniel can stay with Bud and Peg while I'm gone, you're on . . . pal."

His answering smile made liars out of both of them. The warm humor in his eyes told her that he knew they would never be just pals. The way her breath caught and her toes curled up inside her boots forced her to admit she didn't really see him in a platonic light, either.

Of course, that didn't stop her from trying to deny the truth. And, she sternly reminded herself, even if she did have certain . . . romantic—well, all *right*—lusty feelings for the man, she was an adult who could keep such things under control. She managed to preserve that illusion until she found herself standing in her underwear in front of her closet two hours later, flipping hangers back and forth on the rod as if she thought it would magically produce something decent to wear.

Nuts. She should have bought herself a new shirt or two, and maybe a pair of jeans the last time she was in Missoula. She was always so worried about saving every dime and making sure Daniel had everything he needed to be like the other kids, she hadn't realized just how sparse her own wardrobe had become. If you could even call this ratty collection of jeans, T-shirts and work shirts a wardrobe.

Oh, everything was clean and serviceable, but there was nothing...nice. Okay, okay, nothing...feminine. Not that she'd ever had that kind of stuff since her mother had died. Or any real need for it.

There wasn't much call for panty hose and high heels when all of your waking hours went into working a ranch. And why bother with makeup, jewelry and hair doodads when you had no man to please and you weren't trying to attract one? She simply didn't have any time, energy or money to put into primping, right?

Right!

So why was there still this sad little part of her that would have sold her soul for a crisp, colorful new blouse—blouse, not shirt—to wear into Wisdom this evening?

Disgusted at her own inconsistent idiocy, Kelly grabbed the very next shirt and pair of jeans she came to, yanked them on and slammed the closet door. Then she couldn't decide whether to leave just the top shirt button undone, or the top two. And should she wear her hair up in its usual ponytail, or leave it down around her shoulders?

The worst part was, the more she told herself it didn't matter, the more it did. Blast it, she wanted to look nice. Not just for Steve, but for her own self-respect, too. Surely one new outfit a year wouldn't put enough of a dent in her finances to deprive Daniel of anything terribly important.

She gathered up her hair in one hand again and reached for a ponytail holder with the other. If she fastened it lower, like at the top of her neck ... Oh, damn the man. She'd been content with her life until he came along. Reasonably content, anyway.

And now ... well, now she was spending too much time thinking about things, wanting things, that just weren't meant to be. Not for Kelly James, anyway. Sighing in resignation, she let go of her hair and shook it out. This was as good as she was gonna look, and Anderson could think what he dang well pleased.

Daniel came in from taking Wyatt and Wild Bill out for a run. When it came to moving cows, neither of the big dogs was worth the lead it would take to shoot him. Kelly always penned them up when that particular job was on the agenda or if she had to be gone from the ranch. One of Daniel's after-school chores was to help them blow off excess energy.

While he washed up for supper, Kelly fed the dogs and refilled their water bucket as she always did. She had to keep their food dishes separate because Wild Bill was such a hog and so much bigger than the other two, he'd gulp it all down before Pat and Wyatt even got close to the kibble.

Straightening away from the spigot, she rolled her tired shoulders, rubbed the small of her back with both hands, then froze in place when a creepy, somebody's-watching-me tingle slid up her spine. With a nonchalance she didn't feel, she twisted to her left, then to her right, hoping it would look to anyone watching as if she was just stretching out the kinks from a long day in the saddle. Then, moving slowly, she turned completely around, propped her hands on her hips and took a good, long scan of the surrounding area.

She didn't see anyone or anything unusual, and the uncomfortable sensation faded. But, thinking about it now, she realized she'd had that same feeling a couple of other times lately. She looked around again.

Nothing moved. The dogs were acting normal. Aw, he—ck, she was just getting paranoid because of Jay's letter. Well, enough of that nonsense. Tonight was hers, dang it. Jay and

Johnny had already ruined enough of her life. Once and for all, she was done with the James clan.

Daniel hurried out of the trailer, and chattered all the way to the main house. Kelly listened with only half of the attention she usually gave him. The other half was taken up with a sense of anticipation that just plain refused to go away, no matter how many times she told it to. For once, she was going somewhere on a Friday night. With a handsome man. To have some fun. Now, *there* was a concept.

The aroma of Peg's three-alarm chili greeted her at the back door. Sniffing appreciatively, Kelly followed Daniel inside. Peg was bent over the oven, poking a toothpick into a pan of corn bread.

"I hope that's ready," Kelly called across the kitchen. "I'm so hungry, I could take a chomp or two out of Daniel, 'cept he's bound to taste nasty. Like dirty socks."

"Oh, yeah?" Daniel retorted, grinning at the game they'd played for years. "Well, you'd taste like an old horse blanket."

"Oh, yeah?" The phone rang, saving Kelly from having to come up with something else that would be revolting enough to tickle a nine-year-old boy without being gross enough to ruin an adult's appetite.

Peg slid the corn-bread pan back into the oven, picked up a wooden spoon and stirred the chili. "Get that, will ya, hon? If it's for me, tell 'em I'll call back after supper."

As she'd done a hundred times before, Kelly cheerfully answered the call. "Haystack Ranch."

"Hello, this is Sheriff Johnson from Pinedale, Wyoming."

Stunned to hear a voice from out of her past, Kelly inhaled a gasp. "Andy? Andy Johnson?"

"Yeah," he replied slowly. "Who's this?"

"It's Kelly. Kelly, uh . . ." She shot a glance at Peg, saw that she was looking out the window and running water in the sink, but automatically lowered her voice, anyway. "Kelly James. Remember me?"

"I sure do," he said, his tone warming enough to tell her he was smiling. "How the heck are ya? And how's that boy?"

"Fine, Andy. We're both doin' fine. I'm the foreman here, and Daniel's gettin' real good grades in school."

"That's great, Kelly. Hey, your dad was back in town a while ago. You haven't had any problems with him, have you?"

"Just a letter. It was forwarded a few times, though, so I don't think he knows where we are."

"Good," Andy said. "Keep it that way. I'm not surprised to hear you're doing so well, Kelly."

She gave a derisive laugh. "Well, you're about the only one in Pinedale who wouldn't be. Everybody else who remembers me probably thinks I'm servin' time somewhere."

"Not everybody. My wife expected great things from you."

A lump formed in Kelly's throat at the memory of Ginny Johnson's kindness to her and Daniel when they lost the ranch. "How is Ginny?"

"Busy chasing after the kids. Was little Bill born yet when you left?"

Kelly shook her head, then, realizing he couldn't see her, said, "Nope. All I remember's a little girl."

"That's Ellie. She's five now, and her little brother's three. They're both hellions, just like their mother."

Despite his words, there was such immense pride in the sheriff's voice, Kelly felt a pang of envy. While she didn't have much use for cops, she considered Andy Johnson to be a true gentleman. Tough, but fair, he'd always treated her with respect. He'd also helped her get custody of Daniel and change their last names when Jay and Johnny were sent to prison.

"That's great, Andy. Congratulations. Now, uh, what can I do for ya?"

"Well, let's see here." She heard a squeak that probably came from his office chair and a crackling noise that sounded like paper rustling. "We've been out of town on vacation and I'm catching up on my phone calls. I was trying to return one from a guy named Steve Anderson. Note says he's a deputy of some kind?"

The man in question chose that moment to enter the kitchen. Wearing a white polo shirt and new jeans, and with his face scrubbed and freshly shaven, and his hair all slicked back from his shower, he exuded a hearty vitality that made her want to...well she wasn't exactly sure what, but it would involve getting close to him. Mighty close.

He smiled when he saw her. His gaze drifted down over her body in an approving once-over, then rose to meet hers. Her heartbeat stumbled for a second before accelerating into over-drive, and she felt her face grow warm. He raised one eyebrow in question. She gulped.

"Kelly?" Andy said. "You still there?"

Suddenly realizing what this call meant, Kelly wrenched her gaze away from Steve. It shouldn't have hurt so much. Hell, she'd *told* him to contact Andy. She just hadn't thought he would actually go ahead and do it. She'd thought he might be starting to trust her.

She had to clear her throat to make her voice work. "Yeah, Andy, hang on. He's right here. Go ahead and tell him whatever he wants to know."

Laying the receiver on its side next to the phone, she looked back at Steve. "It's for you, Marshal."

While he came to take the call, Kelly crossed the room, quietly told Peg she'd lost her appetite and slipped out the back door. She was running away and she knew it, but there was no way she could watch Steve's eyes fill with disgust when Andy told him about her dad and brother.

She paused at the top step of the trailer and looked out over the valley. A lump clogged her throat and her chest felt tight enough to bust wide open. Her eyes burned and a wave of shame scorched her face. But she would not cry, dammit. She'd choke first.

This wasn't a big deal, really. Just another one of those un-pleasant lessons she should have learned a long time ago. Like, life just wasn't fair. Only the good—like her mama—died young. It didn't pay to reach too far above yourself. Like ought to stay with like.

If there were any more clichés to fit the situation she didn't know them. But she did know one thing. If there ever was a man for Kelly James, he sure as hell wouldn't be a lawman.

* * *

The man on the ridge stood, stretching his back and screaming thigh muscles when the woman and the kid went into the main house. Then he lit a cigarette and took a long, hard drag to get some nicotine back into his system. Daniel was one lucky boy to have that old lady feeding him three squares a day. Kelly never could cook worth a damn.

The so-called meals ol' Kelly had slapped on the table were bad enough to gag a maggot on a gut wagon. The slop they'd served in prison had been better. Shaking his head at the memories crowding in on him, he inhaled another deep drag.

Well, he'd watched this place long enough to know all the basic routines. It was just about time for the fun to start. Time for Miss Snot-nose—

The back door slammed open and Kelly charged out like she had a swarm of wasps after her. Dropping back to a crouch, the man quickly stubbed out his smoke and picked up his binoculars. Damn, she was just standing there, looking out over the valley again. *Had* she seen him before? He hadn't thought so, but...

He finally got the binoculars refocused. No, she wasn't just looking. She was holding back tears. He hadn't thought she was human enough to cry, but somebody must have hurt her feelings real bad for her to get upset enough to miss a meal.

Other than the kid, did she care that much about anyone? Like, maybe that big blond dude, for instance? It was an interesting thought. Possibly a useful one. Maybe he'd better watch her a little longer before he took his boy back. And his treasure.

Of course, that didn't mean he couldn't enjoy rattling her cage a little now. Hell, when he got through with her, she'd have a stiff neck from lookin' over her shoulder all the time.

"Damn woman," Steve muttered the next afternoon. Gratefully accepting an ice-cold can of pop from Aunt Peg, he sat on the ground beside the cooler, stretched out his legs and leaned back against the corral fence. He popped the top on the can and guzzled half of its contents, then sighed with satisfaction.

"Got any idea what's eatin' her?" Peg asked, inclining her head toward the other side of the corral.

Steve looked over at Kelly, and had to bite his tongue to keep from cursing in front of his aunt. Kelly had already been working when he'd come down for breakfast at six this morning. It was now four o'clock, and she hadn't stopped once. Not for lunch, or for a cold drink, or even a bathroom break. Since she'd handed him the phone last night, she hadn't spoken a word to him that didn't pertain to branding, either.

Without taking his gaze off her, Steve nodded. "Yeah, I've got an idea."

Peg huffed at him, a sure sign she was struggling to hold onto her patience. "Well, wouldja mind sharin' it?"

"Yeah, I would," Steve said, giving her an irritated glance. "Don't worry, I'll fix it."

"Hmmph!" Peg said. "Looks to me like maybe you already did. I just hope you didn't fix it for good."

Steve hoped so, too. He hadn't meant to hurt Kelly's feelings by calling Andy Johnson, but he obviously had. And, now that he'd talked to the sheriff, he could understand why she'd been so adamant about maintaining her privacy. To an extent. After all, *she* wasn't a criminal, which the sheriff had gone to great pains to make perfectly clear.

What he couldn't understand, however, was why she was practically killing herself with work just because she was angry at him. At the moment, he wouldn't mind shaking her until her teeth came loose and telling her to grow up. Stubborn little cuss.

He'd apologized. Or tried to. More than once. And what had she done? Turned up her nose and pretended she hadn't heard him. Clamped another calf onto the tipping table, turned him onto his side and castrated him with way too much pleasure on her face for any man's comfort. Worked one calf after another with such focused intensity, you'd think she was doing brain surgery.

Dammit, branding was always hard work, but it used to be fun, too. They'd have all the neighbors over and put everybody to work. When the calves were taken care of, they'd sit down to a big potluck dinner, eat and visit and even have a barn dance sometimes.

Now, though, technology had caught up with ranching. You didn't need a whole crew anymore. With a metal squeeze chute for the cows and a tipping table to hold the calves down, propane heaters for the branding irons and vaccine guns, two people could brand, vaccinate, dehorn, tag the ears and castrate the males in short order. And Kelly had been going at it all day long with the ruthless efficiency of a machine.

Steve gulped the rest of his soda, then pushed himself to his feet, slapped the dirt off his butt with his leather gloves and pulled the brim of his hat down to give his eyes more shade. He appreciated Kelly's work ethic, but he'd had about enough of her brooding, humorless attitude. Hell, if he wanted to put up with that, he'd go hang around Secret Service or FBI agents.

As if she sensed a change in the atmosphere, she looked up when he started back across the corral. Since her hat brim was pulled low, too, he couldn't see her eyes, but the tight slash of her mouth and the rigid set to her chin and shoulders told him nothing had improved during his break. Bud, who had stepped in to cover Steve's side of the table, held out the vaccine gun as he approached.

Steve shook his head, walked over to Kelly and pulled on his gloves. "It's your turn for a break," he said, stepping between her and the branding irons.

"I don't want one." Scowling at him, she shifted to one side, as if she planned to go around him. He shifted right with her, intentionally blocking her path. "Now, if you'll get out of my way—"

She shifted the other direction. He followed. Her scowl heated to a glare. "What the hell do you think you're doin'?"

He grinned. "Relieving you of duty. Go have a sandwich and a cold drink. Maybe it'll sweeten your disposition."

"If you don't like my disposition, you can—"

"Ah, ah, ah," Steve said, shaking an index finger at her. "Just sit down for fifteen minutes, will you? We can handle it for that long."

The fury in her eyes made him glad he couldn't read her mind. Not that he really needed to, of course. Man, if looks could kill, he'd be doing some hard and fast repenting. When he didn't flinch or look away, she turned to Bud.

"Will you please tell your nephew to let me do my job?"

Bud's bushy white eyebrows came together in a worried frown. "Well, now, I guess I'll have to side with Steve on this one, hon. You've been workin' so hard, we'll have this job licked in a couple of hours. No need to kill yourself over it, anyhow."

Kelly opened her mouth, closed it. Opened it again. Closed it again. Then she stomped off to the cooler. Chuckling at the steam he could almost see billowing out of her ears, Steve picked up a branding iron and applied it to the calf's hide.

"What the hell's goin' on, Steve?" Bud asked when he'd returned the iron to the heater and picked up the dehorning paste. "This ain't like Kelly. Not at all."

"Well, for one thing, she's acting damned immature."

Bud's gaze sharpened. "What'd you do to her?"

"I didn't do anything. Not really."

"Dammit, Steve, I told you not to upset her."

"Hey, I've already apologized."

"If you didn't do nothin', then why'd you apologize?"

"She'll get over it in a day or two," Steve insisted.

He wasn't nearly as confident as he tried to sound for his uncle's benefit, of course. He hadn't pegged Kelly for a sulker, either, but she'd done a fine job of it today. Damn woman.

The second she stood, crumpled her empty soda can in one fist and squared her shoulders before starting back toward the branding table, Steve knew he was in big trouble. There was something determined about her carriage, her walk, her expression. She'd made a decision. One he wasn't going to like.

As if to confirm his suspicion, she never did look him in the eye again for the rest of the day. She went right back to work as if she'd never stopped and even joined in the small talk at appropriate moments. But when the last calf scampered off to find his mama, and the equipment had been properly stored, she addressed Bud with a sad smile that made Steve's heart plunge to a point somewhere down around his ankles.

"I've really loved workin' for you and Peg, but it's time for Daniel and me to move on."

"Now, hon," Bud said, "if there's a problem, surely we can work it out."

Kelly shook her head. "Don't think so, Bud. Besides, you don't need me since you've got the Marshal here. He's not a bad hand when he tends to business."

"Dammit, Kelly," Steve said, "don't do this. It wasn't personal, you know."

"What wasn't personal?" Bud asked.

"Nothing," Steve and Kelly said simultaneously.

"Well, it sure don't sound like nothin'!" Bud shouted.

Kelly took a deep breath. "Calm down, Bud. Yellin' won't change a thing. We've already stayed longer than I promised when you hired me."

"But I'll be gone in a few weeks," Steve protested. "Hell, I'll leave now, if that's what you want, Kelly."

"My decision's got nothin' to do with you, Marshal. It's just time for us to go. If you'll excuse me, fellas, I've got packin' to do."

Head held high, she walked off toward the trailer, leaving Steve and Bud staring after her in consternation. Then, following a long moment of looking at each other, Bud broke the silence.

"Well, I hope whatever you *didn't* do to her was worth your career, kid. If she leaves, you're not goin' anywhere."

Chapter Six

"I'm not gonna go." Crossing his arms over his chest, Daniel stuck out his chin. "And you can't make me."

"Daniel, please," Kelly said. "Don't make this any harder than it has to be, okay?"

"You haven't given me one good reason we have to leave. Didja have a fight with Bud or somethin'?"

Telling herself an occasional headache was the price she had to pay for teaching the kid to think for himself, Kelly pressed at the throbbing spot over her left eye. "Not with Bud. And it wasn't a fight, exactly."

"You're not makin' any sense, Aunt Kelly."

"All right, I'll tell you the whole thing." Buying a little time to get her thoughts in order, Kelly pushed herself to her feet and strode from Daniel's bed to the open window. This was her favorite time of day, when she could watch twilight settling over the ranch and her love for the land and the animals brought a prayer of thanks to her heart. Dang it, she wanted to stay here as much, if not more, than Daniel did, but there was no help for it.

Shoving her hands into her front pockets, she paced slowly back across the room and sat on the side of Daniel's bed again. "We have to leave because Mr. Anderson did a background check on us. He knows everything."

"So? He won't tell anybody if we ask him not to."

"We can't take that chance, Daniel."

"Why not?" Daniel demanded. "We didn't do anything wrong."

"You know that, and I know that," Kelly agreed softly, "but there's an old sayin' that goes something like, 'If you lay down with the dogs, you're gonna get up with fleas.' When other folks hear about Jay and Johnny, they're just naturally gonna wonder about us, too."

"Well, let 'em wonder," Daniel grumbled. "Besides, my friends wouldn't do that."

Sadly, Kelly shook her head. "This town is even smaller than Pinedale and it's pretty isolated, Daniel. These folks have learned to stick together. As far as they're concerned, we could live here twenty years and still be newcomers. Now, if a crime's ever committed, and everybody knows our dads are convicted felons, who do you suppose they're gonna suspect first?"

"But once they find out we're innocent, it won't matter."

"Not until the next time something happens, and we go right back to the top of the list of suspects again."

Daniel swiped the back of his hand under his nose. "How can you be so sure?"

"I've lived it. I had plenty of friends before Jay went to jail the first time. But it wasn't long after that, every time somebody lost their milk money or misplaced something, they'd all be lookin' at me like I must've stolen it."

"*Every*body?"

Kelly shrugged. "There were enough folks who weren't willing to give me the benefit of the doubt to make my life miserable. It's an awful feeling when other people don't trust you, Daniel. I've always tried to protect you from that."

He rolled his eyes with a real-men-don't-need-protection attitude. Persistence ought to be this kid's middle name. "But couldn't we wait and see if Mr. Anderson tells anyone?"

Again, Kelly sadly shook her head. "He called Sheriff Johnson in Pinedale, and that's where your grandpa's letter came from. If any gossip gets out down there, which it probably will, Jay'll find a way to track us. Besides, now that Mr. Anderson knows about us, I doubt he'll want us to stay here."

"He's not like that," Daniel said.

"He's a *cop*, Daniel. A deputy U.S. marshal. You know what they think of folks like us."

"But I thought you liked him." Daniel gave her a pleading look. "You know, *really* liked him. And I know he likes you. He thinks you're real pretty, anyhow."

Kelly sighed in exasperation. "Hey, I think Anderson's an okay guy, but if you were hopin' for some big romance here, forget it. The guy's a *lawman*, Daniel. It's not meant to be."

"Aw, that's what you always say, even when they're just cowboys." Glaring at her, Daniel jumped off the bed. Then he stomped to the bedroom door and turned around for one last shot at her. "You're the only mom I've got, and I love you, but I want a dad, too."

"Listen, Daniel—"

He cut her off with a shake of his head. "No, *you* listen for once, Aunt Kelly. I've been tryin' to get you a husband for a long time, but you don't even try to look pretty or nothin', and when a guy finally does smile at you, you always chase him off. It looks to me like Johnny's the only dad I'll ever have, so I might as well stay here and hope he'll come find me when he gets out of the slammer."

With that, Daniel ran from the room. Kelly jumped to her feet. "Daniel, come back here right—"

The front door banged open and shut before she could finish the sentence. She started to go after him, then froze when she heard Anderson's voice just outside the window.

"Whoa. Hold on there, kid. Where's the fire?"

"Lemme go," Daniel said, his breath hitching on a sob. "It's all your fault."

Kelly crept to the side of the window and peeked out. Anderson was down on one knee, holding Daniel by the shoulders.

"What's all my fault?" he asked.

"That we have to move again."

"Oh, that." Anderson tipped his hat back on his head and shot a glance at the trailer.

"Are you gonna tell everyone we're crooks?" Daniel asked. "Because our dads are?"

The anxiety in her nephew's voice made Kelly's heart clench and her fingers curl into fists. If Anderson said anything even halfway mean to that kid, she'd beat him to a pulp. She'd kick him from here to Wyoming. She'd—

"No, Daniel, of course not," Steve said, his voice filled with such conviction, Kelly almost believed him. Whether or not it was really true, she would always be grateful he'd said it, if only for Daniel's sake. "In fact, I came out here to see if I couldn't talk your Aunt Kelly out of leaving."

"You mean it?"

The hope in the boy's voice made Kelly's heart clench again. Of all the low down, rotten things to do! Daniel was already mad at her, and now Anderson was going to make her be the bad guy. As if he could hear her furious thoughts, he shot another glance at the trailer. Then he looked back at Daniel and gave him such a warm smile, Kelly's anger faded and a lump grew in her throat.

"I can't promise anything, son, but I'll do my best."

As if they had a will of their own, Daniel's gangly arms reached out and wrapped around the man's neck in a fierce hug. Anderson hugged him right back, closing his eyes as if the boy's affectionate gesture was a bittersweet experience for him. Daniel looked so small in Anderson's big, strong arms. So small and so... safe.

Damn. This was the kind of a man Daniel should have had for a father. A kind, honorable, *responsible* man, who would automatically protect his child. The thought brought the sting of tears to the backs of Kelly's eyes, and she had to turn away from the window or break down and bawl like a newly weaned calf.

"Thanks," Daniel said, his voice a husky whisper.

Then another thought hit Kelly. If she could hear Daniel's soft reply, anyone hanging around outside the trailer would have heard everything she and Daniel had said to each other equally well. Just how long had Anderson been out there? She hadn't heard any footsteps....

Lord, it would be bad enough if he'd heard her talking about her childhood, but if he'd heard any of Daniel's remarks about her chasing away men and getting him a dad, she would die, absolutely die of embarrassment.

"Peg's baking peanut-butter cookies for you." Steve said. "Go on up to the house, now, and leave your Aunt Kelly to me."

"All right! See you later, Mr. Anderson."

The familiar thud of Daniel's boots hitting the ground from the top step sent a herd of butterflies swooping through Kelly's insides. Which was silly, of course. She'd already made the decision to leave. Deep in her heart, she knew it was the right one—the only one she could make. What could Steve Anderson possibly do or say to change it?

Smiling to himself, Steve watched Daniel run off around the corner of the barn. Then he inhaled a deep breath, turned back to the trailer's screen door and gave it three sharp raps. The trailer remained silent. Damn stubborn woman. She knew darn well he was out here, wanting to talk to her.

Obviously, she didn't want to talk to him. Well, that was just too damn bad. It wasn't as if he'd found out anything bad about her, so he didn't see what the hell her problem was. He knocked again. Harder this time.

"I know you're in there, Kelly. You'd better come out and talk, or I'm coming in there after you."

She walked out of the bedroom hallway a moment later and opened the door for him. As soon as he grasped the door handle, she stepped back and gestured toward the living room. "Come on in then, Marshal. Have a seat."

He settled himself on the old sofa. She took the battered wooden rocker, immediately setting it in motion. It made a soft, homey sort of creaking sound, completely at odds with the waves of tension radiating from the woman supplying the power. They stared at each other for what felt like one heck of a long time. Then Kelly finally spoke, her voice quiet, but with an edge sharp enough to cut wood.

"What do you want, Anderson?"

You. The word flashed through his mind so fast, he was afraid he might have said it out loud. Hell, maybe he should have. The truth was, the minute he'd hung up after talking to Sheriff Johnson, any ambivalent feelings he'd still harbored toward Kelly had dropped away like rocks rolling off a cliff.

He liked her. He was attracted to her. He wanted her.

It was as simple as that. The only complication he could see, was that he wasn't sure how far he wanted to pursue a relationship with her or any other woman. Not until he made a decision about his future, anyway.

Long before his dad had died, his mother had started harping that a man in law enforcement had no business having a wife and kids. He didn't agree with his mother about much, but the divorce statistics for cops backed her up in this instance. And frankly, he wasn't sure he was ready to give up law enforcement.

On the other hand, maybe he *was* ready to give it up. Uncle Bud had offered him this ranch, and he thought—even dared to hope—that something more than a physical attraction might develop between him and Kelly. Maybe a lot more. But he had to convince her to hang around long enough to find out. Otherwise, he would never know for certain.

Deciding a direct approach was the only way to convince Kelly of anything, he looked straight into her eyes. Damn, but he hated that deadpan expression of hers. She wore it like a mask to hide her feelings, and right now, it was working great.

"I want to change your mind," he said.

"About what?"

"About a lot of things. For starters, I'd settle for changing your mind about leaving."

"Why?"

"Because it's not necessary."

She raised a skeptical eyebrow at him. "Well, pardon me all to he—ck, but I happen to think it is."

"Your family secrets are as safe with me as they are with Bud and Peg."

Her mouth tightened to a thin line. "How long were you were out there eavesdropping?"

"Long enough to know you're wrong about me. I don't blame innocent people for crimes their relatives commit." When her eyebrow went up again, Steve leaned forward. "Dammit, Kelly, I'm being as straight with you as I know how to be. I've already apologized for hurting your feelings, but I won't apologize for checking you out. I had every right to make sure my aunt and uncle were safe."

"You had to talk to another cop to figure that out?"

"Yeah. I did. It's nothing personal, Kelly."

Her eyes narrowed and she dug her fingers so hard into the chair's wooden arms, her knuckles turned pale against her tanned skin. "Well, pardon me all over again, but it feels *damn* personal when somebody starts snoopin' into your past."

"If you'd told me yourself—"

"Oh, right!" Rocking forward, she used the natural motion of the chair to propel her to her feet. She stood there in front of him, so furious she was trembling all over. "And as soon as I told you my dad and brother were convicted of dealing drugs, you'd have believed I wasn't involved? Just like that?"

It wasn't easy, but he met her fierce gaze without flinching. "Hell, no. I'd have checked out your story from beginning to end. But once I heard the truth from a reliable source, I'd believe it."

"A reliable source, huh?" She snorted, then rolled her eyes toward the ceiling. "What about Bud? His word wasn't good enough for ya? The fact that I've been workin' this ranch for eighteen months wasn't good enough for ya? Workin' right alongside me yourself for almost three weeks wasn't good enough for ya?"

Steve lunged to his feet and bent down until he was nose to nose with her. "That's right. The only reason I'm alive today is that I've learned to be suspicious of anyone and anything that doesn't hit me quite right. You and Bud and even Aunt Peg have been hiding your background from me since I got here. What else did you expect me to do?''

She looked away, her expression as bleak as a gray January day. "Oh, you did exactly what I expected, Anderson. I'd just hoped that for once in my life..." She paused, then slowly shook her head. "Aw, forget it."

Cupping the side of her face with his palm, he coaxed her to meet his gaze again. "I don't want to forget it. What did you hope for, Kelly?"

"That just once, someone would believe in me...trust me without having to check it out with somebody else first."

"I didn't mean to hurt you," Steve murmured. "And it really wasn't personal. I'd have checked out anybody who gave off as many conflicting signals as you did."

She backed up a step. Stuck the tips of her fingers into her back pockets. Made an abrupt, jerky turn toward the kitchen. When she spoke again, her voice sounded as scratchy as if she'd swallowed a wad of steel wool. "Uh-huh. Well, that's real, uh, decent of you, Marshal. Appreciate it."

Swearing under his breath, Steve went after her. "I'm not getting through to you, am I?"

She shot a wary glance over her shoulder. "Yeah, you're comin' in loud and clear."

"But you're still planning to leave." Without waiting for her to agree or disagree, he grasped her shoulders the same way he had Daniel's and turned her back around to face him. Her eyes practically shot blue sparks at him, but this close, he could see other emotions simmering behind the anger. Pain. Humiliation. Fear.

Clamping her lips together as if she didn't trust herself to speak, she nodded.

His own anger melted at the sight of her distress, which, of course, she was still doing her damnedest to hide. Little wretch always acted like she was tougher than an overcooked steak. Knowing what he did now about her background, he could understand why. Guys like Jay and Johnny James would squash anyone who wasn't at least as tough as they were in a heartbeat.

Consciously gentling his hold, he slid his hands down her arms in a slow, caressing motion, softening his voice at the same time. "Aw, Kel, don't look at me like that. Don't you know I'd never willingly do anything to hurt either you or Daniel?"

Her gaze darted away from his and he heard her swallow. He lifted his right hand and stroked her hair back off her face. "Well, you should. Sheriff Johnson told me you've been raising Daniel since he was just a baby. He's a neat kid, Kelly. You've done a great job with him."

She glanced at him then, as if she wasn't sure whether or not to believe his compliment was sincere. "Thanks."

"You're welcome. You showed a lot of character to accept that much responsibility when you couldn't have been much more than a kid yourself. How old were you?"

"Nineteen." She shrugged, but didn't look at him. "I loved Daniel from the first second I saw him. When his mama died, he was just . . . mine."

"What about his dad? Didn't he even try to take care of him?" Steve asked.

Her laugh had a bitter note to it. "He's one of those guys who thinks real men don't change diapers. There was no way I could trust him to take care of Daniel. Then, when Johnny and Jay went to prison, there wasn't anybody else but me to raise him. I wasn't about to let them put him in foster care."

"Daniel was lucky to have you."

Her grin was quick, but wry. "I wouldn't tell him that. Right now he thinks I'm a hag."

"Nobody ever said parents are always supposed to be popular with their kids. It's your job to tick him off now and then."

"Yeah." Uttering a dry chuckle, she pulled out of his grasp, wrapped her arms around her middle and went back to the rocker. "Well, I seem to do that pretty well."

Steve returned to the sofa, sat back and propped his left boot on his right knee. Lacing his fingers together behind his head he studied her until a flush climbed up her neck and into her cheeks. "Don't leave, Kelly. Bud and Peg need you."

"They'll find somebody else. You could probably handle this place on your own if you wanted. Bud would really love that."

"Not if it means losing you and Daniel, he wouldn't. And I can take orders around here, just fine, but I don't know how to run the whole show. If you go, I'm really gonna be in the dog-house."

"Aha," she said with a soft chuckle. "Now we get the real reason you want me to stay."

Steve lowered his hands to his thighs. "That's not the only reason."

"Oh, yeah?"

"Yeah." He leaned forward, braced his elbows on his knees and loosely clasped his hands in between. "You know I'm still attracted to you, Kelly. I'd like to see where that leads."

Her mask slammed back into place. "To a dead end, Anderson. You know that as well as I do."

"Will you stop being so negative? You've got some kind of a hang-up about my being a cop, but it's not that big of a deal. In fact, I'm thinking about retiring."

"How come?"

"It's a long story. I'll tell you about it sometime if you don't leave."

She gave him a chiding look, but there was a tinge of amusement in her eyes. "It doesn't matter what you do, I still can't stay here."

"Why not?"

Biting her lower lip, she studied him. Then, heaving a resigned sigh, she shrugged. "My dad's out on parole and lookin' for us. It'll be the same story with Johnny when he gets out. I don't aim to let 'em find us."

"Are they dangerous?"

"You mean violent?"

Steve nodded.

"I doubt my dad's got the stomach for that," she said after a moment's consideration. "He's more of a manipulator. I mean, he's the one who cooks up a scam and gets other people to carry it out for him."

"And your brother?"

The sadness that came over her face wrenched Steve's heart. "I don't know for sure. Before Mom died, Johnny was an easygoin' kind of a guy. He was never real ambitious, but he wasn't mean, either. Not like he is now."

"Has he threatened you, Kelly?"

"Not directly. Jay's letter said Johnny wants to see Daniel, but I can't let him. That's bound to make him awful mad."

"Can you legally prevent it?"

"Uh-huh. Andy Johnson helped me get custody of Daniel. Johnny doesn't even have visitation rights."

"Is your brother really that bad?" Steve asked.

Kelly nodded, then cleared her throat. "Somethin' happened to him the first time he went to prison that sort of... twisted his mind. Last time I saw him, he didn't seem to have a conscience at all, nor any sympathy for anybody else. I don't want him within a hundred miles of Daniel. My dad, either."

"You really think they'll come here?"

"The U.S. Marshals Service seized our ranch when the DEA found the marijuana patch Jay and Johnny were growin'. They don't have a home anymore, they're lazy as hell and they've got no job skills to speak of. I'd say it's a safe bet that the first time their probation officers get distracted, ol' Jay and Johnny'll show up on my doorstep shortly thereafter."

Steve shrugged. "Well, give them a few bucks and tell them to hit the road."

"They won't be that easy to get rid of. They'll expect me to take care of 'em the way my mom always did and then I did after she died."

"Running's not the answer, though, Kelly. They'll just keep looking for you."

She stopped the rocker's motion and spoke in a tone that left no room for doubt about her sincerity. "Yeah, well, at least if we're somewhere else when they catch up with us, Bud and Peg won't get hurt. Isn't that what you want?"

"Of course, but we can handle this situation without—"

"*We?* Excuse me, Marshal, but this ain't your problem. It's mine, and I'll deal with it."

"I told you I'd be glad to help. The offer still stands. When they see you're not alone and you're really not going to support them, they'll leave. "

"That's possible, I guess," Kelly said, thoughtfully chewing her lower lip. Then she shook her head. "Nah, Johnny's just too unpredictable. I'd never forgive myself if anything happened to Bud or Peg or this ranch."

Steve chuckled. "Aw, come on, Kelly, I was only worried before because I didn't know who or what you were up against. I've dealt with a lot worse than anything your dad and brother are likely to throw at us. Trust me, will you?"

"That doesn't come any easier for me than it does for you, Marshal. And you *don't* understand what I'm up against. Johnny may be crazy, but he's not stupid. I'd never underestimate him."

"When will he be released?"

"I don't have an exact date, but his sentence was longer than Jay's. Even if he keeps his nose clean, I doubt he'll be out before Labor Day."

"Then stay for the summer. Bud and Peg really do need you. And, maybe, after we've worked together all those days, we'll find out this attraction doesn't lead to a dead end after all."

"What if it does?"

"No matter what happens, I promise you'll still have a job here, and I'll help you deal with your dad and brother so you won't have to spend the rest of your life hiding from them."

"That doesn't sound so bad, but the other part about the attraction and all . . ."

She eyed him with such a doubtful expression, he almost laughed out loud. Lord, the way she was looking at him, you'd think he was some kind of an alien.

"I don't know how smart that'd be," she said.

"Hell, I don't, either." Grinning, he stood, reached out and grabbed her hands, then pulled her up onto her feet and into his embrace. "But playing it safe is for sissies, Jaynes, and you're no sissy."

It felt right to hold her again. Right to feel her warmth and breathe in the rich mixture of smells that was Kelly. Right to kiss her while the earth trembled and starbursts of color painted the inside of his eyelids.

Holy smokes, she made him feel so many things, it would take a lifetime to sort them all out and identify them. One minute he wanted to take care of her and spoil her a little, to protect her from the bumps and bruises life brought with it. The next minute all he could think about was getting her strong, gorgeous body naked and rolling across a king-sized bed, making love until they were both too exhausted to squeak.

Reluctantly releasing her luscious mouth, he rested his forehead against hers while he struggled to catch his breath. Then he pulled back and smiled at the bemused expression in her eyes. "We're really gonna hate ourselves if we don't at least give this a shot, Kel. Stay for the summer."

"All right," she murmured, answering his smile with a shy one of her own. "For the summer."

He bent down to kiss her again, but she planted both hands flat against his chest. "Hold on there, Marshal. I agreed to stay, but not to anything else, so don't go gettin' grabby. At best, what we've got goin' here is a truce. Now, turn me loose, will ya?"

Thinking she looked like a hen with her feathers all ruffled, Steve complied with her demand and wisely swallowed the laughter begging for release. As impatient as he felt to get on to the next step in their relationship, he realized Kelly had just made a huge concession. This was undoubtedly one of those times when discretion was the better part of valor. Still, he couldn't resist saying, "But you do want me, Kelly."

Slowly, grudgingly, she nodded. "I s'pose I do."

"You still don't quite trust me yet, though, do you?"

Her shrug could have meant a lot of things. "Should I?"

"Yeah. I know all your secrets and I still want to be your friend. I still want to kiss you and make love with you."

"That's real nice, Anderson," she said with the barest hint of a smile, "but don't push me. If and when I'm ready for that hanky-panky stuff, I'll let you know."

Chapter Seven

Thump. Thump. Thump. The steady rhythm of a basketball hitting the slab of concrete in front of the machine shop echoed the beat of Kelly's heart. She looked up from the tractor carburetor, saw Anderson wipe one hand down his sweaty chest as he watched Daniel dribble the ball closer to the hoop and felt her pulse lurch. Oh, my.

There were chests and then there were *chests,* and Anderson's was prime. It was broad, of course, and muscular, with just enough definition to give it intriguing contours and a dusting of dark hair that tempted her fingers to explore it. The hair arrowed down to the waistband of his jeans, emphasizing the triangular shape of his torso and the leanness of his flanks.

She didn't even want to think about the way his jeans clung to his butt and thighs, but, of course, she did. Especially at night. When she was in bed alone and wishing she wasn't.

And that smile he was giving Daniel—part encouragement, part challenge, part sheer enjoyment—Lord have mercy, had a man ever looked more appealing? Not in recent memory. He—ck, not in long-term memory, either.

She turned back to the tractor, and, not for the first time, found doubts about her decision to stay on at the Haystack crowding into her head. Anderson had been a perfect gentleman since that last kiss. Over the past two weeks he'd made it absolutely clear that any further contact of a sexual nature between them was strictly her decision. Damn his hide.

Thump. Thump. Thump.

Kelly glanced over in time to see him raise his arms to block Daniel's shot, all that chest and torso stretched out and glistening, the waistband of the jeans riding a smidge lower. And such a tantalizing smidge. Oh, *damn* his sexy hide.

Of course, she didn't have to stay here where she could see so much of it. She'd planned to go check on the cows and calves this afternoon, but it was Daniel's last Saturday before school got out. He'd talked Steve into a quick basketball game, and they were having so much fun, Kelly hated to put a stop to it.

After all, the cows weren't gonna die if she got out there a little late. Still, she supposed she could go by herself. But then Steve would undoubtedly insist on coming with her and she didn't want...

He threw back his head and laughed at something Daniel said, then flung his arms out to the sides, running backwards as gracefully as if he had on sneakers instead of boots. Her mouth went dry and she felt a distinct sensation of warmth curling way down in the pit of her stomach. Oh, Lord.

Well, all *right*. Yes, she *did* want Anderson and his damn, sexy hide. She wanted to stop being tormented by her toes curling and her palms and fingertips itching to feel his warm skin and his hard muscles. She wanted to touch him, dammit. She wanted to fill all those aching, empty places inside of her she'd never even realized she owned. She wanted to find out what it felt like to be a woman.

A real woman.

If only she wasn't so scared. Not that he would hurt her—she'd heard the first time wasn't always much fun, but she was tough, and she'd never seen Anderson act any way but gentle. What worried her was the prospect of making a fool of herself.

Unbelievable as it seemed, here she was, pushing thirty, and she didn't know the first thing about sex. Oh, she knew the mechanics, of course; she'd worked around animals her whole life, hadn't she? There wasn't a thing about reproduction for cattle, horses, chickens, dogs or cats she hadn't observed, discussed bluntly and at length—in mixed company, no less—and even, when the occasion required, assisted.

She just didn't know much about how people did it. She didn't own a TV and rarely went to movies. When she did get to see a movie, she always had Daniel along. His tastes didn't exactly run to romances, and she wouldn't have let him watch a bunch of steamy sex, anyhow.

Most of the books she read were nonfiction, usually something to do with agriculture or training animals, so they were no help, either. Despite Peg's shameless matchmaking, there was no way Kelly would consider asking her for advice about sex when the man in question was her beloved Stevie-boy. It would feel too... indecent.

Anderson would think she was pathetic if he knew how ignorant she was about pleasing a man in bed. She supposed she could always ask him what he liked, but what if he told her and she didn't have a clue what he meant? She would die of mortification.

Thump. Thump. Thump.

Speaking of indecent! There ought to be a law against a grown man running around half-naked like that. It'd serve him right if she was overcome with lust sometime, jumped his bones out behind the barn and had her way with him. The mental picture that thought created made her chuckle. She didn't think he'd work very hard at fighting her off. In fact, once he figured out what she was trying to do, he might just take over and *show* her what he liked. Right?

Well, why not go for it? Anderson was the nicest man she was likely to meet anytime soon. If she was ever gonna try sex, she'd just as soon do it with him as anyone else. Since they both knew she'd be leaving before fall, nobody would get hurt when the relationship ended. And, while she didn't think he was the kind to talk about his sex life, it wouldn't matter much if he did because she and Daniel would be long gone before any gossip could get around.

Yeah. Why *not* go for it?

She glanced at him again. Breathing hard, he had his legs bent a little, his hands on his knees and a grin as wide as Montana. Daniel grinned back, feinting to the left, then to the right. Anderson stayed with him, the muscles in his butt and thighs shifting at every change of direction. And he was moving, moving, always moving.

Then he struck, stripping the ball from Daniel's hands, pivoting and sinking a basket in one smooth, seemingly unhurried motion that left the boy gaping.

"Who was that masked man?" Kelly muttered, wondering if, despite all her self-assurances to the contrary, Anderson might not steal her heart as easily as he'd just stolen Daniel's basketball.

Well, tough. Nobody died of a broken heart. If and when that happened, she'd handle it like she did everything else. And so what if she was still a virgin? She was a take-charge kind of a gal, wasn't she? Damn straight. Next time she went to the library, she'd just read up on human sex in the *S* volume of the encyclopedia. How hard could it be to figure it all out?

"Come on, Harry, don't be shy, hon. Look at those gals, all ready and eager for ya to take care of 'em. Get in there and act like a sex machine."

The massive Hereford bull snorted at Kelly, then turned his rump on her and forged a path through the pasture at a dignified walk. A younger bull started to follow, but Kelly and Babe blocked his path and headed him off in a different direction.

"No, Ferdinand," Kelly said, waving a coiled rope at his nose. "Your harem's over thataway. Go on, now and show 'em what a stud you are. If you don't get busy, Harry'll wander back over here and steal all your prettiest heifers."

Ferdinand gave her a baleful look, but ultimately lost the stare-down contest and lumbered off. A third bull tried to follow Ferdinand, and again, Kelly and Babe intervened, directing him to another corner of the pasture. Toro trotted off with no argument, even strutting his stuff, so to speak, for the cows' benefit. Then he walked right past the cows, plunked himself down under a cottonwood tree and swatted flies with his tail.

Snickering at the rude remark Kelly yelled at Toro, Steve opened the pasture gate, let her out and closed it again.

"Cruel woman," he said. "Poor old Toro's going to have performance anxiety for the rest of his life."

Kelly grinned. "Bulls don't get performance anxiety. Only human males do that."

She turned back toward the bull pen and nudged Babe into a trot. Steve gave Reload his head, and quickly caught up with her, occasionally glancing sideways to feast his eyes on the woman who'd been driving him nuts for two solid weeks. She'd warned him not to push her, and he hadn't.

But it hadn't been easy.

Call him egotistical, but he didn't buy her acting as if, as far as she was concerned, they were just good pals. For one thing, he couldn't forget the kisses they'd already shared, and he didn't believe she could, either. For another, whenever she thought he wasn't paying any attention to her, she watched him constantly.

She was so subtle about it, most guys wouldn't have noticed, but his profession had forced him to develop better peripheral vision than most people. He had also worked harder than most men at learning to read other people's body language for clues to their emotions. His survival, and that of the witnesses he'd been assigned to protect, had often depended on his ability to sense any hostility that might signal an imminent attack.

He wasn't sensing hostility from Kelly, though. There was interest. Wariness. Plenty of frustration. But mostly, when he caught her looking at him, he got an impression of longing. Intense longing. It wasn't hard to recognize it, because he felt the same thing every time he looked at her.

Stubborn woman. Why was she fighting the attraction she felt for him so hard? It was driving him bonkers to wait for her to make the first move in deepening their relationship, especially when he knew he could probably coax her into his bed with a few kisses. The only reason he'd been able to behave himself this long was that she seemed to be expecting him to seduce her.

He didn't want a relationship based on seduction. He wanted her to trust him completely, and he wanted her to want him as fiercely as he wanted her. If he ever had another serious relationship with a woman, he wanted what Anne and John Miller had together.

Anne. He had loved and protected her and Chad for seven years. He only had to think of their names and the ache of loss returned, a gaping wound that even time had refused to heal. What he wouldn't give to see Anne smile at him again. To hear Chad laugh again. Just to be with them again for an hour or a day, and know he was as important to them as they were to him.

It had devastated him to watch Anne go back to her real family, to the ex-husband and daughters she'd been forced to leave behind for their safety's sake. Despite a divorce on paper, however, Anne and John had been equally devoted to their children, equally in love with each other, equally committed to being lifetime mates. Once they finally admitted that, there was no hope for Steve or anyone else to have a prayer of coming between them.

Yeah, when all of the chips had finally landed, Anne and John had shared a rock-solid faith in and loyalty to each other, and their relationship was so strong, Steve couldn't imagine anything besides death that could ever end it. He hadn't been able to help feeling admiration for them, and he'd left knowing that they truly did belong together.

Unfortunately, that didn't mean he'd gotten over losing the two most important people in his life. He'd begun to believe that he never would until he'd come back to the Haystack and met Kelly. Which was why he couldn't wait for her to stop pretending she didn't feel anything special for him.

Kelly gave him hope that it wouldn't always hurt so much. She was the first woman he'd met in two long and lonely years who could make him forget about Anne and Chad for hours, even days at a time. Each new morning at the Haystack was an adventure waiting to happen, and for him, the excitement started the moment Kelly walked into Aunt Peg's kitchen for breakfast.

She was bossy, stubborn and unpredictable as hell. He never knew what would come out of her mouth next, and he'd long since learned that she would do, or at least try to do, almost anything if she thought it would improve the operation of the ranch. After years of working undercover, she was more to him than a breath of fresh air. She was a cleansing breeze of honesty, with healthy doses of earthy humor and innocence on the side.

The horses settled back to a steady walk, and Kelly eventually broke the easy silence. "Say, uh, Anderson. I've got a question for ya."

Thinking her voice sounded a tad strained, Steve studied her closely, intrigued to note a hint of a blush coloring her cheeks. She shot him a glance that had a definite nervous edge to it, intriguing him even more. The Kelly he knew rarely searched for something to say; she either kept her mouth shut or blurted out whatever was on her mind.

"Yeah, what is it?" he asked.

She cleared her throat. Fidgeted in the saddle. Shot him another nervous glance. "Well, um, ya know, Daniel's goin' campin' with Ronnie Cooper's family for the weekend, and Bud and Peg are drivin' up to Kalispell this afternoon for that fiftieth-anniversary party they're goin' to. They're gonna drop Daniel off on their way out of town, and I'll, uh, pick him up around noon on Monday...."

Her voice trailed off and she tightened her grip on the reins as if she was trying to strangle them with her bare hands. Babe danced sideways, and Kelly flushed and eased up. Hardly daring to hope he knew where she might be headed with this line of talk, Steve gave her an encouraging nod.

"And..." he prompted when she still didn't continue.

"And, well...we're, uh, gonna have the whole place to ourselves, so I thought maybe, ya know, ya might wanna come out to the trailer after we get the chores done, and I'll heat up a couple of those dinners Peg's put in the freezer for me and Daniel when she has to be gone."

Disappointment crushed his growing elation like a ton of manure landing on a wildflower. A moment later, however, it occurred to him that there was no reason for Kelly to get so nervous about inviting him over if the only thing she had in mind was supper. He gave her what he hoped was a sexy smile.

"Sounds like fun, Kel. I'll run into Wisdom after we get home and buy a bottle of wine at one of the bars."

Her cheeks turned a shade pinker and she choked the poor reins again. Babe shook her head in warning, but Kelly didn't appear to notice. "That'd be real, uh . . . nice, Anderson."

Interesting. Intending to ask whether they were having chicken or beef, Steve opened his mouth, but didn't get even a syllable out before Kelly halted Babe, then backed the mare up five feet. Cursing under her breath, she dismounted and jogged toward the fence running beside the county road.

Steve climbed off Reload and started after her, finally spotting the section of fence leaning slightly off kilter that must have caught her attention. He turned back to his saddle bags, grabbed some tools and started off again, looking up just in time to see her reach out and tug at a wooden post.

A sharp cracking sound startled a flock of magpies into flight. To Steve's horror, a second crack split the air, followed immediately by a third. Then the three posts closest to Kelly broke off at the base. Steve dropped the tools and ran, praying he could reach her fast enough to prevent a disaster.

The section of fence bounced, then flipped end over end. One of the posts clipped the side of Kelly's head, knocking her backwards into Steve's low-flying tackle. Wrapping both arms tightly around her, he lunged away, rolling again and again, trying to protect the back of her head with his hands.

At the first metallic ping, he flung himself facedown on top of her, desperately covering as much of her body as he could. More pings followed. Steel staples ripped out of the wooden posts and rained onto his back like small pieces of shrapnel. Then the strands of barbed wire snapped with three distinct pops and lashed through the air with a low, almost musical, whanging sound guaranteed to chill a cowboy's blood.

Steve felt Kelly flinch beneath him, but before he could ask what was wrong, the tip of one thrashing wire dug a fiery trench across his left shoulder. Eyes shut tight, teeth gritted, he rode out the pain. By the time he could breathe normally again, the wire had turned its lethal energy in on itself and lay in a tangled rat's nest barely two feet away.

Gingerly raising himself onto his hands and knees, Steve looked down at Kelly. She lay on her side, facing away from him, reminding him of a broken doll. He touched the side of her neck and quickly found her pulse. Okay, her heart was beating. And she was breathing. Breathing was good.

"Kelly. Kelly, can you hear me?"

No response. A sick feeling invaded his gut. He didn't see any obvious cuts or bruises, but she'd taken a vicious hit from that post. He could do basic first aid, but, God, he hoped she didn't have a serious head injury. And he hadn't exactly been careful when he'd tackled her and then jumped on top of her. What if he'd broken one of her ribs and it had pierced a lung? They were so far from help....

He squeezed her shoulder. "Kelly? Sweetheart, talk to me."

No response. Ordering himself to think, dammit, he swept his gaze down over her again and felt his chest tighten when he saw that her shirt sleeve was bloody and torn on the inside of her right forearm. Since the blood was oozing rather than spurting, her arm would keep for a while.

"Kelly, wake up." He brushed her bangs back off her forehead and found a nasty bruise swelling beside her hairline. To his relief, she muttered in protest and rolled onto her back. "That's right, honey. Come on, now, and open those gorgeous eyes for me."

She blinked, shook her head, then winced and closed her eyes. "What the hell? Anderson?"

"Yeah, it's me. Where do you hurt?"

"Where *don't* I hurt?" she grumbled. "Damn, I've got dirt in my mouth."

Steve smiled at her cranky tone. Anybody who could sound so thoroughly peeved was going to make it. "Me too," he said.

"If you'll promise not to move, I'll get the first-aid kit and a canteen."

She raised her head an inch off the ground, winced again and laid her head back down with a soft moan. "No problem. I'm not goin' anywhere."

He climbed to his feet, inhaling a sharp, hissing breath when his shirt rubbed over the wound on his shoulder. Kelly's eyelids opened. Squinting against the sunshine, she frowned up at him. "You all right, Anderson?"

"I'm fine. Lie still, now. I'll be back."

But he wasn't fine. He'd always been Mr. Cool in a crisis; God knew he'd handled enough of them. Gunshot wounds. Bombs. Arson fires. He'd dealt with them all and never lost his composure.

Today, though, his concentration was scattered like buckshot. He dropped the first-aid kit twice. When he finally got it tucked under his arm, his palms were almost too sweaty to hang onto the canteen's strap. Damn, what was the matter with him? He wasn't hurt *that* bad. He'd never been this shaky, not even when Anne had been shot. By the time he got back to Kelly, however, he had himself under control enough to function.

He helped her sit up and rinse out her mouth. He wet his handkerchief and washed the grime off her face. The knot on her forehead looked better than he'd expected, and he silently congratulated himself on maintaining a professional manner.

Then he tried to pull back her bloody shirtsleeve and damn near had a heart attack when she jerked away, spewing a stream of obscenities that would have shocked a prison guard before she keeled over in a dead faint.

Using the last inch of water to loosen the torn fabric, Steve peeled away the cloth and grimaced in sympathy. The wound hadn't bled all that much, but the barbed wire had ripped open several inches of tender flesh. His hands shaking again, he squirted antibiotic cream into the gash and wrapped a strip of gauze around it.

Then he pulled her into the shade of a tree, climbed onto Reload's back and rode like hell for the ranch. She was conscious again by the time he'd called a neighbor for help and got back to Kelly with a pickup. Of course, she tried to give him an argument about going to the doctor, but he was in no mood to listen.

Ignoring her protests, he ground-tied Babe, then scooped Kelly into his arms, dumped her onto the passenger seat, fastened her seat belt and took off for Hamilton.

"Mr. Anderson?"

Steve looked up from the ancient magazine he'd found in the hospital waiting room. Tammy, the plump, middle-aged nurse who had assisted the doctor in tending to his shoulder stood in the doorway. Her anxious expression brought him to his feet. "Is Kelly all right?"

Tammy gave him a strained smile. "She will be. She's being a little...difficult, though, and Dr. Edwards would like you to talk with her?"

Gritting his teeth, Steve nodded and followed Tammy down a hallway. The emergency room staff had his complete sympathy. If there was a more cantankerous patient alive than Kelly Jaynes, he obviously had never visited this particular hospital. No need to ask which treatment cubicle Kelly was in; all he had to do was follow the strident sound of her voice.

"No way, Doc. Go ahead and sew that sucker up."

"Ms. Jaynes, please. I am not in the business of torturing my patients."

"Dammit, I'm *really* tough. I'll hardly even notice a few stitches."

"No shot, no stitches." The doctor's voice sounded weary and exasperated. "I've already given up on convincing you to see a reconstructive surgeon. You do understand there will be a significant scar?"

"I've got plenty of significant scars. One more ain't gonna make any difference."

"Please, Ms. Jaynes, in my opinion—"

Dropping half an octave, Kelly's voice took on a dangerous edge. "Listen, you sawed-off little runt. Since I'm the one that's gonna have to pay the damn bill for this, *my* opinion is the only one that counts. I got more important things to do than hang around this dive, so either start sewing, or get the hell outta my way.''

"Really, Ms. Jaynes—''

Steve rapped on the door and entered the tiny room. Kelly sat on an examination table, her arm propped on a pillow in her lap. Dr. Edwards barely looked old enough to be a college kid, and his shaggy hair and black, horn-rimmed glasses made him look even younger. And he *was* kind of a sawed-off little runt. Too bad they hadn't given Kelly the same, gruff old guy he'd had, Steve thought, shifting his gaze to her mulish expression.

"What's the problem?'' he asked.

Kelly started at the sound of his voice, then flashed him a smile of welcome and inclined her head toward the doctor. "Aw, he wants to pump me full of drugs and I don't need 'em.''

Steve ambled to the examination table, leaned over Kelly's arm and sadly shook his head. "Man, oh, man, I've seen steaks that weren't hurt that bad. Do you really want him to poke around in there without a little something to numb the pain?''

"Don't start with me, Anderson.''

Steve went on as if she hadn't spoken. "You know, if you don't like this guy, I'll be glad to drive you to Missoula. I know the ranch's insurance will cover the bill for a plastic surgeon. Bud would want you to get this fixed right.''

"Forget it. I have chores to do, dogs to feed, and we've probably got cows all over the road.''

"I already called Bobby McCrea and he's going to cover all of that for us,'' Steve said. "There's no reason you can't have the best treatment available. Unless maybe you're scared of a little old needle.''

She stiffened, and her eyes glinted with irritation. "And I suppose you just love 'em, huh?''

Gotcha, Steve thought. Casually folding his arms across his chest, he turned just enough to give her a glimpse of the torn, bloody patch on his shirt.

Kelly gasped. "What happened to your shoulder?''

"Same thing that happened to your arm.'' He turned back to face her. "But I already got my stitches, and I could go home if you'd stop being such a coward.''

Kelly looked away, shut her eyes tight and swallowed hard. When she looked back at Steve, she had an intense expression he would have called pleading if it had been on anyone else's face. Kelly was too damn proud and stubborn to plead.

"I'm not afraid of the needle. I just get really...goofy whenever I have anything stronger than an aspirin. I don't like bein' out of control."

Steve's heart contracted at her quiet admission. Tucking two fingers under her chin, he coaxed her into meeting his gaze. "I can handle goofy, but I can't handle seeing you hurt, Kel. Won't you trust me to take care of you for a few hours?"

"Well, who's gonna drive home?" she demanded. "If you already got your stitches, you must've had a pain shot, and—"

"I did, but it didn't make me goofy at all. Besides, you've been hassling these folks so long, it's already wearing off. If you won't let me take you to Missoula, then just get on with it, all right?"

She studied him for what seemed like an endless moment, then slowly nodded. "All right. Just don't say I didn't warn ya."

Chapter Eight

"Wh-o-o-oa, Nellie. Wouldja get a loada that *sunset*, Marshal? I don' think I *ever* saw *any*thing that pretty b'fore. Did *you* ever see anything that pretty b'fore?" Kelly asked. She turned her head to look at Anderson, and felt her smile widen all by itself. " 'Cept for your eyes, maybe. Didja know you've got damn pretty eyes for a man, Marshal? 'Cept for when ya get mad or suspicious, ya know? Then they get all sorta squinty and mean-lookin'. Scares the livin' hell out me, didja know that?"

"No, but I'll try not to do it anymore," he said.

There was laughter in his voice, but that was okay. At the moment, he could have called her a jackass, and it would've been just fine and dandy. Damn fool doctor.

That first little shot of novocaine, or whatever it was had made her giggly. She'd *told* him that second shot—the Demerol one that *he* insisted would calm her down—would only make her weirder, but would he listen? *Oooh*, no. An' ol' Anderson hadn't helped her a bit, either. He'd stood there an' sweet-talked her into lettin' that sawed-off little runt stick her again.

So, here she was in happy land, actin' like she'd been on a booze-guzzlin' binge, an' he was just gonna have to put up with her whether he wanted to or not. Right? Damn straight.

The pickup stopped rolling. While she struggled to find her bearings, Anderson came around, opened the door for her and took hold of her arm to help her get out. What a guy. Actin' like a gentleman for a rough ol' cob like her. Made her want to just kiss his whole face.

Before she could do that, though, her knees and feet decided to go ever' which way, an' she prob'ly would've fallen if he hadn't put his arm around her, God love him. He started half-draggin', half-carryin' her toward the trailer. Oh, yeah, they were home. Damned if that hadn't been one fast trip to Hamilton and back.

For no particular reason, that fact tickled her funny bone, and she laughed until she heard Wild Bill let out a piteous howl. Well, the poor baby'd been locked up all day. At least, she thought he had. Wyatt, too. And just what the hell had they done with Pat Garrett? She'd swear in court he'd been helpin' 'em move those bulls.

Wrenching away from Anderson, she staggered off toward the dog run. He caught up with her, of course. After all, *he* wasn't drugged to the gills.

"Hey, Kel, where are you going?" He grabbed her by the shoulders and wouldn't turn her loose no matter how hard she twisted and thrashed.

"Can'tcha hear ol' Billie?" she demanded. "He's cryin' like a baby. Don'tcha know ya always gotta take care of the babies, An'erson?"

"It's okay, sweetheart. I'll do it for you, just as soon as we get you tucked into bed."

Letting her head flop back against his chest, she smiled and batted her eyelashes up at him. "Okay, *sweetheart.* Whatever you say. You gonna tuck yourself in with me?"

He snorted with laughter and muttered something that sounded kinda like, "Don't tempt me." Then he hauled her up the stairs and into her living room. It seemed like a perfectly reasonable thing to do, to turn around, wrap her arms around his waist and lay her head on his chest. God, but she loved his chest. He was so nice and warm and . . .

"Kelly, honey, you can't go to sleep just yet."

"I ain't sleepin', Marshal, *honey*. I'm workin' up the nerve to seduce ya."

He made a choking sound that worried her. Tilting her head back she studied his face, then grinned at his stunned expression. Looked sorta like a beached trout.

"Well, see, when you an' Daniel were playin' basketball, I decided I was ready for that hanky-panky stuff," she said. "Did I ever tell ya I *really* like your chest?"

He cleared his throat. "No, uh, you never did."

"Well, I do. You knew it, too, you damned hussy, always takin' your shirt off in front of me. Well, I should hope to shout, it worked. Got my poor ol' hormones all riled up and now they just won't settle back down. So, I was gonna feed ya one of Peg's frozen dinners, an' then kinda . . . *lure* ya into my bedroom. Pretty good plan, don'tcha think?"

He cleared his throat again and peeled her off of him. "It was a great plan, sweetheart. And I'm really flattered, but right now, I've got to go check on the dogs, and make sure Bobby did all the chores." Leading her over to the sofa, he pushed her down into a sitting position. "I'll be back in a few minutes. You stay right there, okay?"

"Okay, *sweetheart*. I'll seduce ya when ya come back and tuck me in."

Grinning real big, he backed toward the front door. "Well, you might want to hold off on that a little while, Kelly. At least until those drugs wear off. We'll talk about it later."

"Sure thing, Stevie-boy."

The next thing she knew, he was gone. She rested her head back against the sofa and closed her eyes. Thump. Thump. Thump. It might've been her pulse pounding in her head, but damned if it didn't sound like a basketball hitting concrete. A vision of Anderson playing with Daniel danced behind her eyelids.

Her heart sped up and her breath shortened. Her toes curled and her palms grew damp. Her fingertips itched. Hormones. Yup, it was hormones, all right.

Hell, she'd wanted him long before they pumped her full of drugs, hadn't she? Damn straight. She was prob'ly already the oldest living virgin in America, so why wait? Since she couldn't think of a single good reason, she pushed herself to her feet, waited for the room to stop weaving, then used her wobbly legs to get to her bedroom. She had preparations to make.

Torn between laughter and fear that he wouldn't know how to help Kelly through this bizarre, drug-induced behavior, Steve quickly took care of the dogs and checked around to make sure all was well. He needn't have worried. Bobby McCrea was a good rancher and a great neighbor, and he'd done a fine job of looking after the Haystack.

When he returned to the trailer, Steve paused for a moment and took a deep breath to fortify himself. God only knew what he'd find inside, because Kelly hadn't been kidding when she'd said painkillers made her goofy. Lord, goofy didn't even begin to describe what those drugs had done to her. It was as if every inhibition she'd ever possessed had been erased.

It would have been hilarious—hell, at times on the way home, she'd been so funny he'd practically driven off the road—if he didn't feel so responsible. But he *was* responsible. He hadn't listened to her, and he'd promised to take care of her, and that was exactly what he intended to do. If he had any luck at all, she would have passed out by now. The way her thoughts had been jumping around in the pickup, like a grasshopper leaping from one weed to the next, surely she would have, at the very least, forgotten her plan to seduce him. Please, God, make her forget she ever said anything about that, at least until she sobered up.

Taking another deep breath, he opened the door and stepped into the entryway. The living room was empty. So was the dining nook. And the kitchen. And it was quiet. After listening to Kelly's wild, rambling chatter for so long, and expecting to hear more of the same as soon as he opened her front door, the silence unnerved him.

His heart climbed into his throat and sweat broke out on his forehead. She'd been drugged. Confused. He shouldn't have left her alone.

He looked down the narrow hallway toward the bedrooms. The door to Kelly's room was closed, but he could see a light shining under the bottom edge. Maybe she'd gone to bed.

Indecision paralyzed him. If she was asleep, he *really* didn't want to wake her up. On the other hand, he *had* to be sure she was all right. Oh, damn, he was acting like an idiot. All he had to do was walk down there, knock on the door and ask if she was okay.

So why didn't he just do it?

Because he really didn't think Kelly was asleep.

Because he hoped like hell she hadn't forgotten her plan to seduce him.

Because he wanted her so much, he didn't know if he had the strength to be noble if she hadn't.

But, of course, he *had* to be noble. Damn woman was going to drive him stark, raving nuts.

Muttering under his breath, he strode down the hall and tapped softly on her door. "Kelly? You all right?"

"Door's open."

God help him, there was a sultry note in her voice he'd never heard before. He reached out, turned the knob, gave the door a push. And there she was, sitting on the side of her bed, carefully laying out strips of some kind on the nightstand.

A small lamp clamped onto the headboard of her double bed illuminated the room with a warm, rosy light. Freed from its usual ponytail, her hair hung below her shoulders in soft, shining waves. With her head lowered and a serious expression on her face, she looked younger, somehow. More vulnerable. In need of protection and tenderness.

Then she glanced up and flashed him a smile that made his mouth go dry. Uh-oh. She hadn't forgotten anything.

"Come on in, Marshal. How're my babies?"

He stopped just inside the doorway, propping his good shoulder against the casing. "Babies?"

"Wild Bill? Wyatt Earp? Pat Garrett?"

"Oh, they're, uh . . . fine, Kel. How about you?"

"Feelin' no pain, an' it's a good thing, too." Grinning, she shook her head and turned her attention back to the strips. "I got these when I was down in Dillon pickin' up that tractor part last week. Ya know, when you and Bud took Daniel to that Boy Scout picnic? I didn't know what kind you liked best, so I bought a variety. Lady at the checkout counter at the grocery store looked at me like I was one can shy of a six-pack."

"What are you talking about, Kelly?"

"Lord, I was sooo embarrassed, but I just brazened it out." She giggled. "I'm kinda partial to these glow-in-the-dark colored ones, myself, but it's your choice."

"Kelly—"

She giggled again, cutting him off. Two seconds later he couldn't remember whatever he'd been going to say, because she stood, unfastened her belt buckle and the metal button at the waistband of her jeans. Then she pulled out her shirttail and opened the front of her work shirt with the well-practiced yank of someone used to wearing Western clothing. The pearl snaps gave way with a series of pops that sounded like firecrackers in Steve's ears.

He should stop her. He knew he should stop her before she went one bit further, but he felt even more paralyzed than he had out in the entryway. Seemingly oblivious to his presence, Kelly unfastened her cuffs, shrugged out of the torn and bloody garment and tossed it at a straight chair.

Of course, his body couldn't help but respond to the sight of her. Her arms and shoulders were neither soft nor delicate. In fact, her whole body had strong, clean lines, honed down to muscle and sinew from years of hard, physical work. None of that surprised him, and he thought she was absolutely beautiful.

Her white cotton bra had been chosen for support, not seduction, but it made her breasts look full and lush. It wasn't that they were so awfully large, as much as that they were so, well...rounded compared to the rest of her. She sat on the side of the bed and bent forward to yank off her boots, giving him a glimpse of cleavage that would have done a centerfold proud.

He must have made some kind of noise, maybe a groan or a moan, because she looked up again as she pulled off her second boot. She tossed it aside, then standing, she braced her stockinged feet wide apart and tipped her head to the left, frowning at him in confusion.

"What's wrong, Anderson?"

Unwilling to take his gaze off her for even half a second, he slowly shook his head. "Not a blessed thing." Now the jeans, he thought, silently urging her to show him the white cotton panties he just knew she had to be wearing.

As if she'd heard his request by mental telepathy, she reached for her jeans zipper, but paused with one hand on the tab. "Aren'tcha gonna take your clothes off?"

"Take my clothes off?"

She propped her hands on her hips and grinned at him. "Well, you gotta get naked to do it, don'tcha? At least your bottom half."

God, she was gorgeous. He could stand here for hours and just look at her. "Do what, sweetheart?"

"Oh, ya big silly! Here I've been tryin' my damnedest to seduce ya." She turned to the night stand, picked up one of the strips and waved it at him. "I even boughtcha these condo...condu....hell, you know what I mean. These condominium thingies. So, what's the deal, here, Anderson? Ya wanta have sex with me or not?"

Steve gulped. "Of course I do, but—"

Giggling, she sashayed up to him, grasped the front of his shirt and coaxed him farther into the room. "You're not gonna turn shy on me now, are ya?"

His own shirt snaps gave way to her strong fingers, and she was stroking him through his chest hair, making him so hard he hurt. "Well, no, but—"

"Then get those duds off and—"

"Wait a second." He captured her hands before she could go after his pants. "Not like this, Kel."

She gave him a perplexed look. "How else *is* there, Marshal? The encyclopedia didn't have any pictures, but don't you just sorta strip down and get on with it?"

"Sometimes," he said, wondering what the hell the encyclopedia had to do with whatever was going on in her poor, drugged brain, "but I think most women like it better if you take things a little slower."

"How long do you usually take?"

He choked back a startled laugh. Leave it to Kelly to be earthy and matter-of-fact about the subject of sex. "It just...depends. Are you always in this much of a hurry?"

She shrugged, then smiled and shook her head. "Gee, I dunno. It seemed like a good idea to get it over with before the shot wears off, is all."

If this conversation got any weirder, he was going to call that idiot doctor in Hamilton. "Before the shot wears off?"

"So it won't hurt," she said.

"Hurt? To have sex?"

"Doesn't it usually? When it's your first time, I mean?"

"Your first time?" He gulped. "Are you telling me this is your *first* time?"

Sighing, she rolled her eyes. "Have you always been this slow, Anderson? Or did that sawed-off little runt give you a second shot, too?"

That did it. Steve tipped back his head and roared with laughter.

"Shut up, Anderson."

He tried to stop. He really did. Especially when she pulled away from him, grabbed her ruined shirt off the chair and put it on with stiff, jerky motions. But her perplexed looks, those absolutely ingenuous questions and all those strips of "condominium thingies" on the nightstand—combined with one hell of a long, hard, emotional day, they all reached out and tickled him without mercy, and the laughter ripped out of him until his sides ached and his eyes leaked tears at the corners.

Her snaps popped back together like hail on a tin roof. "Get the hell outta my bedroom, Anderson. Get outta my house. Get outta my life."

"Now, Kelly—"

"Shut up." She grabbed his arms, aimed him at the doorway and helped him along with a quick, hard shove. "Forget the whole damned thing and don't ever talk to me again."

"Dammit, Kelly, knock it off." Steve dug his heels into the worn carpet and hung onto both sides of the doorjamb. "I didn't mean to hurt your feelings."

"Where you're concerned, I don't have any feelings." She shoved him again, but this time he didn't move, even though his wounded shoulder was starting to hurt like hell.

"Yes, you do." When she stopped trying to shove him, he turned around and grabbed her hands before she could take a swing at his head. "Now, stop that. We've both got stitches that'll pull out if you keep this up, honey."

"Don't call me honey, you sorry SOB." She twisted and squirmed and pummeled his shins with her stockinged feet. "I may not be much of a lady, but I'm not a slut, 'n' you got no call to laugh at me 'cause I'm still a virgin. It ain't like nobody's ever wanted me, ya know. Dammit, turn me loose or I'll kick your butt so far up between your ears—"

Steve felt as if he had the proverbial tiger by the tail. A murderous rage flashed from her eyes, and he didn't dare let go of her. While she wasn't as strong as he was, she was no wimp, either, and he had a strong suspicion she wasn't above fighting dirty. So, he did the only thing he could think of at the moment.

He kissed her.

Right in the middle of a string of cusswords that would have made his aunt run for a bar of soap, he swooped down and planted his mouth on top of hers.

As if stunned by his audacity, she went absolutely still for a second. But a second was all he needed to get his arms around her and pull her flush against his chest. She jerked her head back and inhaled a deep breath, and he kissed her again. With a little more finesse and passion, if he did say so himself.

Her body softened against him. Her arms slid up around his neck. Her lips parted on a sigh.

But when he flicked his tongue across her lower lip, he tasted salt and realized she was weeping. Tenderness for this woman swamped him. She'd had a miserable day, too. She didn't need kissing or sex or an argument at this moment. She needed peace and quiet and a chance to get her emotions back on an even keel while the drugs finished wearing off.

Cautiously backing up, he coaxed her along with him until he felt the bed behind him. She resisted when he sat on the edge of the mattress again and tried to pull her down beside him.

"It's all right," he said. "I promised I'd take care of you, remember? That's all I'm going to do, Kel. I'll just hold you until you fall asleep, okay?"

She warily eyed the hand he held out to her for a long moment before nodding once. Then her shoulders suddenly drooped, her knees buckled and she collapsed into his arms like an exhausted child. He cradled her against him while he dug the pillows out from under the bedspread. Turning her onto her side, facing away from him, he draped his arm across her waist and curled himself around her bottom, fitting his knees to the backs of hers.

Her breathing slowed and deepened about thirty seconds after her head hit the pillow. His shoulder ached and he wished he'd taken his boots off, but he couldn't bring himself to let go of Kelly long enough to fix either problem. Promising himself he would leave soon, he shut his eyes and pulled her closer.

Ninety-nine percent of the time, she was as ornery and independent as a wild mustang. But right now, tonight, she needed him. She needed him in a way nobody else had in a long time, and he wanted to help and protect her if she'd let him.

Despite all of the earlier weirdness, or maybe because of it, he thought with a smile, it felt good to hold her. No, better than good. Somehow, it just felt . . . right.

Safe. Warm. Cuddled. The sensations were too delicious to give up, just because it was morning. Sighing with contentment, Kelly rubbed her cheek against the pillowcase.

It seemed hotter than usual. The pillow seemed awful damn hard, too. And now that she thought about it, there was something funny goin' on, down around the vicinity of her right breast. If she could just get her eyes open for a second, maybe she could figure it all out. Unfortunately, it felt like she had a couple of pregnant sows sitting on her eyelids.

A puff of air stirred the hair tucked behind her left ear. She wrinkled her nose in irritation, then froze when a soft snore accompanied the next puff of air. *Okay,* she told herself, *no need to panic just yet. Whoever's snorin' back there could've cut your throat last night, but you're still breathin', so how bad can it be?*

With sheer force of will she pried one eye open, then slowly turned her head until she could peek back over her left shoulder. Anderson's face swam into focus. She gulped. Slowly turned her head back around. Looked down. Uh-huh. That was definitely his hand clasping her right breast. It felt nice, too.

What the hell was going on? They were both dressed, so she didn't think they'd actually had sex. Surely, she would know if that had happened. Wouldn't she?

Closing her eyes, she searched her memory, realizing, with a horrible, sinking feeling in the pit of her stomach, that from the time the doctor in Hamilton had stitched up her arm until about two minutes ago, she only had bits and pieces of recollection. And the bits and pieces she could recall were too mortifying to believe.

That is, until she worked up the nerve to glance over at the nightstand and saw the condom collection laid out on display.

Lord have mercy, what had she *done?* Anderson must think she was awful. Since she couldn't die a nice, natural death from embarrassment, she wished someone would take pity on her, haul her out in the boonies somewhere and shoot her. Before Anderson woke up, if she was lucky.

Maybe, if she moved *really* carefully and *really* quietly, she could sort of slide out from under his arm, sneak out of the trailer, throw the dogs in the back of the pickup and hightail it for Mexico. She'd worry about getting Daniel back later. If even half of what she thought she remembered about last night was true, she'd rather be dead than have to face Anderson again.

Slowly, slowly, barely moving a quarter of an inch at a time, she managed to get her right big toe to the edge of the bed. Her arm was beginning to throb but she concentrated on moving her left foot over to her right. She was sweating by the time she got it there, but since Anderson's soft snores continued, she figured her chances of escaping were improving.

The second she tried to move her torso, however, his hand tightened around her breast, his forearm dug into her waist and his voice came out in a deep, sexy rumble. "Where do you think you're going?"

"I, uh . . . well, it's morning, Marshal. I've got chores to do, dogs to feed. Time to rise and shine, ya know?"

"It's barely daylight, sweetheart. Go back to sleep."

He nuzzled a sensitive spot behind her ear and pulled her lower body snugly back against him. Then he reclaimed her breast, giving it a loving squeeze that raised gooseflesh all over her arms and legs. Sleep? Yeah, right.

Telling herself she would use the element of surprise, she silently counted to one hundred, giving him time to fall back asleep. The only problem was, he didn't fall back asleep. Instead, as if he had every right, he moved his hand from her right breast, to her left and down over her belly, the curve of her hip and the length of her thighs in a gentle, leisurely exploration that stole her breath and her desire to leave.

He sighed, nuzzled her ear, nibbled the length of her neck. She felt surrounded, protected, cherished. But that wasn't true. It couldn't be. Hell, she'd offered herself to him last night, about as blatantly as it was possible for a woman to offer herself to a man, and he'd obviously rejected her.

She'd been nuts to think a man like him would ever really want her. The last thing she needed now was to let him get her all hot and bothered again and—

"I don't know what's going on in that head of yours," he said with more than a hint of temper in his voice, "but you're not going anywhere until we talk about last night."

Afraid of what she might see in his eyes, Kelly stared straight ahead at the wall in front of her. "What about it?"

"There's no reason for you to feel embarrassed about what happened."

She cleared her throat. "And, um . . . just what exactly did happen last night, Marshal?"

"You got goofy, just like you said you would. And I took care of you, just like I said I would. Everything you said or did stays strictly between you and me. End of story." A definite smile entered his voice. "Of course, now that I know how much you like my chest, maybe you should call me Steve."

Kelly buried her hot face in the mattress for a moment, then looked over her shoulder and almost laughed out loud at the wicked grin on his face. As long as she had anything to do with this man, she was *never* going to live that one down. "Think you're pretty hot stuff, don'tcha, Anderson?"

"No, but *you* do." His grin faded and his voice dropped to a husky whisper. "And I think you're pretty hot stuff, too, sweetheart. In fact, I think you're wonderful and sexy and—"

"Then, last night . . . why didn't you, um . . ."

"Because it wouldn't have been fair to take advantage of you while you were under the influence. But now that you're in your right mind again, I'm all yours if you still want me."

Searching his eyes for any signs of mockery, Kelly found uncertainty instead. His vulnerability touched her deeply, prompting her to whisper, "Yeah, I do . . . Steve."

"Come here, Kel." He rose up on his right elbow, reached his left hand over her hip and inhaled a sharp, hissing breath.

Concerned for his obvious pain, Kelly turned toward him, pushing her right hand into the mattress for leverage. The dull ache under her stitches exploded into an excruciating stab of agony. The same sharp, hissing noise Steve had made escaped her own suddenly clenched teeth, and she fell back onto the mattress with a surprised curse.

His worried face loomed over her. "Are you all right? Did you pull your stitches out?"

Still struggling to catch her breath, she gulped. "Don't think so. What about you?"

"My cuts weren't as deep as yours," he said. "I just had a twinge."

"Yeah, that looked like some *twinge*, all right. Shoots the hell outta feelin' lusty, don't it?"

Steve chuckled. "Well, I might have to heal up a little first, but Dr. Edwards sent some pain pills home for you."

"Oh, no." Kelly shook her head as vigorously as she dared. "You go ahead and take 'em if you want to, but I'll make do with aspirin and a shower."

"You're not supposed to get your stitches wet."

"Whaddaya think all those antibiotics are for? I'll just tape a plastic bag over the bandage and the doc'll never know."

He studied her for a moment, as if trying to decide just how determined she was to ignore the doctor's instructions. She blandly returned his gaze and suddenly found herself exchanging a conspiratorial grin with him.

"All right," he said, "if you promise not to lock the bathroom door in case you get woozy or something. And if you'll tape a bag over my bandage, so I can clean up too. Deal?"

"Deal."

He climbed off the bed and carefully helped her to stand beside him. "We could always save time and shower together."

Smiling, she slowly shook her head. "Now that I'm sober again, I don't think I'm quite ready for that yet."

"All right." He lowered his head and kissed her until her toes curled into the worn carpet. "But remember one thing, sweetheart. Sooner or later, we *are* going to be lovers. Count on it."

Chapter Nine

Later that afternoon, Steve climbed out of the pickup and walked the fence line, carefully studying the new posts and the ground around them with a growing sense of frustration. "I wish Bobby hadn't hauled the old posts away. I could probably tell if they were tampered with. The cows stomped around here so much, there's nothing left but hoofprints."

Kelly ambled along beside him, paying more attention to the cows and calves in the pasture than to the fence. "It was an accident, Steve. Sometimes stuff like this just happens."

"Yeah, sometimes it does." He paused until she finished counting the animals and looked back at him, then continued. "But after you fell asleep last night, I spent a lot of time thinking about the way those posts snapped. They went off like a booby trap."

"Aw, it was probably some kids out drinkin' and drivin' around in a pickup. They smashed into the fence and weakened the posts. When I shook that middle one, they all just busted."

Steve considered her suggestion, replaying the sequence of events in his mind as accurately as he could remember them. He wanted to ease her mind and say she might have a point, but his conscience wouldn't let him. "I don't think so, Kelly. My instincts are screaming that wasn't an accident. I want you to be careful."

She tipped her head to one side, as if she were giving his warning some serious thought. "Well, you know, that's exactly the crummy kind of thing my brother Johnny would do to get back at me, and he wouldn't really care all that much if somebody else walked into it instead of me. But he's still in prison, and I can't think of anyone else who'd intentionally sabotage Bud's property." She raised an eyebrow at him. "Unless there's somebody after you?"

Steve shrugged and immediately wished he hadn't. Damn stitches were going to drive him nuts. "I can name quite a few guys who'd love to get some revenge. Most of them are still in prison, though, and the ones who aren't wouldn't have any way to trace me here."

Sighing, Kelly looked off toward the ridge above the ranch. It was hot out, but she shivered, then crossed her arms over her midriff and uttered a self-conscious laugh. "Let's get outta here before we both get paranoid."

"There's nothing wrong with a little healthy paranoia. It keeps you on your toes."

As if in response, Kelly's stomach gave a loud rumble. Chuckling at her red face, Steve carefully walked her back to the truck. "Anybody ever tell you, you've got a one-track mind, Jaynes?"

"More like a one-track stomach," she admitted. "Unfortunately, we ate the last frozen dinners for lunch."

"Well, stick with me, li'l lady," Steve drawled. She climbed into the passenger seat, let him shut the door for her and rolled down the window. Bracing a forearm on the opening, he went on with his John Wayne imitation. "I'll make sure ya get fed real good."

"You can cook?"

He laughed at the hopeful expression in her eyes, then walked around the front of the truck, climbed into the driver's seat and started the engine. "When I want to, but I think we're way past due for a night out. When was the last time you had a burger at Fetty's?"

Her eyes brightened with delight. "You wouldn't be tryin' to seduce me through my stomach?"

"Yup." He leaned across the bench seat and stole a quick kiss. "Will it work?"

She grinned and kissed him back. "Guess you'll have to take me to Fetty's and find out."

"Lord, you're cute when you flirt, Jaynes. Anybody ever tell you that?"

"Oh, sure. Thousands of guys."

Chuckling, Steve put the pickup in gear and headed for Wisdom. Though he wasn't sure exactly what it had been, he must have done something right this morning. Kelly had been relaxed, open and even a little playful all day. His niggling sense of worry over the fence posts didn't completely go away, but he'd be damned if he'd let it spoil their first real date.

"Well, now, ain't that just sweet enough to make ya puke?" Johnny James muttered, watching the big blond dude escort Kelly to the pickup. Like she was some kind of a lady who needed help hauling herself in and out of one. Hell! That'd be the day.

That section of fence he'd fixed up for her had been replaced, though, and they were both moving a little slow and awkward, so his surprise must've worked pretty well, he thought, smiling with satisfaction. Too bad he couldn't have been here to see the fun. The way she'd been lookin' all around, he figured Kelly must be starting to feel a little nervous. Which was no more than the betraying little bitch deserved.

He wished he could take the time to really drive her nuts, but after some careful consideration, he'd decided it might be wiser to back off a little for a while. He had plenty to keep him busy right now. One good thing he would say about his sister, he could always count on her to take fine care of Daniel for him.

Once he had his money and had gotten himself settled in a new country with a new name, he could always come back for his boy and torment Kelly some more. Might take a little time to turn Daniel into a real man after Miss Goody Two Shoes'd had him all this time, but the kid was probably a fast learner. He was a James, wasn't he?

First, though, he had to get into that little cracker box of a trailer and find his key, so he could get to his travelin' money. He'd thought it was a stroke of pure genius to hide it in that little toy bear Mama had given Daniel just before she died. Sentimental slob that she was, Kelly never would have thrown that thing away. The question was, where the hell would she have stored it?

Wisdom, Montana, was one of those little, blink-and-you'll-miss-it kind of towns, frequented mainly by the local ranchers, occasional tourists and trout fishermen. In Kelly's opinion, the best thing Wisdom had going for it was a little bar and café called Fetty's, which had made at least one travel writer's list of the ten best places to buy a hamburger in the whole United States.

Whether the burgers were *that* good, Kelly couldn't say, but she thought they were out-of-this-world wonderful. The homemade pies weren't bad, either. Feeling pleasantly stuffed, she strolled out of the restaurant with Steve, enjoying the weight of his arm curled across her shoulders and the speculative glances she sensed dancing along her spine, coming from the folks they encountered.

Within a few hours, the news would be all over the valley that Bud and Peg's nephew was carrying on with the hired help, but she couldn't summon up much concern about it. For one thing, Steve was such a good-looking son of a gun, she was proud to be seen with him. For another, it felt nice to be part of a couple for a change. She didn't have to cope with being hit on or worry that if she smiled at some guy on the street, he'd take it the wrong way and assume she was encouraging him. It was just . . . nice.

They were both quiet during the ride back home, but it was a comfortable kind of quiet. When he topped the last rise before turning into the Haystack's lane, Steve pulled to the side of the road and killed the engine. Then he rested his left forearm across the steering wheel and gazed out over the ranch, a thoughtful-looking frown marring his features.

Kelly unfastened her seat belt, slid to the middle of the bench seat and gently touched his right hand, which lay on his thigh in a loose fist. "What's wrong, Steve?"

He gave her a brief smile, turned his hand over and laced their fingers together. Then he looked back out over the land and slowly shook his head. "Nothing's wrong, exactly. I just can't decide what to do about this place."

"What to do?"

Without looking at her, he nodded. "Bud's offered to turn it over to me in the next few years. I don't know whether or not I want it."

Kelly felt her mouth fall open, and she suspected her eyes were bugging halfway out of her head, but she couldn't have stopped gaping at him if he'd stuck a loaded .45 in her face. "Not *want* it? The Haystack? You mean he's offering to *give* it to you?"

He glanced in her direction, turned back to the windshield, then did a double take and grinned at her. "Yeah, but I'm having a hard time deciding what I should do."

Appalled at his stupidity, she huffed at him. "Are you out of your tiny little mind, Anderson?"

The idiot man actually had the gall to look as if she'd hurt his feelings. "You think I'd make a lousy rancher?"

"No! And you don't, either. I'd probably kill for an offer like that. I can't believe you're even thinkin' about *not* grabbin' it. Do you have *any* idea what this ranch is worth?"

"Hey, I know it's worth a lot of money, but—"

She waved that issue aside. "I'm not talkin' about money. Sure, the Haystack's probably worth a few million on paper. But it takes so much cash to keep it up and keep it goin', you'd never get to live like you were real rich."

"If I wanted to be real rich, I wouldn't be a deputy U.S. marshal," Steve said.

Ignoring his observation, she glared at him in warning. "Unless you're willin' to subdivide it and sell it to movie stars. In which case, the devil can take you and I'll never speak to you again. Ever. And when you die, I'll spit on your grave."

"Okay, okay." He held up his hands in surrender. "It's a beautiful piece of land, Kel, but that's all it is. Just a piece of land. Why get so upset about it?"

Searching for words to describe the undescribable, she tipped back her head and focused her eyes on the mountains to the west. "Ranching's hard, dirty work, with long hours and low pay, but there's... dignity in it. You don't punch a time clock or have some boss breathin' down your neck. Everything you earn comes from your own efforts and ingenuity. You have to be independent and self-reliant and too dang stubborn to give up when you run into a problem."

"You've got the stubborn part down real well," Steve said, his tone dry enough to make her smile. "But so far you haven't convinced me the dignity you're talking about is worth the hard, dirty work, long hours and low pay."

Kelly wrinkled her nose at him. "It's a vanishing way of life, Anderson. Lots of guys can be cops, ya know? But how many really get to be cowboys anymore? *Real* cowboys?"

"Cops help people."

"Cowboys feed 'em. And if they're worth a damn, they take good care of the land while they're at it. I'm not talking about some pissant little five- or ten-acre spread, but hundreds, even thousands of acres."

Steve nodded. "Agreed. But what if a guy's really not cut out for ranching?"

"Aw, heck, Anderson, you're cut out for it just fine. Every time we ride out to work, I can see how much you love this place. And you're patient, you know how to handle animals and you like workin' with your hands."

He nodded again. "So? That doesn't mean I should change careers, does it?"

"Doesn't mean you shouldn't, either. Now, be honest. When you came here as a kid, didn't you love the freedom? Didn't you ever dream about owning a ranch some day, or pretend you owned this one?"

A wistful smile curved his lips. "Well, yeah. I guess I did. But that was before my dad died. After that, I never wanted to be anything but a cop."

"How did that change your mind?"

"It's a little . . . complicated," he said slowly. "I'm not sure I can explain it."

"Hey, I've got all kinds of time. Give it a shot."

He shifted around on the seat until his back leaned against the door's arm rest and his legs stretched past the gas pedal and the gear stick. "All right. See, my mother never liked my dad's being a cop. She hated the hours and the low pay and worrying about him all the time."

"They fought about it?" Kelly asked.

Steve rolled his eyes. "God, yes. Whenever she'd start in on him, Dad would always say, 'Being a cop is not what I do, Evelyn, it's who I am.' If he hadn't been killed in the line of duty, I think they would have divorced before very long, anyway."

"How old were you when he died?"

"Thirteen."

"That's a tough age." She shook her head in sympathy. "It was hard enough when my mom passed away, and I was almost nineteen."

He nodded. "Yeah. I was closer to Dad, anyway, and Mom was so angry and bitter, she could never say anything good about him. She was always ranting about how he'd gotten himself killed. Like he'd planned it just to spite her."

Kelly took his hand in hers again and gave it a squeeze. Steve squeezed back, then rested his head against the seat and gazed off into the distance as if he was looking at old, painful memories.

"Two years later, she married this nerdy little accountant and started having my three half-sisters," he said. "If it hadn't been for me, I think she would have erased Dad from her life as if he'd never existed."

"So you became a cop to remind her?" Kelly asked.

Steve shrugged his right shoulder, then gave her a wry grin. "I suppose that might have had something to do with it. I always thought Dad would be proud of me for going into law enforcement, so it was a good way to honor him, too, you know?"

"And a good way to help people," Kelly added. "You seem to like doin' that."

"Yeah, I like to feel useful," he agreed. "Once she started her new family, my mother sure didn't need me anymore."

"How often do you see her?"

"I don't. Not unless we happen to run into each other at a family wedding or a funeral. She doesn't approve of my being a cop, either." His laugh had a bitter ring to it, and he swung back around to face the windshield with short, jerky movements. "I'll be damned if I'll quit just to please her any more than my dad would have."

Her heart aching for him, Kelly studied Steve for a long moment. "So why are you still a cop? To spite your mom? To honor your dad? Or because deep down inside, that's what *you* really want to be?"

He scowled at her. "Hey, don't try to play shrink with me. I've worked hard to get this job, and I'm damn good at it."

"Never said you weren't. But it doesn't seem like you've missed it much since you've been here. If bein' a marshal makes you so happy, how come you're takin' a whole summer off?"

"I needed a break."

"Two weeks is a break. A month is a long break. A whole summer is time to do some serious thinkin' about whether or not you still want to be a cop. Maybe you need to quit to please yourself."

"And become a cowboy?"

She corrected him with a smile. "A rancher. There's a big difference between ownin' a ranch and just workin' on it. I still miss havin' my own place, and probably always will."

"What was your ranch called?"

"The Tumbling A." A jagged lump formed in her throat, and she had to gulp hard to be able to talk around it. "It was in my mom's family for four generations by the time she inherited it."

"What was it like?"

"Oh, it was a great little spread for Wyoming." Kelly sighed. Smiled. "Ten thousand acres with plenty of pure water and great grass. Even had a fair-sized stand of timber. Mom and I had some good times, workin' it together. Jay got it when she died, but I was the one who ran it, so I always figured it was more mine than his or Johnny's."

"Your dad and brother didn't help you?"

Shaking her head, Kelly found it was her turn to let out a bitter laugh. "Heck, they weren't interested in any kind of *work*. If they'd have just robbed banks or stolen cars or something, the government couldn't have seized everything. But those dang dirty drugs were another story. I'll never forgive either one of 'em for plantin' that damn marijuana on our land."

"I'm sorry you lost it," Steve said.

"Yeah, me too, and not just for myself. I'd give almost anything to be able to pass that ranch on to Daniel. If he stays in this business, he'll never know what it's like to be the owner, now. He'll always be the hired hand."

"Is that really so awful?"

"Not when you've got somebody like Bud and Peg to work for. But, with fewer family farms and ranches every year, there's not much future in it. That's why I'm always after Daniel to do his schoolwork. I'm savin' up to get him a computer, too, so he can do somethin' else for a livin' if he wants."

"People are always going to need food."

"Yeah, but agriculture's goin' corporate," she said with a resigned sigh. "These days, any rancher who wants to stay in business really has to look ahead and see what's comin' down the pike. That means usin' computers and any other kind of technology that'll save time or money. You can't just work hard anymore, you've gotta work smart."

"And you think I can do that? Kelly, I don't have a degree in agriculture."

"I don't, either. But I can damn well read and learn and talk to other folks in the business, and so can you. Shoot, it could even be an advantage that you haven't been doin' this your whole life. Might make you more open-minded about tryin' new stuff or doin' things a different way."

Steve looked at her as if he wanted to believe her, but didn't quite dare. "What if I don't make it, though? Bud and Peg have put their whole lives into this place. I'd really hate to disappoint them."

"Your aunt and uncle know the odds. They could go under next year or the next, same as anyone else. If you stay here and give it your best shot, they'll be proud of you no matter what happens."

"You really think I could do it?"

"Hell, yes! You could build somethin' special here." Kelly punched his arm in encouragement. "Believe me, the Haystack's got everything you need to succeed, where some other places I've worked just plain didn't. And it's your *home*, Steve. You belong here. It's not like you'd have to do it all alone, you know? Bud'll be around to help you get started."

"Would you stick around?" he asked.

"After the summer?" She tipped her head to one side and thought about it. "I don't know. Daniel and I really love this valley. Guess I wouldn't mind stayin' if I could keep Jay and Johnny off my back, and things don't get so, uh...uncomfortable between you and me that we can't work together."

He gave her the charming, boyish grin that made her insides feel all warm and squishy, then leaned down and kissed the tip of her nose. "That'll never happen."

"You don't think so? If you want me to stay on as your foreman, you might want to rethink this bein' lovers stuff. It doesn't always pay to sleep with the hired help."

"You're more than hired help to all of us, and you know it," he scolded. "A lot more."

He kissed her again, a long, sweet kiss on the mouth that left her feeling overheated, ruffled and breathless when he pulled back a minute later. Looking as if he was in about the same condition, Steve cleared his throat, started the pickup and pulled onto the gravel road. Instead of sliding back over to the passenger seat, Kelly stayed beside him.

Bud, Peg and Daniel would all be home tomorrow. She wanted to enjoy every second of privacy they had left. If that last kiss had meant to Steve what it had meant to her, tonight was gonna be a very special night.

They arrived back at the ranch, and by unspoken, mutual agreement, did the evening chores together. Then Steve went to check on the main house while Kelly let the dogs out to play. They were always excited to get out of their pen and run around, but tonight she thought they acted particularly rambunctious.

Well, she hadn't given them much attention the past two days and Daniel hadn't been around to play with them, either. She figured they'd all settle down just fine when everyone got back into their normal routines. Then she saw Pat Garrett coming around the far side of the trailer.

Crouching in a Blue Heeler's typical, dog-with-a-mission slink, Pat zigzagged across the yard, sniffing as if he was on the trail of a wayward cow. Every now and then, he'd pause for an extra sniff or two and growl. When he came to the trailer's front steps, he sat in the middle of the bottom one, head up, ears perked, like a soldier on sentry duty.

Kelly walked over and stroked his neck, feeling a twinge of uneasiness when her fingertips encountered fur bristling with tension, and the dog uttered a soft whine. "What is it, boy?"

Pat glanced at her, whined again, then trotted up the steps and scratched at the front door. Kelly looked toward the main house, hoping to see Steve heading her way. No such luck. Well, shoot, she'd never waited around for a man to do her dirty work or take care of her before. She wasn't about to start now.

Since she'd lived out in the country her whole life, she'd never learned to lock her doors, and it had never been a problem. Until now. Remembering what Steve had said about the fence posts going off like a booby trap, however, she looked around for a long stick. With the right tool, she could pop the latch from a distance.

She found an old broom handle lying in the tall grass beside the trailer's skirting. Then she had to coax Pat away from the door, which proved to be no easy task. By the time her normally obedient Blue Heeler submitted to her commands to "Come, sit and stay," she was convinced *some*thing unusual had happened here while she'd been gone.

Then Steve returned, and when she explained the situation, he insisted on going back to the house for his .45 before she opened the damn door. Kelly found her curiosity warring with her natural sense of caution at yet another delay in unraveling the mystery. She was almost disappointed when she finally used the broom handle on the latch and nothing happened.

Of course, being a man and a cop, Steve also insisted on going inside the trailer first. Kelly didn't like his bossy attitude much, but decided this wasn't the time to argue about it. Besides, somebody needed to hang onto Pat's collar until the trailer had been checked, and she feared the dog would bite anyone else who tried to interfere with his canine duties. The moment Steve stepped over the threshold, Pat pulled hard against her restraining hand, his mottled hide quivering all over.

"Good boy, Pat," she crooned, scratching behind his ears. "You did a good job of warnin' us."

Steve appeared in the doorway, his expression grim. "Brace yourself. Somebody left you a mess."

"A mess?" she muttered a moment later, tiptoeing her way through the debris scattered across her living room. "What do you call a tornado, Anderson? A little wind?"

Every storage space in the trailer stood wide open, the contents ransacked and emptied. No corner or cubbyhole had been spared, from the linen closet in the hallway, to Daniel's bookshelves, to the drawer under the stove and the cardboard box on the shelf above the clothing rod in her bedroom closet where she kept Daniel's A-plus papers and art projects from school.

When she'd seen all the devastation and returned to the living room, Steve came up behind her and gently kneaded her shoulders. "Do you have any idea what he might have been looking for, Kel?"

Kelly shook her head. "God knows I don't own much of anything worth stealin'." Then she shot him a questioning look. "What makes you think he was lookin' for something and not just out to trash the place?"

"Vandals usually break more stuff, like all the mirrors and dishes and furniture. It could've been a lot worse."

"Oh, really?" Infuriated, Kelly shrugged off his hands, kicked a sofa cushion out of her way and stomped over to the side window. "Some jerk stuck his grubby hands in my underwear drawer and threw my tampons all over the bathroom floor, Marshal. How could it have been any worse?"

Steve's voice rose in volume to match hers. "He could've come in here while Daniel was home alone, doing his homework. Do you want to hear more?"

Kelly's throat closed up. Wrapping her arms around herself, she turned away from Steve's angry gaze, blinking against the burning sensation at the backs of her eyes. Dammit, she would *not* cry. She'd be fine in a second. Just fine.

Well, she would've been if that big lug, Anderson, hadn't come over and put his arms around her.

"I'm sorry, Kel," he said. "I know you must feel violated. Anybody would. But when you've seen some of the things I have, you realize nothing's that bad if nobody died."

She pushed herself away from him, curled her fingers into fists and lowered them to her sides to stop herself from reaching for him. "Don't do this to me, Anderson. For God's sake, don't be so damn nice."

"Why not?"

"Because, I . . ." She paused, took a deep breath, swallowed hard. "Just, don't, okay?"

"No. It's not okay," he said. "You know, you don't have to be tough all the time. You *are* allowed to lean on somebody else once in a while."

Shaking her head in protest, she took another step back. "No way." she said. "You're gonna make me cry if you don't cut it out."

"So? What's wrong with crying?"

"It doesn't solve a blessed thing, and it makes a person weak. I've gotta stay strong, Anderson," she said, thumping her sternum with her index finger. " 'Cause I'm all Daniel's got."

"No, you're not, sweetheart." He came closer, holding out his arms, tempting her with a silent offer of comfort she craved. "I'm here, and I won't let anything happen to either one of you."

"You can't guarantee that." Palms raised, she backed up again. "Nobody can."

"That's right. But I've had lots of training and experience at protecting people, and I really am damned good at it, if I do say so myself. You're not alone, Kelly."

She looked up into those sincere, almost...loving, gray eyes, choked, thrashed her head back and forth. She wouldn't give in, dammit. *Couldn't* give in.

But it hurt to breathe, and he had her cornered against the sofa and there was everything she'd worked so hard to provide for Daniel and herself tossed around like it was so much garbage. Her eyes stung and her knuckles ached because she'd curled them into such tight fists again and dammit, she was afraid. *Afraid!*

She'd been worried before. Worried sick about paying bills and raising Daniel right and what would happen to him if she got hurt or sick. But it wasn't the same thing at all as knowing some...creep thought he could just waltz back into their home, dammit, and do whatever the hell he pleased.

Dear God, what if Daniel *had* been here alone when that creep had showed up? She couldn't be with the kid every living minute, and he was way too young to pack a gun around with him. He could've been hurt, molested...murdered. Nobody would've heard him cry for help.

She shuddered, dragged in a deep breath and choked on it. Glaring at Steve, she swiped the first tear away with the back of her hand. He groaned, reached for her, and the next thing she knew, she was in his arms, clutching at the front of his chambray shirt with both hands. Against her will, a few more tears trickled out from under her scrunched-up eyelids.

Once the floodgates loosened, all the emotions she'd stuffed down inside her broke free, forced their way to the surface and gushed down her cheeks. Steve held her and stroked her hair. She kept telling herself to stop blubbering, suck it in and stand on her own two feet, but her body and soul refused to listen.

They kept her right there, in his arms, soaking up all that damned warmth, affection and security. Where it felt like...home. Of course, by the time she finally found the strength to pull away, it was way too late to save herself.

God help her, she was already falling in love with him.

Chapter Ten

"You're not alone," Steve said.

He held his breath while Kelly stared at him, her eyes wide and wary. She reminded him of a wounded animal who desperately needed help, but was too fearful of abuse to allow anyone to come close enough to give it aid and comfort. Well, by God, she was going to have to trust him this time.

He didn't like the smell of this situation one bit, and he'd be damned if he'd let her face any kind of danger by herself. He'd stand here, feeling like an idiot and holding his arms out to her until they fell off if he had to. He'd felt alone and lonely for one hell of a long time. Kelly could snarl and snap about her independence all she wanted, but he wasn't going away. Dammit, she needed him.

Then, with no warning, her features crumpled. She grabbed the front of his shirt and slammed into his chest, rocking him onto his heels. Accompanied by harsh, gut-wrenching sobs, her tears flowed in a soaking torrent that made him suspect it had been years since Kelly had allowed herself to cry.

That she would let go of such fierce defenses with him, humbled him. Tenderness nearly swamping him, he gathered her close, stroked her dark hair, murmured soft, comforting words. And still the tears flowed, making him wonder what all this grief was about.

Losing her mother? Losing the Tumbling A? The father and brother who should have protected her instead of stripping her of the only home she'd ever known and leaving her to raise a child alone, when she'd been little more than a child herself?

Seeing her hurt so deeply enraged him and hurt him, as well. Dammit, he would find the jerk who had made this mess and terrified her, and then he would feed the son of a bitch to Wild Bill for breakfast. Nobody messed with the people he loved and got away with it.

And he loved Kelly Jaynes. Really loved her. More than he'd loved anyone before. More, even, than Anne. Maybe because Kelly needed him more than Anne ever had.

Anne had needed him to protect her and Chad. She'd needed him to be a male role model for Chad. She'd needed him to be a friend and a cop, but she'd never needed anything more from him. She'd always had a family of her own—with a man and other children she loved with all her heart—to go back to someday.

There were similarities between the old situation and this new one, of course. Kelly needed him to protect her and Daniel. She needed him to be a male role model for Daniel. She needed him to be a friend. But she was as alone as he had always been, and though he doubted she would admit it, she was every bit as lonely. She needed him as a man.

A man who would love and cherish her for herself. Who admired and respected her courage and her strength, her work ethic and her determination to make a decent life for herself and the boy who depended on her to give him a home and values nobody had bothered to teach her.

A man who would love her beautiful, strong body with the tenderness and respect she deserved. Who would see her "significant scars" as the honorable badges of hard work they really were. Who would delight in teaching her the wonderful things that could happen between a man and a woman she would never learn from the *S* volume of the encyclopedia.

A man who would love her because of her generous spirit. Lord, how could she have felt genuinely excited on his behalf when she'd found out her own lost dream of owning a ranch was dropping into his lap like a gift from heaven? But she had. He'd seen it in her eyes, heard it in her voice, felt it in the encouragement she'd given him.

He still wasn't sure he wanted to give up law enforcement and spend the rest of his life as a rancher. Whatever his future held, however, he wanted Kelly to be a part of it. Daniel, too. And maybe some kids of their own someday. Well, in all honesty, forget the maybe.

He liked being around kids. Liked seeing how their minds worked. Liked watching them learn. Since the day he'd witnessed Chad Miller's birth as Anne's labor coach, he'd wanted to be a father, and nothing, including colic and dirty diapers, tantrums and potty training, skinned knees and ear infections, fear of monsters hiding under the bed and endless requests for glasses of water—had ever changed his mind.

Yeah, he wanted children, and he wanted Kelly to be their mother. She had a few rough edges, all right, but she had so much heart and integrity, any kid would be lucky to have her. The thought of watching her belly grow with his baby made him smile and turned him on at the same time.

She pulled away from him then, brushing at his soggy shirt and avoiding his eyes as if she'd committed a shameful act. He considered coaxing her into talking about it, but decided a low-key approach might be more productive in the long run. As independent as Kelly was, her head was probably bursting with regrets over showing him a "feminine" weakness.

Convincing her to admit she was attracted to him had been hard enough. Convincing her to admit she was in love with him was bound to be even harder. And at this moment, convincing her to agree she wanted to marry him and have his children looked daunting, if not downright impossible.

Well, tough. Fishing his handkerchief out of his back pocket, he mopped up her face, handed her the cloth and turned away in order to give her a little privacy while she regained her emotional equilibrium. One day soon, she was going to learn, not only to accept his comfort when she needed it, she was going to learn to expect it. Maybe even demand it.

The thought made him smile again. One way or another, they were going to be together for a very long time. All he had to do now was convince her of that.

Unnerved by her loss of control, Kelly gulped, sniffled and swiped at her eyes. Then, cursing under her breath, she crammed Steve's hanky into her back pocket. Damn. She couldn't believe she'd done that. She sure as hell didn't want to talk about it.

Straightening her shoulders, she glanced at Steve, saw him set the kitchen chairs upright and shut the cupboards beside the stove. Yeah, he had the right idea. Just get to work and put this stuff away. Leaving Steve to tackle the living room and kitchen, she stomped down the hall to the bathroom.

If she slammed a brush into a drawer, banged a plastic shampoo bottle around and cussed a blue streak while she restored order to her home, nobody else had to know about it. Damn. She *still* couldn't believe she'd bawled like that. And in front of Steve. Aw, hell! Gritting her teeth, she moved on down the hall, cleaning up the linen closet and the bedrooms.

She'd thought she had her emotions neatly tucked away along with everything else, until she found the last bit of damage in her bedroom. It wasn't that much, really, the only monetary loss being the cost of the cheap picture frame that had been smashed on the floor beside her dresser. And yet, it disheartened, even scared her, in a way nothing else had done.

Dragging the cardboard box she'd been using for a trash can along, she slowly sank to the floor, sat cross-legged and carefully reached for the mangled pile of glass, paper and wood.

"Ready to pack it in for the night?" Steve asked from the doorway.

Kelly started violently, dropped the frame and jerked around to stare at him. "I didn't hear you coming," she said with a shaky laugh, her heartbeat suddenly hammering in her ears. "You're lucky I don't keep a loaded gun in here."

Steve crossed to her side in four long strides, then knelt beside her. "I'm sorry, Kel." He touched her cheek with the backs of his fingers in a caress that soothed the raw hurt inside her. He nodded at the frame. "What have you got there?"

"It's nothin'." She scooped up the mess and dumped it into the box. "Nothin' important, anyhow."

Steve glanced around the room as if he'd never seen it before. Of course, knowing how wacko she must've been last night, Kelly figured he probably hadn't had much time to notice the lack of decor. She hadn't noticed it, either, until now. Between moving so often, taking care of Daniel and working a more-than-full-time job, she'd given up unpacking the few feminine doodads, keepsakes and knickknacks she owned. It made her room look awfully Spartan, but with all of that stuff stored in Bud and Peg's attic, she had less to dust.

Ignoring her warning to be careful, Steve reached into the box, and retrieved the picture frame. Broken glass fell out, followed by half of a snapshot and four paper scraps. Fishing out the photo, he carefully picked it up by the edges. "Nice picture of you. Did you tear this up?"

Kelly winced inwardly. Mr. Nice Guy had vanished and here she was again with the cold-eyed marshal. "No. It was already like that when I found it."

"What was on the other half?"

"Daniel. Peg took it when I got my General Equivalency Diploma in the mail last winter. That's what those pieces of paper used to be."

"Was the diploma torn before?"

She shook her head.

"Did you touch anything but the frame?"

Kelly shook her head again, then paused in indecision. "I didn't just now, but I did when I put it all together. Why?"

"Might be able to lift some fingerprints and identify your intruder. We'd have to print you first so we can eliminate—"

"Won't be necessary, Marshal." Unable to meet his piercing gaze, Kelly studied the edges of the bandage on her arm. "I know who did this. Most likely, he did the fence posts, too."

"Your brother?"

"I'd bet a month's pay on it. I don't know how he got out this early or how he found me, but I can't think of anyone else who would do this."

Clearing her throat, she lifted her chin and, though it was difficult, looked at him. "You saved me from getting ripped to shreds by the barbed wire. What if Bud or Peg had noticed those posts were sittin' a little funny? Or Daniel? My God, they could've been killed or maimed, and it's all my fault."

He cupped her face between his palms. "You're not responsible for what your brother does. Don't blame yourself."

"Well, who else is there? I knew Daniel and I should have left as soon as school got out, but we were both too comfortable here. Too attached to Bud and Peg. As soon as Daniel gets home, we'll go. I don't know where, but—"

"You're not going anywhere." Steve lowered his hands to her shoulders and gave her a shake. "Remember? You promised to stay for the rest of the summer."

"I've changed my mind. I thought if Johnny ever came after us, he'd just try to get money out of me. Or try to see Daniel. But now..." She waved her right hand toward the box, feeling infuriatingly helpless. "Well, I never realized before how much he must hate me."

"Because he tore up the diploma?"

Kelly nodded. "It practically killed me when I had to drop out of high school to work the ranch, 'cause I was afraid I'd never be able to go back and finish. Johnny knows exactly how much gettin' my G.E.D. means to me, and tearin' it up was just pure spite. He's doin' things mainly to hurt me, but like with the fence posts, he won't give a rip if somebody else gets hurt, too. God only knows what he'll do next."

Steve squeezed her shoulders. "We'll handle him, sweetheart. I promise."

Kelly shook her head. "*You* might be willin' to take chances with Bud, Peg or Daniel's safety, but I'm not."

"Wait a minute. We really don't know if it's Johnny. I'll call my boss in the morning and have him find out about Johnny's status. If he's been released, we'll get the fingerprints checked. One step at a time, Kelly. We'll take precautions to keep everybody safe."

"Oh, yeah? Like what?"

"Like you and Daniel are moving into the main house. In terms of security, the trailer's a joke. A five-year-old kid could break into this thing."

"Yeah, but with the dogs sleepin' inside, I always thought we were pretty safe."

"Under normal circumstances, you probably were. But your brother's already gotten past them once to get in here tonight."

"They were locked up tonight," Kelly protested. "Of course he got past 'em."

"Granted," Steve said. "But how did he know they were locked up? I think he's been watching the ranch, learning everybody's routines. He might have even seen us drive off to Wisdom. He might also have spent some time wooing the dogs with treats while we were gone, so they won't jump him when they're not locked up."

Remembering the creepy, somebody's-watching-me feelings she'd been having lately, Kelly shivered, then climbed to her feet, slowly nodding in agreement. Johnny was sly enough to do everything Steve had suggested. "You still think he was looking for something?"

Steve stood, too. "Have you thought of anything he'd want? Other than Daniel, of course. A keepsake, maybe, or—"

Kelly rolled her eyes. "He's not sentimental enough for that. We didn't get to keep much when the marshals took the ranch, but Johnny didn't even try to take anything of Mama's. Of course, Dad's letter said he wanted to see Daniel, but he wouldn't have to trash the trailer to find him."

"And Daniel's room got off the easiest," Steve said with a thoughtful scowl. Then he shook his head as if to clear it and offered his hand. "There's nothing more we can do here tonight. Grab your toothbrush and let's go. We'll get whatever else you need tomorrow.''

Exhaustion, more mental than physical, suddenly washed over her, and she leaned against the dresser to steady herself. After a moment's rest, she dug out the oversized T-shirt she usually slept in. When she turned back, she caught Steve using the hand he'd offered her to filch a strip of condoms from the nightstand.

''Mind if I bring along a few of those condominium thingies?'' he asked.

''I didn't call 'em *that*,'' Kelly protested, her face feeling awfully warm all of a sudden. ''Did I?''

He just grinned in reply, and the look in his eyes was so...wicked, she couldn't help chuckling at him. After so much tension, it felt good to laugh a little, and she appreciated his efforts to lighten the mood.

Determined to do her part, she raised an eyebrow at him. ''You really think we'll need 'em?''

His expression grew serious for a moment. ''That's up to you, Kelly. I know this has been pretty upsetting.'' Then he gave her that wicked smile again. ''But I can always hope, can't I?''

''Yeah, you can always hope, Stevie-boy. Bring the glow-in-the-dark kind.''

Of course, her use of his aunt's pet name produced a bellow of outrage, which in turn produced a line of good-natured bickering that continued while they closed the trailer, penned up the dogs again and walked back to the main house.

Used to sleeping in the trailer, Wild Bill and Wyatt had a mournful howling contest when Kelly locked the dog run. Pat Garrett remained silent as any self-respecting Blue Heeler would, but he did give her an unmistakably disgusted look. Unfortunately there wasn't a thing she could do to help the dogs.

She wasn't about to leave three big animals alone in her trailer, and she knew Peg wouldn't appreciate having them in her house, whether or not Kelly was there to ride herd on them. Since they would either make pests of themselves camping out on the front porch or entertain themselves by bothering the stock, she couldn't let them run free around the ranch, either. It took a solid ten minutes of expressing their protests for the dogs to finally give up and settle down for the night.

When the noise died down outside, a new, not entirely unpleasant brand of tension escalated inside the house. For Kelly, the tension was part sexual attraction, part anticipation and part fear of the unknown. She wasn't sure what Steve had to feel tense about, seeing as how he had more experience at this sort of thing than she did, but he acted as restless as a mare getting ready to give birth.

He offered her something to eat. She declined. He offered her something to drink. She declined again. He invited her to sit on the living-room sofa. She accepted, but, to her disappointment, instead of joining her, he paced over to the entertainment center and offered to turn on the TV, the radio, the stereo. Wishing he would just shut up and kiss her, she declined all three.

After he'd checked the locks on all the doors and windows downstairs at least twice, Kelly decided she'd had enough of this nonsense and asked him where she was supposed to sleep. His eyebrows shot up in surprise, and a dull flush climbed his neck and on up into his cheeks.

"I thought, I mean . . . I hoped, you'd want, to sleep with me," he said, "although we probably won't actually sleep all that much. At first, anyway. If, uh, that's what you want?"

Kelly grinned. "Anderson, you big faker. You're as nervous as I am. Are you a virgin, too?"

A stunned expression flitted across his face, and then he let out a shout of laughter that echoed through the big, empty house. "Not hardly." His expression sobering, he leaned down, picked up her left hand and pulled her to her feet. "I haven't had sex with hundreds of women, but I'm not a complete rookie."

"Then what's wrong here?" Kelly asked. "If you've changed your mind about bein' with me like that, all you've gotta do is say so and point me to an empty bedroom."

"No!" He shook his head, chuckled, then shook it again and wrapped his arms around her waist. "That's the *last* thing I want to do. I want you so much I'm about to lose my mind."

Perplexed and a little irritated with his laughter, Kelly braced her hands against his chest and frowned at him. "Well, I don't get it. If you want to have sex with me so much, why're you goin' on and on about food and TV, and stompin' all over the house like you've got ants in your pants?"

He kissed the tip of her nose, rested his forehead against hers and pulled her closer. "I was afraid I might scare you if I pounced on you the minute we walked in the door. I was trying to slow down, and, well, show a little finesse and charm."

"That's really sweet," she murmured.

Despite the disgruntled note in his voice, she figured he must be telling the truth. His heart was thudding fast and heavy against her palms and a hard ridge behind his jeans zipper pressed against her belly. Her own heart jerked into a higher gear in response, and she felt a delicious warmth slowly moving through her limbs.

Yeah, she remembered feeling like this when she'd kissed him before, all right. Only this was the place where they usually stopped, instead of where they were just getting started. Gazing into his eyes, she suddenly felt entranced...almost as if he'd hypnotized her.

Maybe he had. The longer her eyes met his, the less the word "sweet" seemed to fit him. In fact, it seemed as if, in the space of a heartbeat or two, he changed from a warm, easygoing, sexy kind of a guy into a hot, intense, demanding male animal who only had one thing on his mind.

Mating.

With her.

Now.

She gulped. Tried a smile. Threw in a little nervous chatter. "I don't know a whole lot about charm, but as far as I can tell, you're doin' just fine."

He smiled.

Lord, those weren't butterflies in her stomach; they were bats. And they weren't just fluttering; they were swooping and swan diving. She'd only felt this much anxious anticipation once before. Back when she was a kid, they'd owned a buckskin colt she'd been expressly forbidden to ride.

The colt was a corker from day one, a natural-born bucker destined for the rodeo circuit. Knowing she'd never get a crack at him once the stock contractor picked him up, she'd paid Johnny a month's allowance to hold the bronc long enough for her to scramble up the corral fence and jump aboard.

Her landing had been swift and painful, but she would never forget those heart-pounding seconds when she'd been poised over the saddle, feeling the animal's seething energy and leashed strength, knowing all hell was gonna bust loose when Johnny let go of the rope.

The funny thing was, when she thought back on that escapade, it wasn't the pain of getting bucked off she remembered. Nope, she remembered those magical moments on the colt's back. It hadn't lasted long at all—a few seconds at best—but it had been one hell of an exciting ride while it lasted. She'd never regretted it, never felt so alive before or since.

Until now.

In his own way, Steve represented as much risk to her heart as that colt had to her body. She was older and wiser, but she could no more turn away from him than she could have turned away from the colt. She might get hurt, and hurt real bad, but she wouldn't pass up an opportunity for the ride of a lifetime.

She leaned into him and raised both hands to the back of his head, weaving her fingers into his hair. Everything she remembered about kissing him was still there—the gentleness, the tenderness, the affection—all of which seduced her. But this time, instead of the built-in, gentlemanly restraint she'd always sensed in him, she encountered a primitive, masculine determination that excited her beyond anything she'd imagined.

Opening her mouth wider, she deepened the kiss even more. He groaned in response and slid his hands from the back of her waist down over her hips, cupping her buttocks with his palms, holding her closer, moving against her in ways that aroused and frustrated her at the same time.

Her knees turned mushy. Mindful of his sore shoulder, she crisscrossed her wrists behind his neck, unfortunately banging her stitched forearm in the process. The pain made her gasp, which immediately ended the kiss.

Steve inhaled a deep, shuddering breath, then blew it out and gave her a lopsided grin. "Why don't we go upstairs, find a bed and do this right before one of us rips out our stitches?"

Accepting his outstretched hand, she accompanied him to the second floor and down the hallway to his bedroom. Unlike hers, it was filled with books, pictures and boyhood keepsakes such as arrowheads and birds' nests, a rock collection and attempts at whittling that required imagination to figure out what they were supposed to be.

Before she could begin to absorb it all, however, he shut the door and came to her, guiding her to the side of the queen-sized bed. Pushing her to a sitting position, he tugged off her boots, then sat beside her and tugged off his own. From there, she put her trust and her body into his capable hands, allowing him to take the lead.

She hadn't spared the time for many romantic fantasies, but he fulfilled every single one she'd ever had, undressing her between slow, mind-bending kisses, caressing her with such tender approval, she felt no embarrassment at all. It only seemed natural and fair to return the favor, and he obviously liked the process of being undressed and caressed as much as she had.

Once they were both naked, she wasn't sure what to expect, but his eyes promised delights she'd probably never heard of. He didn't disappoint her. Suddenly, he was no longer a cop or a cowboy; he was now an erotic explorer, searching her body for sensitive spots, stopping at each one to kiss and pet and ask if she liked being touched this way or that way better.

She answered when she could find the breath to speak, nodded when she couldn't. He wouldn't let her try to return the favor, insisting that this time was just for her pleasure, promising he would catch up with her at the end, no problem. Taking him at his word, she gave herself up to the incredible sensations he created with his hands and his mouth.

Her concept of time became fluid, stretching out in delicious expectation one moment, contracting to a stinging pinpoint of need the next. He made her sigh and gasp, ache and demand, steadily building a heat and a restless, seething energy and an insatiable hunger she didn't know how to satisfy.

She thrashed her head back and forth on the pillow, whimpering with frustration, grasping at his hips, instinctively trying to pull him inside of her to fill the emptiness and the hunger and that huge, lonely spot up under her heart.

Soothing her with kisses and soft words, he stroked her tangled hair back from her face, then knelt between her thighs and slowly, ever so carefully, united their bodies. Any discomfort she might have felt was quickly swallowed in the first flash of knowledge that her ultimate ride finally had begun.

Unlike the colt, however, the man hovering over her remained absolutely still. She looked up and saw that his eyes were squeezed shut as if he was in terrible pain. His jaw was clenched, making the tendons in his neck stand out in harsh relief. The muscles in his arms, shoulders and chest were equally rigid.

Desperate to end his agony, she reached up and cupped the side of his face with her palm. His eyelids flew open so suddenly she flinched in surprise.

"What is it?" he demanded. "Am I hurting you?"

"No," she whispered, "but it looks like I'm hurting you."

His quick, wicked smile eased her fears. "I'm fine, sweetheart. I don't think I could stand it if I felt any finer."

Confusion filled her. Was this all there was to it? He felt great but, while she definitely liked this physical intimacy, she still felt edgy and itchy for heart-pounding excitement or at least *some*thing else to happen.

Restless for any kind of movement, she instinctively flexed her hips. New sensations flowed from where their bodies were joined, lifting the cloud of disappointment she had begun to feel. "Oh, wow," she whispered.

Ignoring the masculine groan above her, she flexed her hips again. He reached down and grasped her waist, holding her still for an excruciating moment. Then he let go and all hell broke loose. She felt as if she was back on the colt, responding to each powerful buck, hanging on for dear life with her thighs and her hands, knowing she was going to fly off into the sky, but loving every precious moment of contact, shouting with the pleasure and excitement of it.

Her voice blended with his, and then she did fly off into the sky, but this time there was no bone-jarring crash at the end, no explosion of pain, no humiliating, derisive hoot of her brother's laughter at her failure.

No, this time, she came back to consciousness with sweet, fervent kisses all over her face, neck and shoulders, with a husky, masculine voice telling her how wonderful she was, with warm, strong, loving arms holding her as if they never, ever, wanted to let her go.

If this was some kind of weird dream, she never, ever, wanted to wake up. Purposely keeping her eyes shut, she snuggled into those strong, loving arms and told herself to go to sleep. The last thing she heard was Steve murmuring into her ear as he pulled her close against his side.

"I love you, Kel. Sleep tight."

For a moment, that disturbed her. Then, deciding it was a just a wistful dream after all, she settled back down for some sorely needed rest.

Chapter Eleven

Steve awoke early the next morning with Kelly's naked, curvy little butt snuggled against his side, a feeling of delight and satisfaction at finding her there and a powerful temptation to roll her onto her back and make love to her again.

As if his lusty thoughts had disturbed her, she scrunched up her face, turned onto her stomach and buried both hands under her pillow before settling back into slumber with a soft sigh. Steve grinned and told himself he was probably far too proud of his performance last night. A modern, sensitive kind of a guy wasn't supposed to feel so . . . well . . . *macho*, for lack of a better word.

Well, tough. He usually tried not to act like a jerk around women, but at heart, he wasn't really all *that* modern or sensitive. Truth was, at the moment, he felt downright primitive. Studly. As if he wanted to leap naked from the bed, beat on his chest like Tarzan, then jump back into that bed and make love to Kelly again and again until she admitted she belonged to him. So much for centuries of civilization.

Last night had been the best damned night of his life. Once they'd gotten past the barrier of her virginity, Kelly had met him with an earthy enthusiasm that had made him feel like the hottest lover ever born. She made love the way she did everything else—with a whatever-works practicality that transformed the entire experience into an honest, fun, utterly natural pleasure.

He leaned over for a better view of her face and felt his heart give an odd lurch. Last night she'd been a wildcat in his arms. Now, she looked so... defenseless. She was anything but, of course; Kelly had more defenses than a cactus.

What she needed was to feel secure enough to drop those defenses and let her softer side show through more often. She needed someone who could make her laugh and let her cry when she had to. Someone who was bigger and meaner than she was, who was on her side and completely unimpressed by her criminal relatives. Someone like him.

Yeah, she needed him, he assured himself. She wouldn't admit it yet, but he had reason to hope that someday she would. Coming from Kelly, that would be almost the same thing as an admission of love. His chest tightened when he realized how much he wanted to hear her say those words to him.

Jeez, he had it bad. For seven years with Anne he'd been Mr. Patient, willing to wait however long it took for her to resolve her feelings about her ex-husband before giving her a clue he wanted more than a professional relationship. With Kelly, he was Mr. *Im*patient, always wanting to push and coax, tease and beg, even drag her, by the hair if necessary, farther along the road to intimacy.

Judging by the randy reaction a certain part of his anatomy was displaying at the moment, he would undoubtedly end up becoming extremely intimate with her if he didn't get out of this bed in the next sixty seconds. The shadows under her eyes convinced him, however, that a more thoughtful man would let the lady sleep. He could always slip out, do the morning chores and bring a breakfast tray up here. With Kelly well rested, well fed and, hopefully, still naked, he figured all sorts of interesting things might happen.

Easing away from her, he silently climbed out of the bed, grabbed a clean set of clothes and tiptoed from the room. After a quick shower and a shave, he dressed, put on a pot of coffee and went out to do the chores. The coffee was ready by the time he came back into the kitchen. He found potatoes and an onion in the pantry for hash browns, then poked around in Aunt Peg's cupboards for utensils, seasonings and cooking oil.

During his search for a skillet, he glimpsed the stove's clock. An automatic calculation of the time difference between Montana and Chicago told him Noah was probably just sitting down at his desk with the first cup of rotgut coffee of the day. There would never be a better time to catch him.

Deciding breakfast could wait, he pulled a chair over to the wall phone, poured himself a steaming mug of his own brew and dialed Noah's private line. It was his first contact with the office in five weeks. While he waited for the call to go through, Steve realized Kelly had been right—he hadn't missed his job much at all. In fact, he really enjoyed the slower pace of life at the ranch.

"Solomon."

The sound of Noah's voice, gruff and harried even at the start of the day, made Steve smile. "Whoa, boss, sounds like maybe *you* could use a vacation."

"That you, Anderson?"

"Yup. How'dja guess?"

Noah's laugh boomed from the receiver. "It's that cowboy drawl. So, what's up? You finally getting bored out there with the cows and the sagebrush and the coyotes?"

"Hell, no. I think we've got a couple of two-legged coyotes running around here, and they're making me nervous. I need some information from your magic computer."

"Trouble?"

It was easy to slide back into cop jargon. Steve briefly explained what had been happening. Before he'd finished telling everything he knew about Kelly's father and brother, he could hear Noah clicking away on his keyboard. It had always amazed him to watch his huge boss's beefy fingers race over the little buttons with the speed and accuracy of a concert pianist.

"Hold it, hold it, hold it," Noah ordered, his voice tinged with barely controlled excitement. "You're talking about Jonathan Frank "Johnny" James. Age thirty-three. Arrested Pinedale, Wyoming. Convicted of growing and sale of marijuana?"

"That's him."

"He was released three months ago. Skipped on his P.O. two months ago and dropped out of sight. Plenty of people looking for him. File's flagged. Hang on a sec, and I'll see what that's all about."

Steve poured himself another cup of coffee and listened to more clicks. Then Noah came back on the line.

"Amazing. Guy was connected with some major players on the west coast, the Reyez brothers. Seems there's still a big chunk of cash unaccounted for, and the DEA thinks your pal Johnny knows where it's at."

"He's not my pal," Steve muttered.

"Well, if he's there, you're probably going to have a lot of company. DEA was hoping he'd take them to the money, and will they ever be glad to get a lead on him. I'll bet the boys on the coast'll know he's out by now, so they'll be looking for him, too. Be careful, man. You ask me, the whole deal smells bad."

"Yeah. It reeks."

Kelly wandered into the kitchen. Wearing her nightshirt and nothing else as far as he could tell, she looked sleepy, tousled and sexy as hell, and the smile that crossed her face when she saw him raised his temperature at least ten degrees. He patted his lap in invitation. She grinned, shook her head and headed for the coffeepot. Entranced with following her every move, Steve lost track of what his boss was saying.

"Anderson? You still there?" Noah demanded.

"Oh, uh, sure, Noah," Steve said. "Sorry, I got distracted. What did you say?"

"I said, when are you coming back?"

"I don't know."

Noah was silent for a moment. The man had such an uncanny knack for picking up subtle nuances in another person's voice, Steve had often accused him of being psychic. As a result, he wasn't terribly surprised when his boss asked his next question.

"You *are* coming back, though? Right, Anderson?"

Carrying a mug of coffee, Kelly strolled over to Steve and playfully ruffled his hair before reaching around him to get the sugar bowl from the counter. God, she smelled all warm and womanly, and he could see her breasts move freely beneath the soft cotton of her nightshirt as she stirred her coffee. He had to clear his throat to speak.

"Uh, I don't know, Noah. My plans are pretty, uh, indefinite right now."

Noah's voice softened. "What did you say that cowgirl's name was? You know, your uncle's foreman? Johnny's sister?"

"Kelly." She looked at him, an eyebrow raised in query. Steve smiled and patted his lap again. "Kelly Jaynes."

"She wouldn't have anything to do with your plans being so, uh, indefinite, now, would she?"

"Uh-huh," Steve admitted. "She's a beautiful woman."

To his delight, Kelly blushed, then set down her mug and accepted his invitation. He wrapped both arms around her waist. She looped her arms around his neck and rested her head on his shoulder. Contentment washed over him.

Noah laughed, but his voice held more than a hint of exasperation. "I sent you out there to get over a woman, so you'd be of some use around here. You're not supposed to fall in love with another one."

"Well, boss, I'm afraid it's already too late."

"Damn it, Anderson, you sure know how to pick women. Why can't you ever like one who's not up to her eyeballs in trouble?"

"Just lucky, I guess," Steve said. "Thanks for the info. Let me know if you hear anything else."

"Yeah, yeah. Watch your back, man."

"Who was that?" Kelly asked as Steve hung up the phone.

Nuzzling the crook of her neck, he breathed in the scent of her skin. "My boss. You smell good this morning." He hugged her close. "Feel good, too."

She kissed his cheek, then exhaled a soft sigh when he turned his head and gave her a deep, wet, better-than-caffeine good-morning kiss. "Mmm," she murmured, "you taste good. So, what were you telling your boss about me?"

"Nothing much. That you're beautiful." He filled his palms with her breasts. She moaned and arched against his hands. "But you already heard that. How're you feeling this morning, sweetheart?"

"Frisky, sweetheart. Dang frisky." She climbed off his lap, turned around and straddled him. Then she slid her fingers into his hair and kissed him with enough steam to blow off the top of his head.

Steve sank his fingertips into her hips, rocked her back and forth on his aching groin and promised himself he'd tell her all about his conversation with Noah. Soon. Right now there was only one way he wanted to communicate, and it wasn't verbally. Kelly didn't seem to mind.

Nor did she object when he slipped his hands up under her nightshirt. He'd been right; she was naked as a newborn under this thing. He caressed soft, bare skin all the way up her body until the nightshirt came off. He tossed it aside and reveled in her whimpers as he made love to her luscious breasts.

Lord, she was luscious everywhere, and he wanted to see, touch and taste all of her. If she'd only hold still... But, as he'd learned last night, this woman didn't know how to be a passive lover.

She tugged his shirt open and gently raked her short nails down his chest, sending shivers of pleasure straight south. Of course, with her sitting on him, there was no way she could get his pants off, and...oh, God, he was gonna die if he didn't get inside her. Clasping her thighs to his sides with his elbows, he grabbed her waist, surged to his feet and lifted her bottom onto the countertop.

Their harsh, choppy breathing echoed in his ears while she fumbled with his belt buckle and zipper. He should slow down. Slow down. Slow down. Make it last.

But she was shoving at his jeans and shorts with her hands and then with her bare feet until they ended up somewhere down around his knees. And she was stroking him. Fondling him. Making him dizzy and short-circuiting his brain with her touch and her kisses, her naughty whispers and giggles. He could feel her excitement—her wanting him as much as he wanted her—and it was the most erotic thing he'd ever known.

She pulled him close, and when he was buried deep inside, she clamped her strong thighs around his hips. Cradling her in his arms to protect her from the hard counter, he laid her back, kissing her eyelids, her lips, her neck, shoulders and breasts. He couldn't think, didn't want to think. He only wanted to feel. To make her feel.

And then they were moving together, pleasuring each other again and again. Her sweet cries became gusty shouts, urging him on, driving him higher, making him tremble with the effort to hold back. This was where he wanted to be. It was ecstasy. It was heaven. It was home.

He didn't want it to end. Couldn't let it end when he'd only just found it. And when he finally had the whole world within his grasp, her body tightened around him, triggering a release that didn't stop until he collapsed on top of her, sweating and shaking, and calling her name.

Her arms enfolded him. Her fingers stroked his hair. Her soft words soothed him, guiding him back to full consciousness. His racing heart slowed. His lungs remembered how to function. Strength returned to his muscles.

Propping himself up on his elbows, he gazed down into her eyes, felt his lips curve in response to her radiant smile. "You're wonderful," he said. "Absolutely incredible."

She tenderly laid one palm against the side of his face, cleared her throat and instantly went rigid all over at the familiar sound of Bud's pickup pulling into the drive. They exchanged a horrified look, then separated in a mad, laughing, cursing scramble for clothing and at least a modicum of decency, since dignity was undoubtedly beyond them.

By the time Bud and Peg walked through the back door, Kelly had her nightshirt on—inside out and backwards, but covering all the necessary bases, so to speak. Steve had managed to yank up his pants and fasten his shirt, but it wasn't tucked in and his belt and zipper both hung open. Noting the way Kelly's hair was sticking up in the oddest places, he smoothed one hand over his own hair, then forced a grin for his aunt and uncle.

"Hi. Welcome home."

Aunt Peg took one look at the two of them and stopped in her tracks as if she'd run into an invisible wall. Uncle Bud barreled right into her, rocked back on his heels and grabbed her shoulders to steady her. He looked at Steve, then at Kelly, then at the floor, covering his mouth with a loosely curled fist to smother a sudden coughing fit.

Feeling his face heating up, Steve snuck a sideways glance at Kelly and cringed inwardly. Her face was so red, it was a wonder it didn't burst into flames. He wanted to put his arm around her, comfort her somehow, but he suspected she'd probably deck him. Well, hell, it was an embarrassing situation, all right, but they were both consenting adults. There was nothing left to do but brazen it out.

As casually as if he got caught doing this kind of thing every day, he shoved his shirttail into his jeans, zipped them and buckled his belt. Then he picked up the onion and the sack of potatoes he'd dug out of the pantry what seemed like hours ago and carried them over to the sink. "We were just getting ready to fix breakfast," he said while he washed his hands. "Have you guys eaten yet?"

"It's a little late for breakfast, ain't it?" Bud muttered.

Peg elbowed him in the ribs. "We had a little something in Missoula, but we could probably eat again." Then she spotted the bandage on Kelly's arm. "My word, Kelly, what happened?"

Kelly gave her a blank look, shook her head as if to clear it and expelled a nervous laugh. "Oh, uh, nothin' much, Peg. Just had a little accident with a fence." She started inching toward the stairway. "Steve took good care of me."

"Yeah, it sure looks like it," Bud said, scowling at Peg when she elbowed him again.

Steve shut his eyes and silently counted to ten. When he opened them, his aunt and uncle had come farther into the room and Kelly had vanished. "So," he said. "How was your trip?"

Bud poured himself a cup of coffee and retreated to the kitchen table. Peg joined Steve at the sink, washed her hands and, chattering away about the anniversary party they had attended, proceeded to take over the cooking and nudge him out of her way. More than happy to give her back her turf, he dumped the coffee dregs and started a fresh pot.

Kelly returned freshly showered and fully dressed, just in time to help him finish setting the table. He gave her a reassuring wink and felt great relief when she responded with a shrug and a sheepish grin. As if by magic, Peg produced platters of crisp bacon, fried eggs, hash browns and toast. Steve filled the coffee mugs and they all sat down to breakfast.

If the kitchen seemed quieter than usual, Steve told himself it was because Daniel wasn't home. By the end of the meal, however, he had to admit that tension was the real conversation-killer in the room. He didn't know whether to ignore it, which was kind of like trying to ignore a dead skunk lying in the middle of the table, or just go ahead and talk about what had happened that morning and get it over with.

Before he could decide, Bud asked Kelly about her accident. She told him what had happened with the fence and that someone had broken into her trailer. With typical blunt honesty, she went on to confess her suspicion that her brother might somehow be involved with both incidents. Realizing he hadn't yet told her about his conversation with Noah, Steve recounted the information he'd received earlier.

Kelly turned pale at the news. "So it *was* him." She heaved a discouraged sigh, then looked at Bud and Peg. "I'm sorry. We should have left a long time ago, but—"

"You hush up right now, Kelly Jaynes," Peg ordered. "We're not gonna listen to any of that kinda talk."

Bud nodded vigorously. "That's right, you've got nothin' to apologize for, Kelly. You told us the truth about yourself, and we've wanted you to stay all along. I'm just glad ol' Stevie-boy's here to help us handle this." He turned his gaze on Steve. "What do you think we should do?"

"It's a situation with some nasty possibilities, Uncle Bud." Steve considered the alternatives before continuing. "I'd hate to tip Johnny off by changing our routines much right now. If we can hang tough for a couple of weeks, the DEA will probably nab him and he'll go back to prison for violating his parole."

"Well, that doesn't sound too bad," Bud said.

Steve shrugged one shoulder. "Depends on how you look at it. We'd have to be on our guard all the time. Because of the fence, I wouldn't put much of anything past him. And if his drug-running partners show up, anything could happen."

"I've got to get Daniel out of here," Kelly said. "Johnny never accepted having his parental rights terminated. He'll grab Daniel if he gets half a chance, I know he will."

"There's some church camps up on Flathead Lake," Peg said. "Maybe we could send Daniel to one."

"He wouldn't go by himself." Kelly got up and paced between her chair and the window. The anxiety in her voice grew more distinct with every step. "And he's been askin' about his dad lately. If he knew Johnny was anywhere around, I'm afraid he'd go lookin' for him. He was so little when Johnny went to prison, he just doesn't understand—"

Steve casually reached out, looped his arm around Kelly's waist and pulled her onto his lap. She shot him a dirty look. He put his other arm around her waist and hugged her tighter in response. "Of course he doesn't understand, sweetheart, and it's perfectly normal for him to be curious about Johnny."

"But he can't see him, Steve. He's still too young."

"I agree, and I think you're right about getting him out of here. I also know that kid adores you, and he won't go anywhere if he thinks you're upset about something. We'll figure out a way to take care of him, I promise. Will you trust me enough to believe that?"

She looked so long and so deeply into his eyes, Steve almost expected her to say no. He knew trust was the most difficult thing for Kelly to give, and the more he learned about her background, the more he could understand why she felt that way. If their relationship was to go even one step further, however, she had to trust him now.

Gazing into Steve's eyes, Kelly thought he could make her believe in just about anything. Last night she had trusted him enough to share her body with him in the most intimate way possible, and he had responded with more passion, tenderness and affection than she could have imagined. When his aunt and uncle had come home early enough to know what the two of them had been up to, he'd continued to treat her exactly the same way, and had made no excuses or apologies for his behavior.

He would never know how deeply he had touched her by acting as if his having a romance with an ignorant cowgirl like her was only natural. And Bud and Peg, God love 'em both, they'd just played right along with him. If she didn't work pretty dang hard at staying realistic about her station in life, she was liable to start daydreaming about ridiculous things that weren't going to happen, no matter how much she might want 'em to.

Things like engagement rings and weddings. A husband and a home of her own nobody could ever take away from her. And babies. Lots of babies to love and cuddle and enjoy. She'd never told anyone how much she wanted to have her own kids. Heck, the only way she could justify keeping such useless critters as Wild Bill and Wyatt around, was to admit they were substitutes for the kids she'd never have.

"Kelly?" Steve hugged her again, making her realize she still hadn't answered him.

"I'll try, Marshal. I know you're right about me stayin' calm for Daniel's sake. I just feel real guilty, for bringin' all of this down on you folks. It shouldn't be your problem."

Peg reached across the table, took Kelly's hand and squeezed it. "Hon, around these parts, we take care of our own. As far as we're concerned, you and Daniel qualify. Whether you like it or not, you're part of our family."

Tears welled up in Kelly's eyes. Before she could blink them back or wipe them away, Bud leaned forward, propped an elbow on the table and made matters worse.

"That's right, young lady, and don't you ever forget it." Then a wicked grin that reminded her an awful lot of Steve's spread across his face. "Besides, from the way you two keep lookin' at each other, I suspect you really *are* gonna be part of the family before very long. I can't think of anything that'd make us happier."

Kelly opened her mouth to set him straight, but Steve cut her off. "We haven't gotten quite that far yet, Uncle Bud, but I'm working on it."

Turning back around to frown at him, she found herself facing a man with a confident smile and an unnerving, determined glint in his eyes. Good Lord, he was serious. Probably felt responsible for her since he'd slept with her, or some such noble nonsense. He was an incredibly decent guy at heart.

Well, she'd have to save Steve from himself, eventually, but first she had to deal with Johnny. Damn his mangy, miserable, insane hide. And damn Jay's selfish, lazy, cowardly hide, too. Talk about comin' from the shallow end of the gene pool. Why, if the Jameses were cattle or horses, she'd have the whole bunch put down due to inferior breeding.

"Okay, Anderson," she said. "I can tell you've got a plan, so let's hear it."

He winked at her with obvious approval. "All right, here it is. You and I need to stay and keep working the ranch so Johnny won't suspect we're onto him, but the fewer civilians we have to get in the way, the better the DEA boys will like it. The best way Uncle Bud and Aunt Peg could help, would be to take Daniel on a vacation."

"A vacation!" Bud shouted. "Boy, have you lost your mind? Somebody's threatening my foreman and my ranch, and you want me to just take off? Hell, I'm not afraid of those bastards and I'm still a better shot than most of—"

"I know that," Steve interrupted, "and I'm not questioning your courage, Uncle Bud. But right now, I don't have any idea who's out there. It could be Johnny and Jay. It could be the Reyez brothers. It could be all of them. Noah will get some backup in here as soon as he can, but until they get here and we know exactly what's going on, it'd be a lot easier if I knew you were keeping Aunt Peg and Daniel out of danger."

Bud still looked as if he wanted to argue, but Peg laid her hand on his forearm and said quietly, "Steve's right, hon. We can get Daniel to come with us without gettin' him all upset. We could go to Virginia City, and the Lewis and Clark Caverns. He'd go nuts over that big new museum in Bozeman that's got the dinosaurs, and I don't think he's ever been to Yellowstone Park, has he, Kelly?"

Fighting a lump in her throat, Kelly shook her head. "No. We lived real close to it all those years, but we never did go play tourist."

"How long do you want us to stay gone?" Bud asked.

"A week. Maybe two," Steve answered. "And you're gonna have to stay on your toes. Keep an eye out for anyone following you. If you get any weird, suspicious feelings, I'll want to hear about it."

Bud looked at Peg and a reluctant grin tugged at one side of his mouth. "Oh, all right," he grumbled. He pushed himself to his feet and propped his hands on his hips. "I'll go clean out the camper and you organize some food. I'm bringin' the fishin' poles, so don't forget the corn meal. We'll leave first thing in the mornin' if that's soon enough?"

Steve nodded, nudged Kelly off his lap and stood. "I'll give you a hand, Uncle Bud."

The men went out the back door, already deep in conversation before it closed behind them. Suddenly finding herself alone with Peg left Kelly feeling unusually exposed and uncertain of what to expect. Her relationship with the older woman had always been warm and friendly, but that was before this morning.

While Peg had seemed pleased about Steve and Kelly's romance, such as it was, that had been while Steve had been around to protect her. Now she was on her own, and the piercing expression in Peg's eyes made Kelly damn nervous.

Never one to beat around bushes, Peg came right to the point. "You love my nephew, don't you?"

"Yeah. But don't go gettin' your hopes up, Peg." Kelly picked up Steve's dirty plate and her own, and carried them to the sink. "About anything . . . permanent happenin', I mean."

Peg's eyebrows climbed halfway up her forehead, and she followed with another load of dishes. "Why not? He sounded interested in something permanent to me. He's not some jerk of a ladies' man, you know."

"How could I know something like that?" Kelly asked with a shrug. "I only met him a few weeks ago."

"Well, he's not," Peg said. "He's a good, solid man, and he'd make a wonderful husband."

"Probably so." Her lips clamped in a tight smile, Kelly sadly shook her head. "But not for me. It just wouldn't work."

"You don't know that," Peg protested.

"Yeah, I do. I come from a line of crooks that goes back over a hundred years. He's a cop, Peg. A *lawman.*"

Her eyes narrowed, Peg studied Kelly for a long, breathless moment. Then she smiled, propped one hand on her hip and pointed the index finger of her other hand at Kelly's nose. "Well, get over it, gal. He can't help it and I won't stand for you actin' like such a dang snob. My Stevie-boy's plenty good enough to marry you, even if you are a James."

Chapter Twelve

The next four days were nothing short of a revelation for Kelly. Once Daniel, Bud and Peg took off on their trip, she found out it could be a lot of fun to live with a man. During the day, she worked beside Steve just as she had before, but instead of spending most of her time trying to avoid or ignore him, it now seemed as if she couldn't talk to him enough. Or laugh with him enough. Or touch him enough.

Every new thing she learned about him fascinated her, and he appeared to feel the same way. And there was so dang much to like about him, she figured he was at least a different breed of male, if not an entirely different species than her dad and brother, and every other cop she'd ever met, except for Andy Johnson back in Pinedale. She spent a lot of time trying to figure out why he appealed to her so much, and finally came to the conclusion that he really did see and treat her as an equal.

For instance, he picked up after himself. Didn't seem like such a big deal on the surface, but life was a lot more pleasant when you weren't constantly tripping over somebody else's messes. He really could and did cook most of their meals, and didn't act like she was some kind of freak because she'd never learned. He didn't expect her to wait on him, but if she did happen to bring him something out of convenience or politeness or whatever, he always noticed and said, "Thanks," and even returned the favor on occasion.

And then, there were the nights. Kelly smiled to herself every time she remembered the first time they'd made love and she'd thought it would be the "ultimate" ride for her. Hah! It had been good, all right, much better than she had expected a "first time" to be. But she hadn't even begun to imagine the variety of possibilities the phrase "making love" might include.

So far, at least, it had been a different, more delightful experience every single time they'd done it, and God knew, they'd done it plenty of times, in plenty of ways and in plenty of places. It was a good thing Daniel and the Ryans were gone, because she and Steve just couldn't seem to keep their hands off each other. Considering how little sleep they were getting, it was a wonder they had any steam at all left for work.

That didn't turn out to be a problem, however. In fact, she'd never had more energy. When every moment together was so precious and exciting, sleep became a waste of time.

Though one part of her mind insisted this was just sort of a honeymoon period that would eventually have to end, Kelly refused to listen. She had never felt so wonderful before, doubted she would ever feel so wonderful again and she wasn't about to spoil one second of it worrying about the future. She intended to store up as many memories of being in love with Steve Anderson as possible, like a squirrel stashing a supply of nuts for the winter. The future would undoubtedly show up plenty soon enough, thank you very much.

She'd privately been hoping for at least two blissful weeks alone with Steve. She figured she'd be lucky to get ten days. When reality intruded after only four days, she felt downright cheated, not to mention royally ticked off.

They'd spent the day in the national forest, fencing the acres Bud leased from the federal government for summer pasture. It was hot, dirty work, but with Steve's help and company, the hours had zipped by at twice the normal speed. They carried on and teased each other about who should get the first shower all the way back to the ranch.

After parking by the back door, Steve unfastened his seat belt, slid across the bench seat and hauled her onto his lap with the stated intention of kissing her until she agreed to share. Of course, Kelly *had* to refuse, if only for the sheer pleasure of letting him try his best to change her mind, which, of course, she'd planned to do all along.

It was silly, playful, high-school-kid behavior, but it was fun, and she hadn't had nearly enough of that when she was growing up. She suspected Steve hadn't, either, and she enjoyed seeing this relaxed, carefree side of him.

The sight of a white car rolling up the drive trailing a cloud of dust was an irritating interruption at best. Biting back a disgruntled sigh, she followed Steve out the driver's door and stood beside him. He slung an arm around her shoulders with an air of affectionate camaraderie she—the woman who had once thought she didn't like to be touched by anyone but Daniel—had come to love.

Then the car stopped. The driver's door opened and one of her worst nightmares emerged into the late afternoon sunlight. Her breath caught, her gut clenched and her mouth went dry when she recognized her dad.

Other than a lot more gray in his dark hair, Jay James hadn't changed much in the nine years since she'd seen him. His face was still relatively unlined, and his shirt and slacks looked crisp, new and expensive. He'd always taken pride in his physique and had obviously made use of the prison's athletic facilities to maintain it. He even had a tan, although it wasn't nearly as dark as it used to be.

Pulling away from Steve, Kelly raised her chin, straightened her spine and propped her fists on her hips. "What do you want, Jay?" she demanded, putting enough icy steel into her voice to daunt anyone who wasn't packing a gun.

His ingratiating smile hadn't changed either, except that it no longer held the power to charm her. "That's not much of a welcome after all this time, Kelly."

"That's because you're *not* welcome here," Kelly replied. "How'd you find me?"

Shrugging one shoulder, he maintained his smile, though Kelly thought it was starting to look a tad forced. "You know how small towns are. A tidbit of gossip here. Another one there. It wasn't terribly difficult."

"Yeah, I'll bet. What do you want, Jay?"

Jay's gaze traveled to Steve, who had come to stand directly behind Kelly. "Won't you introduce me to your friend?"

Before Kelly could refuse, Steve rested his hands on her shoulders, and gave what she interpreted to be a warning squeeze. "Steve Anderson," he said. "My uncle owns this ranch."

"It's a pleasure to meet you, Steve," Jay replied. "I'm Jay James, Kelly's father."

"Yes, I know," Steve said, his voice neither welcoming nor discouraging. Kelly shot him a quelling glance, but if he saw it, he ignored it. "Kelly's told me a lot about you and her brother. Was there something we can do for you?"

Jay spread his hands, palms up, in a "what-can-I-say?" gesture. "Not really. I just wanted to see my daughter again. And my grandson. Daniel is still with you, isn't he, Kelly?"

Kelly gave him a stiff nod. "He's not here right now, though, and I wouldn't let you see him if he was."

Jay's smile faltered. "Now, Kelly, there's no need to hold a grudge. I'm a changed man, sweetheart. I've made some terrible mistakes, but I'm still your daddy. We'll always be a family—"

"No, we won't," Kelly interrupted. "Daniel's a *good* kid, Jay. He works hard in school, he's never been in trouble with the law, and he's got a future that doesn't include jail cells. I will be *damned* before I'll let you or Johnny get anywhere near him."

One side of Jay's mouth kicked up, forming a taunting grin. "Have you heard from Johnny lately?"

"I think you know the answer to that," Kelly said.

"Do you know where Johnny is?" Steve asked, his tone calm and bland as a bowl of vanilla pudding.

Jay glanced down, then back up at Steve before answering, the movement so quick most folks would have missed it. Kelly didn't miss it, however, and she'd seen it enough times to know it always preceded a lie. "As far as I know, he hasn't been released yet."

"You're a changed man, huh?" Kelly scoffed. "You wouldn't know the truth if it bit you on the behind. I've got nothin' more to say to you. Not ever."

"You don't mean that, Kelly," Jay said.

Steve squeezed Kelly's shoulders again. "What does Johnny want besides Daniel?"

"I'm sure I don't know what you're talking about."

Noting Jay's telltale gesture again, Kelly snorted in disgust. "Like hell you don't. Well, you just tell Johnny for me, that if I catch him trespassin' on this ranch again, I'll shoot him down like I would a rabid skunk. And the same goes for you . . . *Daddy*."

Jay's composure finally slipped. Stepping away from the car, he gave Kelly a glare hot enough to singe hair. "That's enough, you little b—"

Moving as if he wouldn't hurry if his pants were on fire, Steve gently pushed her behind him and advanced toward Jay, who was a good four inches shorter and twenty or thirty pounds lighter. Though the volume of Steve's voice stayed the same, a distinctive note of threat entered it. "I wouldn't call her that if I were you."

Jay backed up, stretched as tall as he could and cast a denigrating look over Steve's dusty Stetson, jeans and boots. "Why don't you mind your own business and excuse us, cowboy?"

Steve crossed his arms over his chest and tipped his head to one side as if he was giving the suggestion serious consideration before slowly shaking his head. "I don't think so. If you two were to get physical, she'd probably beat the living hell out of you, and I'd hate to have to save your mangy hide."

Jay leaned to the left and glared around him at Kelly. "You can't hide behind this big goon forever. Don't try my patience any further. It's your own fault Johnny is so...angry with you."

"Why, you low-life scumbucket." Enraged, Kelly tried to get in front of Steve, but he easily blocked her attempts.

"Dammit, Kelly, be reasonable," Jay said. "I need to talk with you about Johnny. Alone. *Now*. I can help you deal with him."

"I don't need your damned help." Since pounding on Steve's back hadn't moved him out of her way, Kelly pinched his right buttock. Hard. He yelped, and when he reached back to rub the injured spot, she dodged around to his left, finally managing to step in front of him. She glared over her shoulder at him. "And I don't need yours, either, Anderson."

"Ah, such brave words." Jay's smile mocked her. "But will you be as brave when your brother catches up with you? It *was* your turn, Kelly. You owe us. Big time."

Kelly turned back to face Jay and forced herself to speak in a deadly quiet tone of voice. "I don't owe Johnny, you or anybody else squat, and I meant every damned word I said. You two are no kin of mine or Daniel's. Don't bother us again."

A dull red flush climbed into Jay's face and he answered Kelly in the same, deadly quiet tone. "You'll regret this."

"I doubt it. I'm not afraid of either one of you anymore, so stop tryin' to push me around." Maintaining eye contact with him, she pointed toward the drive. "Get the hell off this ranch and go find yourself a big flat rock to crawl under."

Jay glared at her a moment longer, then stomped back to his car, climbed in and roared off. As if to expose her bravado for what it was, a shudder raced up Kelly's spine.

"Hey, Kel, don't hold back." Uttering a soft chuckle, Steve moved up beside her again and slid his arm around her waist. "Tell him how you really feel."

Humiliated that Steve, of all possible people on the planet, had been a witness to that pathetic, disgusting exchange between her and her miserable excuse for a father, Kelly elbowed him in the ribs. He let her go with a startled "Oof," then rubbed his side and frowned at her.

"What was that for?" he asked.

She frowned right back at him. "I meant what I said to you, too. I don't need you to handle my own family."

"Oh, really?" Scowling, he tipped back his hat and scratched his head in a gesture of mock confusion. "Well, gee-whiz, Ms. Kelly, weren't you the one whose only idea of how to handle those guys was to cut and run?"

His sarcasm infuriated her. His being right didn't endear him to her, either. "Well, you didn't exactly put the fear of God into my old man, Marshal. He'll be back."

"I'm counting on it," Steve said. "Next time he shows up, see if you can control that temper of yours a little better. Get some information out of him."

"Like what?"

"Like where he's staying. Where he got the money for that car and those clothes he was wearing. Any kind of clue that might help the DEA guys find your brother."

"Yeah, well, if they want him so much, where are they? Why aren't they already out here? Then they could just follow Jay, and I'll bet you fifty bucks he'd lead 'em right to Johnny."

"They'll be here tomorrow, Kelly. It takes time to set up a good surveillance operation. Especially out here in the boondocks where there's no network in place and so few good places to hide."

Kelly rolled her eyes and huffed with impatience. "Johnny's managed it so far, and, believe me, he's no mental giant."

"He's just one guy. He doesn't have to bring in any special equipment or even get all that close to us." Steve gestured toward the foothills in the national forest to the west of the ranch. "He could pose as a backpacker, sit up there on a ridge with a pair of binoculars and nobody'd think anything of it."

The hair on the back of Kelly's neck prickled at the thought of her brother watching her whenever he felt like it, and she shot an uneasy glance in the direction Steve had indicated. "What'll your pals from the DEA pose as? Boy scouts?"

Steve shrugged. "Tourists, fishermen, ranch hands. Telephone linemen. A new bartender in Wisdom. Whatever they think they can get away with that won't draw undue attention."

"They'll contact you, won't they?"

"Probably. From what Noah said the last time I talked to him, though, they want Johnny to lead them to that money so bad, they're willing to pull out all the stops."

"Which means?"

"Which means, they'll be extremely careful to avoid tipping him off. They'll make contact, but they won't tell me everything they're doing."

"Well, now, *that's* certainly comforting." Wrapping her arms around herself, Kelly turned away.

"It'll be all right, Kel," Steve said. "These guys are pros. I trust them and so can you."

She tipped back her head and let out the bitter laugh that would have given her heartburn otherwise. "Right. Last time I had anything to do with you feds, I lost my land, my home, my stock, and I came damn close to losin' Daniel. Pardon me all to hell if I have misgivings about gettin' involved with any of this."

"Do your misgivings include me?"

Kelly turned at the waist and met his challenging gaze head on. "Yeah."

"Why, Kelly? After all we've shared—"

"All we've shared? Oh, you mean the bed? The kitchen countertop? The living-room rug? What's our havin' sex got to do with anything? You're still a lawman, Anderson. And I'm still a James. If push comes to shove, whose side are you gonna be on?"

"I don't understand what you mean. You don't have anything to worry about from me or any other lawman, sweetheart. You haven't done anything wrong."

"I didn't do anything wrong the last time, either, but I still lost everything." She turned away again. Swallowed hard, but couldn't get the husky note completely out of her voice. "Nobody wanted to believe I didn't know what Jay and Johnny were doin'. If it wasn't for Andy Johnson, they probably would have sent me to prison, too."

He came up behind her, and gently squeezed her shoulders. "Nothing like that will happen this time, Kelly. I promise I'll take care of you."

Old habits truly did die hard. Despite his reassurance, the cold, tight little seed in the pit of her stomach sent out poisonous tendrils of fear. They choked out the truth in her heart, in her mind, leaving room for little but a foggy, unreasoning sense of panic whenever she had to think about Jay, Johnny and lawmen at the same time.

She whirled to face him, then slowly backed away. "I don't need you to take care of me, Marshal. I don't need anybody."

She turned and ran toward her trailer, but not even the dogs' exuberant greetings from their pen could block out the words Steve shouted after her.

"We didn't just have sex, Kelly. We made love, and you damn well know it."

Chapter Thirteen

While Kelly did the dishes that night, Steve stepped onto the back porch, stuck his .45 into the waistband of his jeans at the small of his back and put on a denim jacket to cover it. Then he walked outside, put his hands in his front jeans pockets and ambled across the barnyard. Maintaining a slow, easy pace, he scanned the area around the house and outbuildings with a critical eye, looking for signs of intrusion.

He'd felt uneasy since Jay James had left. Though he saw nothing out of place now, the back of his neck tingled, his survival instincts kicked into gear, and he knew Johnny was out there somewhere. Watching. Steve had expected as much.

After the way Jay had insisted on speaking to Kelly alone, Steve had assumed Johnny must be nearby, waiting for his father to come back with whatever it was they wanted from her. Until he knew what that was, Steve intended to patrol the ranch as often and unobtrusively as possible. His DEA backup could take over when they arrived. Of course, that wasn't the only reason he'd wanted to get out of the house right now.

He had a slew of questions he wanted to ask Kelly, but he was still too angry and hurt over the things she'd said to risk getting into anything more than polite chitchat with her just yet. On an intellectual level, he could understand her reluctance to trust anyone, especially federal law-enforcement officers. She'd been poorly treated and justice had hardly been served by taking away her heritage and her livelihood for a crime she hadn't committed.

On a more personal, emotional level, however, he couldn't understand her inability to trust *him*. During the past few days, they had been as close as any man and woman could be. He wasn't a cop when he was with her; he was a lover and a friend.

Damn her suspicious hide, she *knew* he loved her. How could she still doubt him so much? How could she believe for one second that he would ever allow anyone, law-enforcement officer or not, to do anything bad to her or Daniel? After that confrontation with Jay, how could she say she didn't need him?

A chain-link fence rattled off to his left. He started, then looked over at the dog run. Wild Bill stood on his hind legs, front paws hooked into the diamond-shaped holes in the steel mesh, long, skinny tail wagging, a hopeful, canine-type grin on his muzzle. Steve couldn't help grinning back at the beast. Wild Bill barked and wagged his tail harder. As if he'd called them over, Wyatt Earp and Pat Garrett stood and shook themselves, then trotted up to the fence and copied the wolfhound's stance.

Steve laughed out loud. "Okay, guys, I'll spring you. You'll need another run before bedtime, anyway."

He opened the gate. Wyatt and Pat ran out, but Wild Bill darted to a far corner and returned with his favorite toy, a fat hunk of rope with a knot tied in both ends. He galloped through the opening, turned back around and spat the toy onto the ground at Steve's feet. Lowering his front end in a blatant invitation to play, the hound let out a thunderous bark.

Laughing again, Steve picked up the rope and heaved it as far as he could. Wild Bill raced after it, brought it back and, growling deep in his throat, shook it at Steve. Digging the heels of his boots into the dirt, Steve grabbed the other end and

played tug-of-war until he thought the beast would yank his
arms out of their sockets.

"Let go," he said. "Drop it, you dopey mutt."

Growling again, Wild Bill thrashed his massive head and
pulled harder. Steve leaned back, using his entire weight for
leverage. Wild Bill pushed against the ground with his huge
paws and stiffened his legs, but slowly, slowly, he started to
slide. With a grim smile of satisfaction, Steve strained every
muscle and sinew, reeling in the wolfhound.

In a strange way, this contest of physical strength with Wild
Bill reminded him of the contest of wills he continually found
himself waging with Kelly. Worthy opponents, they both challenged him to his limits and demanded his respect. They were
bighearted and lovable on one hand, strong and stubborn as
hell on the other. Both would occasionally loosen up enough to
let him hope he might win. Then they'd turn right around and
come at him from a different angle, letting him know he might
win a battle now and then, but they were far from beaten.

While he thoroughly enjoyed his rough-and-tumble play with
the dog, Kelly's resistance worried him. What would he have to
do to convince her he would always be on her side? Propose to
her? He'd already hinted at that more than once and been po-
litely slapped down every time. Quit his job? The idea reminded him too much of his mother.

Granted, he was already thinking about quitting for other
reasons, but he needed Kelly to trust him whether he was a cop,
a cowboy or a carpenter. And he needed her to admit she loved
him because she wanted to, not because he'd pressured her into
saying the words. Dammit, all of these ambivalent emotions
floating around confused and confounded him. Falling in love
should be a happy sort of thing, shouldn't it?

"C'mon, Bill, drop it," he said. "I'll throw it for you again.
Listen, fur ball—"

"Try ticklin' him under his chin," Kelly suggested.

Surprised at the sound of her voice coming from somewhere
close behind him, Steve looked over his shoulder. Wild Bill
immediately released the rope and ran to greet her, prancing
around and demanding attention at the same time. Still pull-

ing on his own end of the rope with all of his strength, Steve suddenly felt himself toppling over backward.

He heard Kelly let out a startled yelp and take two running steps toward him, and then he smashed into the ground with enough force to drive the breath from his lungs. Slightly out of focus, Kelly's worried face hovered over him. He could see her mouth moving, but couldn't hear her words over the ringing in his ears.

Wild Bill's shaggy head appeared beside Kelly's. Before Steve could raise a hand to fend him off, a long, rough tongue lashed across his lower face, drenching his mouth with dog slobber. His lungs screaming for oxygen while he sputtered and violently shook his head, Steve struggled to sit up. Kelly shoved her hands under his shoulders and lifted, roaring at Wild Bill to, "Sit, you idiot dog!"

Wild Bill sat. Kelly knelt behind Steve, held him up with one hand and whacked him between the shoulder blades with the other, ordering him to, "Breathe, dammit, will ya?"

Steve breathed. Relief was instantaneous and he quickly realized he hadn't really hurt anything besides his dignity. He wiped the back of his hand across his mouth, took one look at the crestfallen expression on the wolfhound's face and exhaled a shaky laugh.

Kelly heaved a relieved sigh, then sat on the grass behind him, stretched her legs along the outsides of his and put her arms around his torso, silently coaxing him to lean back against her chest for support. It was an offer he wouldn't dream of refusing, and when he tipped his head back to thank her, she leaned down and, ignoring the possibility of picking up dog spit from his mouth, planted a sweet, sensuous kiss on his lips.

"M-m-m-m, what was that for?" he murmured when it ended.

She hugged him, then rested her chin against the side of his head. "I just wanted to, and . . . well, I guess it was sort of an apology. I'm sorry I, uh . . . hurt your feelings. You didn't deserve what I said to you after Jay left."

Surprised and touched by her words, Steve directed his gaze toward the barn. This discussion would be easier for Kelly if she didn't have to look him in the eye, and he was more than willing to help her any way he could. "Apology accepted."

"You'll forgive me just like that?"

He nodded. "I'd like to understand more about what made you so mad, but I know none of this is easy for you."

She sighed again and hugged him again. "I guess part of it was just the shock of seein' Jay. It brought it all back. The arrests. The trials. Losin' the ranch. And he was so dang... smarmy and he was such a liar...." She paused, shuddered, then slowly shook her head. "I felt real, uh, ashamed for you to even meet him."

Her voice wobbled on the last sentence. Steve glanced back at her and felt his heart wrench at the sadness in her eyes. She immediately looked away, of course, but not before he saw tears well up. Shifting around to face her, he clasped her cheeks between his palms.

"It's not your fault, Kel. You're not responsible for Jay or Johnny."

"You keep tellin' me that, but—"

"But nothing. We can't change the past. We can't change who our families are going to be or where we come from. We can only change where we're headed and what kind of people we want to be by making our own choices. The ones that feel right to us."

"I know. I've tried to do that, but sometimes I can't help worrying it won't last." She swiped under her eyes with her fingertips, sniffled and gave him a watery smile. "I'm afraid there's some weird, genetic defect that keeps getting passed down from one generation of Jameses to the next. That no matter how hard I try, Daniel and I won't be able to escape it and we'll end up in jail, too."

"That's hogwash." Steve got his feet under him, then took her hands and pulled her up with him when he stood. "Criminal behavior isn't genetic, it's learned. It can turn into a vicious cycle in some families because nobody teaches the kids any other way to live. You've already fixed that, sweetheart. You've broken the cycle for both you and Daniel."

"You sound so sure of that," she whispered.

She met his gaze and he suddenly understood what it meant to see someone's heart in their eyes. He could see Kelly's hope warring with doubt and fear, and it nearly broke his own heart to see such pain in the depths of hers. He wrapped his arms around her and held her close, cupping the back of her head when she rested her cheek against his shoulder.

"I've never been more sure of anything," he said. "You're already a wonderful person in your own right, Kel. And Daniel's as honest as kids come. He's going to be just fine."

She snuggled closer and put her arms around him. They stood there holding each other for what felt like a long time. While the sun slowly dipped behind the mountains to the west, Steve felt a sense of peace and completeness sinking into his soul. The beauty, the isolation, the serenity of the ranch and Kelly in his arms were more than enough to make him happy.

He nuzzled her ear. She tilted her head back, aligning her mouth with his. He would have kissed her, but as their lips met, an indignant "Woof!" drew his attention. Wild Bill sat right where Kelly had left him, his eyes pleading, his hide trembling with impatience and pent-up energy.

"We forgot somebody," Steve said.

Kelly giggled. "Okay, Wild Bill. Go on and run."

The wolfhound galloped off to join Wyatt and Pat. Steve watched for a moment, then turned back to Kelly. She met him halfway, sliding her arms around his neck and kissing him with a sweet eagerness that made him tingle clear down to the soles of his feet.

This time, the kiss had a poignant flavor to it, as if they both realized an important barrier had been crossed. As if they both realized they really *could* find a common ground on which to build a future. As if they both also realized just how fragile and iffy that future might be.

The back of his neck tingled again, reminding him this was neither the most private time nor the best place to start making out with Kelly. In an odd way, he almost hoped her brother and dad *were* watching them at this moment, if only to get it through their thick heads that Kelly was no longer alone. But he didn't intend to give them any more of a show than this.

Regretfully pulling back, he waited for her to regain her equilibrium. Then, keeping his arm around her waist, he set off to finish patrolling. Kelly easily matched her steps to his, saying very little while they penned up the dogs again and headed back to the house. At the bottom of the porch steps she paused, looked off toward the west and shivered, and he knew she felt the silent threat of the watchers as keenly as he did.

As if she'd given herself a private pep talk, she raised her chin, squared her shoulders and marched into the house. Admiring her courageous spirit, Steve followed her inside, shut and locked the kitchen door and found her waiting there for him, ready and eager to slide into his arms.

"Make love to me, Steve," she whispered. "Please."

Darkness had invaded the house while they were out. Deep shadows made familiar objects look weird, even frightening, reminding Kelly of how Johnny had loved to scare her when they were kids. Wherever she went, whatever she did, she'd always had to be on her guard in case he would jump out at her from behind a boulder, a bale of hay or a big chair, and then laugh his fool head off when she screeched in surprise.

In the years since she'd left Wyoming, she'd gotten over most of the fear he'd instilled in her. But not all of it. Never all of it. At this moment, she remembered every bit of that fear so vividly, she couldn't bring herself to move until Steve turned on a light.

While the idea of such cowardice shamed her, Kelly found herself instinctively turning to the man beside her. "Make love to me, Steve," she whispered, telling herself she really wasn't looking to him for protection. Not *just* protection, anyway.

Steve was the one person who could make all the bad stuff go away. For a while, at least. When she was in his arms, everything else—memories, responsibilities, worries—faded away before the magic they always created together.

Was it such a crime to want a little of that magic when it felt like every bad memory she'd ever had was about to crash down on her at once?

If so, they might as well come and lock her up right now, because she wanted ... well, okay, she *needed* him, with a desperation that defied all sense of reason. Johnny and Jay would come after her soon enough, and she would deal with them when they did. But for these few stolen moments, she would allow herself the excitement, the forgetfulness, the ... comfort only Steve could give her.

She sidled closer to him, slid her palms up his chest and linked her fingers together behind his neck. "Please."

Smiling, he leaned down and kissed her senseless. Then he squeezed her left buttock, whispered, "Last one to the bedroom's a rotten egg," and took off running. His rumbling laughter trailed behind him, luring her to chase him through the house and up the stairs, shedding fears and inhibitions as fast and easily as they shed their clothes.

By the time his arms closed around her again and he tumbled her to the mattress, all of the shadows were gone. The magic surrounded them, lifting them to the golden place where pounding hearts and sweaty, tangled limbs turned into groans of pleasure and soft, satisfied sighs. Where giving became receiving. Where lusty desires mixed with earthy pleas, producing wild, ecstatic climaxes, the warmest, gentlest caresses and emotions so sweet and deep they brought tears to her eyes.

Afterward she sprawled across him in a blissful, boneless heap, finding utter contentment in stroking his chest hair with the tip of her index finger. His heart thumped out a reassuring rhythm beneath her ear. One of his hands made long, slow sweeps from her nape to the backs of her knees.

This was what she had wanted and needed from him, these soft, lazy, moments of closeness, in which she didn't have to do or say or be anything in particular. All she had to do was lie here and enjoy being with him, which came as naturally to her as breathing.

Best of all, nobody could ever take these moments away from her. Whenever she felt sad or lonely or scared in the future, she would always have these memories to hang on to. No matter how bad life got, she could always tell herself that at least once, a kind, decent, wonderful man had known all about Jay and

Johnny and her other creepy ancestors and relatives, and he'd loved her anyway.

As if that last thought had conjured an evil spell, a blood-chilling cry from the kennel shattered the quiet night. Before Kelly could even identify which dog had howled in distress, Steve was on his feet, yanking on jeans, boots and shirt. Then he picked up his .45 from the dresser and said, "Stay here," before he headed out the door.

She scrambled into her own clothes, muttering, "In your dreams, Marshal."

Through the open window she could hear Wyatt barking and yelping, calling for her as clearly as a screaming child. Pausing only to grab her old .22 rifle and a box of shells from the pickup, she ran toward the barn. When she slowed down to skid around the southeast corner, a hand reached out of the deeper shadows, latched onto her forearm and practically yanked her out of her boots.

"What the hell do you think you're doing?" Steve whispered.

"I'm goin' to my dogs," she whispered back, furiously resisting his hold. Besides Wyatt's hysterical barking, now she could hear terrible whimpers that sounded as if they must be coming from Wild Bill. "Dammit, turn me loose."

"Stop it, Kelly." He pointed to the big yard light that stood between the barn and Kelly's trailer. "You'll make a perfect target out there."

"They won't shoot me."

"You don't know that."

"Jay wants somethin', remember? He's smart enough to know he won't get it if I'm dead."

"Then why did you bring the rifle?"

"Because I don't know if Johnny's that smart, and I don't want him to think I'll go down easy, all right?" Fearing she might explode with impatience, Kelly stopped struggling and forced a note of calm into her voice. "Now, will you *please* let go of me?"

"All right. But let me go fir—"

The instant he relaxed his grip, she twisted free, whipped around the corner of the barn and sprinted for the kennel. She heard him curse under his breath and come after her, but she charged ahead. Wild Bill sounded like he could die if she waited for Steve to go through all of his careful-cop rigmarole.

It took two seconds to figure out what was wrong with the wolfhound—one to identify the wrappings of a pound of hamburger, the other to read the label on the box of rodent poison lying outside the chain-link gate. Strychnine. The word alone was enough to cause visions of hideous suffering.

Kelly picked up the box and shoved it at Steve's midsection. "Read what it says about accidental poisoning."

She turned back to the gate and yanked it open. Wyatt and Pat jumped around her, begging for attention, but she shoved them aside and hurried to Wild Bill. Whining, he paced back and forth, his movements stiff and agitated. When Kelly reached for his collar, he jerked away and went back to his pacing.

"Easy, boy," she crooned. "I just wanna help you."

Wild Bill whined again as if in apology, but his agitation increased every time Kelly tried to touch him. By the time she finally managed to get hold of him, he was trembling all over and panting as if he'd just come back from a long run.

"What's it say, Steve?" Kelly asked, forcing the urge to panic deep down inside herself. "Do we induce vomiting or not?"

"Yeah. But how the hell do you make a dog vomit?"

"There's some syrup of ipecac in the trailer. Top shelf over the stove." Wild Bill's breathing turned choppy. His neck and his belly became rigid, his ears stood straight up and his lips pulled back from his teeth in a canine version of a grimace. His eyes rolled with terror. Intending to tell him to hurry the hell up, Kelly turned back to Steve, but he was already running for the trailer.

Wild Bill relaxed for a few moments. He whimpered and panted and whimpered some more, like a little kid trying to tell his mommy how rotten he felt. Kelly stroked his head and neck and kept trying to soothe him. Then Steve slammed back out of the trailer and, as if in reaction to the noise, the wolfhound's whole body seized up, every muscle contracting so violently he toppled over.

Steve ran into the kennel and handed the small bottle to Kelly. When the seizure passed, he lifted the huge dog to a semi-sitting position and helped Kelly coax his powerful jaws apart long enough for her to pour a dose of the syrup down Wild Bill's throat. The wolfhound fought and fussed, but Steve hung on and managed to clamp his jaws shut and keep them shut until the medicine did its job.

Once Wild Bill's sides started to heave, Steve released him. The poor dog staggered to a corner of the kennel, hung his head and retched repeatedly. Keeping an eye out for signs of another seizure, Kelly asked Steve to go call the vet and bring the pickup around. While he was gone, she cleaned up the vomit so Wyatt and Pat wouldn't get into it and poison themselves, consciously reining in her emotions as she worked.

She continued to do so throughout the long, nerve-racking night. Wild Bill suffered more seizures and more misery than any animal should ever have to endure, and she had to keep a clear head to cope with the situation. But a cold fury grew deep in her gut with every whimper the dog made, and she promised herself if she ever managed to get her hands on Johnny, she would beat him within an inch of his worthless life.

The sun was already up by the time the vet sent them home with repeated assurances that Wild Bill would be fine and she was only keeping him at the clinic for observation as an extra precaution. She could keep him calm and sedated enough to recover from his ordeal. Though she hated to leave him, Kelly had to admit he wouldn't get much rest at the ranch, what with Wyatt and Pat and God only knew what other distractions he would encounter.

Physically exhausted and emotionally drained, she hauled herself into the passenger seat, slumped down until the back of her head rested on the seat cushion and closed her eyes, wanting nothing more than to make the world go away.

She couldn't, of course. She'd already tried that last night in Steve's bed, and look what had happened. If she'd been in her own trailer, tending to her own business, she would have heard the dogs fussing long before Wild Bill had gotten himself into such serious trouble.

It was time to go back to the life she'd worked out for herself and Daniel. Time to quit playing around with pipe dreams about being in love. Time to deal with Jay and Johnny before they hurt anyone else.

Steve aimed the pickup down the gravel road to the ranch, then glanced over at Kelly and wondered what was going on in that hard head of hers. Though her eyes were closed, he knew she wasn't sleeping; there was too much tension floating around the truck's cab for any activity that peaceful. Besides, her lips were tightly crimped, she had a deep, vertical wrinkle between her eyebrows and he could almost hear the wheels cranking furious thoughts around and around in her brain.

And no wonder. Damn, what a miserable night they'd spent. He'd never seen an animal in such distress before and prayed he never would again. Wild Bill obviously had been terrified by the effects of the strychnine, but when the vet explained that the slightest noise, touch or movement might set off another seizure, they couldn't even try to comfort the poor beast.

Of course, that had damn near killed Kelly. Big and ugly as he was, Wild Bill was still one of her "babies." When he suffered, she suffered. About the only blessing Steve could see in this whole mess was that Wild Bill had been a hog and had downed the poisoned meat all by himself, unwittingly saving the other dogs from suffering the same agony.

Man, oh man, he didn't even want to *think* about what it would have been like to have Pat and Wyatt helping Wild Bill to give him a whole new perspective on the phrase "sick as a dog."

Steve glanced at Kelly again, and immediately disliked the grim expression on her face. Every time her mouth curved down in that particular way, she made a decision that drove him nuts. Hell, it wouldn't surprise him to find out she was sitting over there, silently plotting her brother's murder.

Not that he would blame her. Anyone who would inflict such torment on an animal deserved a good shooting. Unfortunately he was still obliged to uphold the law, meaning he would have to protect Johnny James from his sister's rage, no matter how justifiable it was.

He supposed getting her to talk about what had happened was his best hope to prevent her from committing homicide. Which, judging by the scowl on her face, would probably be about as easy as getting Wild Bill to drink syrup of ipecac again any time soon. Even with his belly full of poison, the dog was strong as a bear, and Kelly wasn't much different.

All this mess with her dad and brother was like strychnine in her soul. While he sensed she'd told him more about her family than she'd ever told anyone else, he also sensed she still hadn't told him everything. Well, it was time to get at the rest of it, purge it and let her get on with her own life. With him, he hoped.

Taking a deep breath, he tightened his grip on the steering wheel and forced a casual tone into his voice. "Hey, Jaynes, I've been wondering about something."

She opened one eye and replied in an equally casual, and, he suspected, an equally forced tone. "Oh, yeah?"

"Yeah. What did your dad mean when he said you owed him and Johnny big time?"

Kelly shut her eye again, turned her face toward the side window and, with a subtle change in posture, seemed to close in on herself. A thick, sticky silence pulsed through the cab, dragging on and on. For one mile. Then two. Telling him more plainly than words he'd struck pay dirt the first time. Pay dirt, that is, if she ever answered the damned question.

When he felt as if he only had one nerve left and it was shredding fast, she straightened her spine and heaved a sigh that sounded as if it had come all the way up from her toenails. She still refused to look at him, but she did start to talk.

"He was talkin' about an old family...well, I guess you could call it a tradition. Jay claims it's an old James tradition, anyhow. I don't know if that's really true, or if it's somethin' else he just made up because it was convenient, but he always made a big deal out of it. It's what he, uh, used to get Johnny into the business."

"What's the tradition?"

"Whenever somebody in the family got caught breakin' the law and it was a sure thing he was gonna have to do time for it, then whoever had the cleanest record was supposed to step forward and claim he was really the guilty one, because he was sure to get a shorter sentence."

She swallowed. Cleared her throat. Shook her head. "Johnny didn't seem to mind all that much when he just had to go to the county jail or to a juvenile home for a few months. But after mom died, Jay started takin' bigger and bigger chances, and Johnny ended up doin' two years in the state pen.

"When he came home that time, Johnny was real . . . different. Harder. Meaner. More willing to fight with Jay. He had terrible nightmares for a long time."

She shot him a tortured look. Steve reached across the bench seat and squeezed her left hand in reassurance. Her skin felt cold to the touch. "Go on, Kel."

"Then he met Cindy, Daniel's mom, and I thought he'd settle down, 'cause he was real excited about the baby. But after Daniel was born, Cindy got awful restless and started partyin' a lot, and she was always complainin' there wasn't enough money. I think she was the one who got hooked up with the drug crowd over in Jackson first. Before long, she started sellin', and she was drivin' a big new car and wearin' flashy clothes.

"I guess Johnny felt like he had to keep up with her. I started takin' care of Daniel, 'cause they'd just go off and leave him. Pretty soon Jay was in on it with 'em, and they were all really livin' it up. And then Cindy tried cocaine."

"She got hooked?" Steve asked, more to keep her talking than because he couldn't guess how the story would end.

Kelly nodded. "Oh, yeah. And they were right back to never havin' enough money. That's when Jay got the harebrained idea to plant marijuana on the ranch. Then Cindy overdosed and died and the feds found the marijuana patch, and Johnny and Jay got into one hell of a fight over who had to take the fall this time."

She closed her eyes and exhaled a deep, shuddering sigh, giving Steve the impression she was reliving that fight. "With their records, neither one of 'em was gonna get off easy. I was mad enough to kill 'em both, and I opened my big mouth and told 'em they deserved to get twenty years apiece. And then Jay looked at me and started to laugh, and he said, 'Well, we're not gonna do any time, Miss Kelly. You are.'"

"It was your turn, huh?"

"That's how they saw it," she agreed. "Johnny got real excited about the idea, 'cause I didn't have a record at all. He kept tellin' me I'd probably get off with probation. That's why he's so mad at me now, see? If I'd have just taken my turn like I was supposed to, he wouldn't have had to go back to prison. I thought about doin' it, and maybe I should have."

"No way." Steve pulled over to the side of the road. "You did the right thing, Kel."

"Did I?" Her laugh was sharp, bitter and carried a trace of hysteria. "I don't know anymore, Steve. I keep tellin' myself I couldn't leave Daniel alone with those idiots, but maybe that's just an excuse. Maybe I was just too damned chicken. And now my brother's gone totally wacko and it's all my fault."

"Stop it, Kelly. It wasn't your job to take care of your brother. Your dad was supposed to do that and he didn't, so he's trying to blame you. There wasn't a thing you could have done to save Johnny from prison in the long run, but you've given Daniel a great chance to make a decent life for himself. You should be proud of that and proud of him."

"I am. But I still feel so…guilty and so damned helpless. I don't know what to do next."

"What does Johnny want, Kelly? If we knew what he was looking for when he trashed the trailer—"

"I don't know!" she wailed. "I've been racking my brain, tryin' to figure that out. Hell, I'd give him anything but Daniel to make him happy."

Steve took her upper arms in his hands and gave her a gentle shake. "You won't have to do that, sweetheart. Remember, you're not alone this time. You've got me."

"Johnny can sit up in those hills and pick us off whenever he feels like it. And he'll do it. After last night, I know he will." She pushed him away, then wrapped her arms around herself. "And if he's seen you kissin' me like you're always doin', you'll probably be his next target. I don't want to be responsible for you gettin' hurt."

"Hey, I'm a professional, remember? And I'm not alone, either. I called the sheriff last night when you were helping the vet with Wild Bill. He promised to send a deputy out to the ranch and leave him there until we get back if he didn't have any big emergencies. That should make Johnny think twice before he does anything else."

"Yeah, but a deputy can't stay forever."

"We won't need him to, Kel. Our DEA backup will be in place today. It's all going to work out, I promise."

Though she nodded and murmured, "All right," there was a resigned expression in her eyes that said she'd heard those promises too many times without seeing any positive results. Releasing her, he slid back behind the wheel and headed for the ranch, silently vowing to restore her faith in law enforcement. He had to, or she would never have any faith in him.

When they got home, everything looked fine on the outside. The promised deputy, complete with a shiny green-and-white patrol car, sat in the middle of the barnyard. Pat and Wyatt ran out of the kennel in good health and good spirits. The horses came up to the pasture fence, demanding their daily ration of oats.

Steve and Kelly took care of the morning chores together and went up to the house for breakfast, showers and, hopefully, a nap. Kelly went first, took one look at the kitchen and stopped dead in her tracks with a muttered curse. Steve thumped onto his heels to keep from plowing into her, then muttered his own curse when he saw the room.

It had been trashed in much the same manner as the trailer had been, no doubt before the deputy had arrived to stand guard. In addition to the usual mess, however, Johnny had left a red, spray-painted message on the wall beside the refrigerator. In big, misshapen block letters, it said, "Give back my son and the bear."

The note went on, trailing down the wall, calling her every vile name Steve had ever heard. But the P.S. froze his blood.

"You have to pay for what you did, Kelly," it said. "You really do have to pay."

Chapter Fourteen

After poisoning Wild Bill, trashing Bud and Peg's house and painting a weird message on the kitchen wall, Johnny left Kelly alone for the next eight days. By June fifteenth, she didn't know what to think or expect from him. Figuring that was exactly what he'd wanted all along, she continued to work the ranch as if nothing was wrong and moved the cows up to summer pasture.

Steve objected, of course. If he'd had his way, she would have hidden in the house with all the doors and windows locked until Johnny was in custody, but there was no way she could do that, even if she'd wanted to. Which she darn well didn't.

For one thing, she had a nephew, three dogs and two horses to support. For another, the stock needed her and she owed Bud a day's work for a day's pay. And for another, she refused to give her brother the satisfaction of knowing he'd made her miserable.

She'd go stark raving nuts if she had to stay inside all day. To her way of thinking, it would have been like letting Johnny put her in jail for however long he pleased. Heck, for all she knew, her brother already could have left the state for good. She doubted it, but she could always hope, couldn't she?

Right.

And one of these days, Babe was going to sprout wings and fly like Pegasus.

On the other hand, there was no sense in borrowing trouble, and she made a conscious effort to enjoy whatever time she had left to be alone with Steve. After Johnny's last "visit," however, life wasn't the same. It was as if her brother had tainted the atmosphere around everything he'd touched. Just like old times.

Never knowing when or where he might show up again made it impossible for her to relax. Steve obviously felt the same way. He wore his "cop" face and his .45 all the time and stuck to her like a suction cup on glass. Receiving the official word that the DEA backup team was in place only increased her tension, because now the I'm-being-watched sensation she used to feel only once in a while, never went away.

If all of that wasn't quite enough to cool the lusty passion she and Steve had shared, Bud, Peg and Daniel's return finished the job. When the camper unexpectedly rolled into the yard late on a Friday afternoon seven days later, Kelly gave up trying to recapture the magic. She wasn't sophisticated or sneaky enough to hide an affair for long. Therefore, it had to end. Now.

It was one thing to carry on with a man when she had plenty of privacy; it was something else entirely when she had an elderly couple and an impressionable boy living with her.

Of course, the more discreet she tried to be about her relationship with Steve, the more openly affectionate he became. She'd swear the man had been born perverse. No matter who was around, he couldn't walk past her without touching her, couldn't greet her without hugging her, couldn't leave her for more than five minutes without kissing her.

Delighted with the show they were continually provided, Bud, Peg and Daniel teased Kelly unmercifully every time she blushed and cheered Steve on at every opportunity. When she accused him of raising false expectations, he looked her right in the eye and told her he'd be happy to fulfill any expectation she wanted to name. The wretched man.

Didn't he know how much she wanted to believe in the promises and determination she saw in his eyes? Didn't he know how much she wanted to say yes to all the questions she saw in Bud's, Peg's and Daniel's eyes? Didn't he know how much she wanted a future with him?

Of course he did. And he shamelessly used everything she wanted against her. According to him, she didn't need to worry about Johnny and Jay anymore. If she would only put her troubles into his capable hands and allow him to, as he put it, "take care of her," why, they could just ride off into the sunset together and live happily ever after.

Right.

The man was not only perverse. He was also tetched. *Really* tetched, if he honestly believed she could do that.

She appreciated the way he cared, even worried about her safety. What he didn't understand, was that she couldn't help worrying about his safety, too, and feeling responsible for it. If it was in her power to prevent it, it would be one mighty cold day in Hades before she'd let him get any more involved in her problems with Johnny and Jay. Steve had already done more for her than she could ever hope to repay.

Whenever the temptation to give in to his pressure tactics grew unbearable, she reminded herself of the vow she'd made the night Wild Bill had been poisoned. She had to figure out a way to deal with Johnny and Jay before they hurt someone she loved. She had to do it soon, and she had to do it by herself. The only question was, how?

Engine roaring, the ancient pickup bounced and jolted across the meadow. Bracing himself with one hand on the dash, Steve looked over at Kelly and would have laughed out loud if he hadn't been so busy hanging on for dear life. He loved the big grin on her face, and it pleased him tremendously to see her pitting her skills against the rough terrain like a stunt driver making a truck commercial.

What she could do if she had a rig that was twenty years younger, God only knew, but the phrase "hell on wheels" came to mind. Braking to a stop, she leaned out the window and pointed toward a grove of aspens. "How about over there, just to the east of that big rock?"

"You've got it." Steve opened his door, jumped to the ground and lifted a salt block out of the pickup's bed. The cows grazing on the lush grass ignored him. Eager to return to Kelly, he ignored them as well, set the big white cube on the ground and hustled back to the truck.

Barely allowing him time to get his door shut, Kelly took off again. Steve settled in for the rough ride, making a quarter turn sideways so he could watch her. She'd been exceptionally quiet and preoccupied since Bud, Peg and Daniel had come home and it felt good to have some fun with her again.

He knew she was surprised and embarrassed that he wasn't trying to hide how he felt about her in front of the others. If life had been following a more normal course, he would have been at least a little more circumspect about his intentions toward Kelly. Life *wasn't* taking a normal course, though, and the tension inherent in their situation provided fertile ground for misunderstandings to sprout and grow between them.

He'd had to work long and hard to convince her to make love with him in the first place, and he wasn't about to take any unnecessary risks with their relationship now. Therefore, he wasn't about to give Kelly any reason to doubt his feelings for her. She meant too much to him.

He wished she would be equally open about her feelings for him, but he had to settle for whatever encouraging signs he could get. A big smile from her qualified, and he'd do just about anything to provoke one. Even ride along in her ratty old truck and play delivery boy to a bunch of dumb Herefords.

If only Bud and the others had stayed away just a few more days... Well, there was no use wishing for the impossible. Eleven days alone with Kelly didn't seem like much to ask, but Steve knew that for a rancher like Bud to be away from his land and his stock, it must have felt like a lifetime.

Cranking the wheel hard to the right, Kelly skidded around a pine tree and onto a dirt track winding farther into the forest. Then she barrelled across a shallow stream and braked on the opposite bank. Steve swung out of the cab to unload another salt block, heard a sharp crack and instinctively dove behind a tree stump that had been blackened by a long-ago fire.

A bullet ricocheted off the pickup's tailgate and thumped into the ground, kicking up a little puff of dust five feet to his left. Kelly turned around, surprise crossing her face when she didn't see him. He rose to his knees and motioned for her to get down.

Her eyebrows climbed halfway up her forehead. She opened her mouth, but before any questions could come out, another crack sent Steve ducking for cover again. This time the bullet lodged in the tree stump in front of him. Making a rough triangulation from the two rounds already fired, Steve guessed the sniper was lying in the bushes on an outcropping thirty yards behind and twenty feet above the pickup. There was no way he could get a clear shot at the guy from here, but if he wormed his way around—

To his horror, the pickup's engine stopped rumbling. The driver's door opened and slammed shut. Then Kelly's voice cut through the sudden quiet.

"Johnny! Johnny James! I know it's you."

The sniper replied by firing another bullet into Steve's sheltering tree stump.

"Dammit, Johnny, cut that out!" Kelly stomped around to the back of the truck, making a perfect target of herself. She even pounded her sternum with two fingers, as if to invite the next bullet to kill her. "I'm the one you want, you big dumb jackass. You want to shoot somebody so bad, shoot me. But leave my dogs and my friends alone."

Steve pitched his voice loud enough to reach her ears. "Kelly, get down. *Now.*"

She didn't even glance at him. Instead, she raised her chin and then opened her arms wide, hands up beside her ears. "C'mon, Johnny, I know you're madder'n hell at me, so take your best shot. What's the matter, you scared of me?"

Steve gathered his feet under himself, preparing to tackle her before the sniper, whoever he was, accepted her offer.

"I ain't scared of you, Kelly." The answering voice was deep, with the gravelly texture of a heavy smoker. It also held enough amused admiration to make Steve pause before launching himself at Kelly.

She lowered her hands and propped her fists on her hips. Though her voice softened, her tone implied she had better things to do than stand around talking with him. "Then what do you want?"

"Besides my son?"

"Daniel's fine, and he belongs with me. I know you already know that, so what do you really want?"

"I told you, sis. I want the bear."

"I had to throw Daniel's teddy away years ago, Johnny. One of the dogs chewed his nose off and all the stuffing came—"

"Not *that* one. The little blue one Mama gave him."

"I don't know what you're talkin' about," she said.

"Sure, you do, sis. You'd better find it, too."

"Or else what?"

Johnny's soft chuckle sent a chill racing the length of Steve's spinal column. "Or else I'll have to plug ol' loverboy behind the stump there with my trusty rifle. And then, I'll pick off those old folks you work for. One at a time."

Kelly stiffened and her neck and cheeks turned red. "Dammit, Johnny, if I've still got it at all, I don't have any idea where it would be."

"*Find* it." There was no mistaking the threat or the implacable fury in that voice now. Steve had the impression that if he could see Johnny James, there'd be a maniacal light in the man's eyes, as well. "Otherwise, you're gonna have to pay for what you did to me. Prison's not a nice place."

"All right, I'll look for it," Kelly said. "Supposin' I can find it, how do I get hold of you to hand it over?"

"You don't. When I'm ready for it, I'll let you know."

The bushes on the outcropping rustled. Steve looked up, but couldn't see the man. Then the voice came again, sounding farther away. "Oh, and Kelly?"

"Yeah, Johnny?"

"Daniel's still *my* kid."

Kelly raised one hand and pointed her finger at the voice. "Leave him alone, Johnny. I mean it. Don't even think about getting him involved in one of your stupid—"

"He's *mine* and I'll do what I want with him. Don't ever forget that."

"*You* forget it, Johnny. When did you ever really give a damn about that kid, huh? The judge—"

Johnny expressed his opinion of the judge with a bullet planted squarely between Kelly's feet. She jumped back, banged one elbow on the tailgate and swore under her breath while she rubbed the injury. Though she called to him several times, Johnny never answered her again. Just to be on the safe side, however, Steve grabbed her uninjured arm and dragged her back behind the stump.

"Dammit, Kelly, have you lost your mind?"

She turned on him, her eyes glinting with temper. "No, but I think you have."

He took a deep breath, giving himself a moment to let his gut-wrenching fear for her safety subside. When he spoke again, his voice was husky, but lacking the anger of the previous moment. "You could've been killed."

Her expression softened. "Aw, Johnny was just tryin' to scare me."

"Did he succeed?"

"Yeah." She gave him a grudging nod. "A little."

"Well, good. Maybe now, you'll listen to reason."

Her hands went back to her hips, her chin came up and her attitude turned sour. "Meaning?"

"Meaning, you can't be out here anymore. It's too dangerous."

"Now wait just a danged minute," she said. "Out here is where I work, Marshal."

He knew better than to argue with her when she called him that; it was one of several ways she used to put distance between them. Unfortunately this time, he wasn't in any mood to back off. This time, his palms were still sweating, his knees were still trembling and his mind was still rolling out terrible pictures of what could have happened if Johnny's aim had been even a little bit off.

Propping his own hands on his hips, he got right down in her face and forced his response through gritted teeth. "Not anymore. We'll hire extra help to handle the cows."

She let out a derisive snort. "Good luck findin' anybody reliable. And it's almost time for hayin'. Case you didn't notice, my big brother's one hell of a shot. You think he couldn't pick me off a tractor just as easy as he could get to me out here?"

"You're not going to help put up the hay, either."

Her nostrils flared. "Like hell I'm not."

"Dammit, Kelly, will you be reasonable?"

"You're the one who's not bein' reasonable. Johnny won't hurt me."

"Maybe not, but what if his drug-dealing pals are out here, too?" Steve asked. "They're completely unpredictable and you know it. What will happen to Daniel if you get killed?"

She opened and shut her mouth, but no sound came out. Finally she clamped her lips together in a grim, hard line, turned around and stalked back to the truck. Steve tried to talk to her all the way to the ranch, but all he got out of her was a few grunts.

After parking near the back door of Bud and Peg's house, she climbed out, went inside and stalked right on upstairs to her room. Though he wanted to continue the argument until he won her agreement to let him handle this situation in his own way, Steve decided it would be better to give her a little time and space first.

Shoving his hands into his front pockets, he hustled out to the barn, hoping to find his uncle. After Johnny's threats, he had to get Bud, Peg and Daniel out of here again. It would be a lot simpler to convince Kelly he knew what he was doing if he had a solid plan to offer. Then maybe she could learn to rely on his judgment the way Anne eventually had.

Of course, when he thought back to the beginning with Anne, he remembered some times when she hadn't followed orders very well, either. He'd better get in touch with his DEA contact and let him know Johnny was definitely in the area. He couldn't watch Kelly every second of the day by himself. Anyone would need a little help doing that.

Damned, independent women would be the death of him yet.

Kelly stood to the side of her bedroom window, watching Steve stomp across the ranch yard. The second he disappeared into the barn, she headed for the attic steps at the end of the hallway. Now that she knew exactly what Johnny wanted, it wouldn't be hard to find it.

Mama had given Daniel the little stuffed bear just before she'd died. Johnny had been so wrapped up in his drug dealing back then, Kelly hadn't thought he knew anything about it. She'd stored it in a box with the other keepsakes she was saving for Daniel, which was up in Peg's attic.

This was likely to be her one chance to gain control of the situation and she wasn't about to blow it. Steve would remember the bear before long, and when he asked about it, she intended to protect him any way she could. Even if she had to lie through her teeth to do it.

It was not a decision she made lightly. The number-one value she had always tried to instill in Daniel was the necessity of telling the truth under any circumstances. The thought of Johnny sighting in on Steve, however, turned such ethical issues into luxuries in pretty darn short order.

She didn't care if she was hiding evidence in a criminal case, obstructing justice or committing a felony, she wasn't about to hand the bear over to a bunch of cops. They'd just fiddle around with it and stick it in a forensic lab or an evidence room, where it wouldn't do anyone a bit of good. If whatever was in the toy was this important to Johnny, it was a potential bargaining chip, and Kelly intended to hold on to it.

Fumbling in her haste, she pulled the chain on the hanging light bulb, then tugged the box out from under the eaves and sat cross-legged beside it. She hadn't opened it in five years, but she remembered the contents with perfect accuracy, right down to the faint scent of her mother's lilac sachets embedded in the tissue paper wrapped around each treasure. Smelling that fragrance again was like ripping a scab off an old, festering wound that refused to heal.

It hurt to touch Mama's things. Of course, if she'd had time, she would have unwrapped every item and dredged up all the associated memories, anyway. She wouldn't have been able to resist the temptation to revisit these pieces of Mama's life, no matter how painful it might have been.

Even through the paper, she could identify Great-grandma Bridget's favorite thimble, the one Great-great-great-grandma Maeve had brought to America from Ireland over a century ago. And here was Grandpa Grady's straight razor and Great-grandpa Gunnar's pocket watch. The blue bear was crammed inside a dented tin cup that had come halfway across the continent in a covered wagon with the Swedish branch of Mama's family.

Lord, she needed to label all of this stuff, or Daniel would never know who had owned what, or how old it was, or why it was important to keep. She should write down all the stories she could remember about these people, too, so Daniel would know at least some of his ancestors had been honest, hardworking people. She would do all of that just as soon as this hassle with Johnny and Jay was over.

The fat little bear was only about four inches tall, but the body was tight and hard for a stuffed toy. She held it up to the light, turning it over and over, looking for signs of tampering. Aha! There was a row of tiny, handmade stitches between the bear's hind legs, and an equally tiny knot under the tail. The second she had time to pull those stitches out, she intended to find out what was hidden inside the toy.

Setting the bear aside, she repacked the box, hesitating over the flat, rectangular bundle she hadn't been able to avoid, though God knew she'd wanted to. She picked it up, turned it over, set it in its place—right on top, where it wouldn't get broken—reached for it again. Oh, hell.

With quick, jerky movements, she stripped away the tissue paper, turned the photograph right side up and traced the delicate pattern of wildflowers Great-grandpa Gunnar had patiently carved into the wooden frame on long winter evenings at the ranch. The faces in the photograph inevitably drew her gaze, bringing a familiar, stabbing pain to her heart.

It was the only formal family portrait they'd ever had taken. She was a pigtailed, gap-toothed first-grader in this picture. Johnny would have been eight. Both of them wore big grins and looked like any other normal American kids back then.

Mama stood behind them, looking at Jay as if he was the most wonderful man alive. Looking back at her with the same besotted expression, Jay had one arm around her waist. His other hand rested on Johnny's shoulder, and Mama had one hand on Kelly's opposite shoulder, completing the circle.

Dammit, they'd been a happy family once. They hadn't been rich, but they'd had everything they really needed. Mama was so pretty and sweet and she'd loved Jay so much. Why hadn't that been enough for him? What had possessed him to ruin all of their lives for the sake of a few easy bucks?

And Johnny. Sometimes she forgot her big brother hadn't always been so awful. When this picture was taken, she'd adored him. He'd taught her how to get on the school bus and protected her from bullies on the playground, dried her tears and bandaged her scraped knees when she'd fallen out of the apple tree. How had their relationship deteriorated into such a sorry state?

Kelly put the box away and smuggled the little bear to her room without being seen, then went back to work. Her inability to find rational answers to those questions haunted her for the rest of the day, however, as did Johnny's threats against Bud and Peg, and the shots he'd fired at Steve. By nightfall, she'd come to a decision, one she would have reached weeks ago if she'd been listening to her head instead of her heart.

She hated to tear Daniel away from this place, from these people he loved, and who loved him almost as much as she did, but it had to be done. She desperately wanted to believe they could stay here and see this thing through without anyone getting hurt, but she wasn't that much of an optimist. The history between the James family and the law was not a happy one.

The Haystack was too big and too isolated for any number of law-enforcement guys to patrol it over an extended period of time. Johnny and Jay were her responsibility, and since she now had a bargaining chip, she should deal with them herself. There was no excuse for exposing the Ryans or Steve to any more danger.

Knowing Steve could help her soften the blow to Bud, Peg and Daniel if he chose to do so, she waited until the others had gone to bed before asking him to join her in the kitchen for a private talk. He came through the doorway behind her, gave her a long, searching look, then crossed the room, pulled a chair away from the table and straddled it. Kelly leaned against a bank of cupboards, crossed one foot in front of the other and braced her palms on the countertop behind her.

His polite, expectant expression remained in place while she struggled to tell him she and Daniel would be leaving in the morning. When she finally gave up trying to find the right words and just blurted it out, he responded with one short, quiet word.

"No."

"Excuse me," she said, "I wasn't askin' your permission, Marshal. I was tellin' you about my decision."

"I don't care what you were doing, sweetheart. You're not going anywhere."

"You can't stop me."

His voice took on a hard edge. "Don't count on it."

She closed her eyes against a wave of weariness, then shook her head before looking at him again. "Please don't give me a hard time about this, Steve. I can't stay here."

"Why not?"

"You heard my brother out there today. He wasn't makin' idle threats, and I can't stand knowin' I'm puttin' you and Bud and Peg and this ranch in danger. It's not your fight."

"The hell it's not."

He climbed off the chair, shoved it under the table and walked toward her. She held up both hands to ward him off. He closed his bigger hands around her fingers and pulled her into his arms. She laid her head on his shoulder and let his warmth surround her, promising herself this would be the last time she would allow him to comfort her.

Emotions flowed between them in the silence. He stroked her hair, tucked a finger under her chin and kissed her. Again and again his lips moved against hers, gently, sweetly, passionately enough to break her heart. When he spoke, his voice carried an echo of the raw need that was eating her alive inside.

"You can't leave, Kelly. I love you."

She shook her head. Tried and failed to pull away. "No, Steve, you can't—"

"It's too late. It's been too late from the first time I saw you smile. I want to marry you, Kelly. Help you raise Daniel. Have some more kids, too. A whole herd, if you're willing."

If she was willing? What had he done? Snuck inside her head and found her deepest, most cherished desires? Why couldn't he be a plumber or an electrician? Anything but a lawman.

If the uneasy feelings in her gut were even halfway accurate, Steve's sense of honor and duty would either get him killed or force him to shoot a member of her family. Yes, Jay and Johnny were still members of her family, dammit. Despite all their faults and their despicable behavior, they were still her dad and her brother, and though she didn't want to at all, a part of her would always love them.

She pulled away again, and he let her go this time. Funny, she'd thought she would have to lie to him about having the bear. She could have done that without the least bit of remorse. But this . . . what she had to do now . . . hell, it was liable to choke her.

Hugging herself for warmth, she backed toward the doorway to the living room. "Sorry." Lord, her voice sounded okay, but her throat felt as scratchy as a lump of steel wool. "I, uh, just can't see myself bein' married to a, uh, cop."

Steve raised an eyebrow. Took a wider stance. Propped his hands on his hips. "I won't be one much longer. I've decided to accept Uncle Bud's offer. You won't be a foreman anymore. You'll be a full partner."

"That sounds real nice, but I don't think so. Thanks for askin', though."

His eyes took on a piercing expression, the one that always made her feel like she was walking around buck naked.

" 'Thanks for asking?' You're going to blow me off just like that? Come on, I know you can do better than—''

"Whaddaya want from me, Anderson?"

"The truth, dammit." He shoved one hand through his hair like a man down to his last ounce of patience. "You love me, Kelly Jaynes. I know it and you know it."

She looked away. Hugged herself tighter. Vaguely heard a door open and close upstairs, but paid no attention to it. "I never said that."

"I can see it in your eyes every time we make love."

She shot him a glance, winced inside at his implacable expression, then lifted one shoulder in a half shrug. "Maybe I just like makin' love with you."

"Oh, you do." His reminiscent chuckle raised gooseflesh on her arms. Softening his voice, he took a step closer. "But that's not all you love, Kelly. Now, stop this nonsense and tell me what's really going on here."

"Nothin's goin' on." Straightening her spine, she forced herself to meet his gaze head-on. "I just don't want to marry you."

"Liar." He took another step closer. Softened his voice even more. "You love me, Kelly Jaynes. Admit it."

His persistence, not to mention his arrogant confidence that he knew her so well, irritated her. "It doesn't matter. We could never make a marriage work."

"Why not?"

"Do I have to spell it out for you?"

He stood directly in front of her now, looking down at her from his superior height, a hefty dose of temper making his eyes glint. "Yeah. Let's hear it."

She inhaled a deep breath and mentally nailed her feet to the floor. She couldn't allow him to see any weakness here, couldn't relinquish one more inch of space. "All right. You're a good man, Anderson. I like you. I respect you. Maybe I even love you, but—"

"There's no *maybe* about it."

"Fine. Whatever. But even *you* should be able to see that's not enough, Stevie-boy." His eyes narrowed at her use of his aunt's nickname, and she silently acknowledged the low blow. But hell, saving this guy from himself wasn't easy, and she was getting desperate here. "We come from real different backgrounds. Almost different planets."

"That doesn't matter, Kelly. I've already told you that."

"Oh, *please*. Cut out the nobility, will you?" Holding her hands out at her sides, she stepped back. "Take a good, hard look at me for once, Marshal. Can't you see what I really am? What I've come from? You deserve better than what somebody like me can ever give you."

"Kelly, stop it." Intensity flared in his eyes, and for a second his gaze flitted to a spot beyond her right shoulder. "Stop it right now."

But she couldn't stop it. She'd uncorked a load of frustration, and there was no holding it back now. "It's this damned James blood. It's like it's . . . tainted. And I won't risk passing it on to another generation."

He vigorously shook his head and reached for her, but she sidestepped him, determined to make her point.

"Can't you understand that? I've worked real hard to keep Daniel on the straight and narrow, but I still don't know if it's gonna take or not. The last thing this world needs is another rotten James kid."

Steve finally got his hands on her arms and gave her one hard shake. "Dammit, Kelly, shut *up*."

Shocked at his roughness, she stared at him for a moment, then realized he wasn't looking at her, but at the doorway behind her. A sick feeling invaded the pit of her stomach. Slowly, she turned her head and came face to face with Daniel.

Though he had a good start on his summer tan, his face looked pale and his dark eyes seemed huge in contrast. She'd never seen anyone with a more stricken . . . wounded expression. His arms were skinny and gangly below the short sleeves of his pajama shirt, his fingers curled so tightly the joints stood out in white ridges. His chest heaved as if it hurt to draw a breath.

It was one of those endless, truly hideous moments in a lifetime. Kelly would have ripped out her own tongue and stomped it to pulp if it would have allowed her to take back what she'd said. But nothing could do that for her. Those hateful, hurtful words hung in the air like the leftover stink of a cheap cigar. Daniel's throat bobbed with an audible gulp.

The boy inhaled a shaky breath, and then fury replaced the pain in his eyes. "Is that why you're always fussin' at me, Aunt Kelly? Readin' me the Bible and that other stuff about virtues? 'Cause my *blood's* tainted?"

Her heart was so full of regret, she could barely get out a whisper. "No, Daniel. I didn't really mean that."

"Yes, you did. And I guess that must mean *I'm* tainted, too." Tears dripped off his chin, but he ignored them. "No matter how hard I try, I'm probably gonna end up just like my dad. Isn't that right?"

"Honey, listen—" She reached for him, but he jerked away as if he feared her touch might burn him.

"I think I've listened to you enough, Aunt Kelly. To hell with you and all of your big ideas about workin' hard and gettin' into college. You don't really think I can do any of that, do you? I might as well give up right now."

"No, Daniel, you can't—"

"That's what you're doin'!" He swiped the back of one hand under his nose. "You think our blood's so bad, you won't even give Mr. Anderson a chance."

"It's more complicated than that."

"Oh, yeah? Well, I think you don't like men at all, no matter how nice they are. So you probably won't even like me much longer, anyway, 'cause I'm gonna be a man pretty soon, too."

"Daniel, I'll always love you, no matter what. And I like men just fine."

"Do not. You sure as hell don't trust 'em."

"What do you expect, Daniel? Two of the most important men in my life have done nothing but let me down and hurt me."

"I haven't. Bud hasn't. Mr. Anderson hasn't. But you don't trust us, either. Well, I'm sick of bein' good all the time. And I'm sick of tryin' to prove myself, when you're never gonna believe in me."

With a strangled sob, he pushed past her and ran out the back door. She started after him.

"Daniel, wait—"

Steve blocked her path. "Give him some time to calm down, Kelly. He'll come back when he's ready."

"Will he?" She felt bleak and gray inside, as if someone had announced the sun would never shine again. "How can you be so sure?"

Steve's only response was a sad smile that did nothing to reassure her.

Laughing silently to himself, Johnny James snuck into the back room on the west side of the barn, pausing just inside to catch his breath and listen. In a minute or two, he'd turn on his flashlight and go to work on Kelly's saddle. He'd rattled her cage but good today. Wait'll she got a load of his next trick.

Raising the flashlight, he found the switch with his thumb, then froze when a door banged on the other side of the building. The footsteps that followed were so light, he almost wondered if he really heard them or just imagined them. A thud directly overhead confirmed the former, and a muffled sob made his heart beat faster.

He stared up through the darkness, desperately wishing he could see through the rough boards over his head. Yeah, dammit, that *was* a kid crying up there. And there was only one kid on this ranch. The last time Johnny had seen him, Daniel had been a toddler.

Emotion filled Johnny's chest. Forget about the saddle. He could always deal with Kelly later. Right now, he wanted to get acquainted with his son.

Chapter Fifteen

Where *is* that kid, Kelly thought, staring at the lid of the dog-food bin through a haze of exhaustion, guilt and worry. Following Steve's advice, she'd given Daniel an hour to calm down last night. Then she'd gone out to the barn to talk to him, but he wasn't in the hayloft.

One by one, she'd tried his other favorite haunts, but she'd found no sign of him. Neither, to her knowledge, had Steve, Bud or Peg, though they'd all been out looking ever since she'd sounded the alarm. Now the sun was poking out from behind the eastern side of the Pioneer Range, and Daniel was still missing.

Nine hours. He'd only been gone for nine hours, but it felt more like nine years. She kept telling herself Johnny had made such a big deal of wanting Daniel back, he must have nabbed the kid. But Johnny wouldn't hurt his own son—would he? She was ninety-nine percent sure he wouldn't.

But what if Daniel *wasn't* with Johnny? What if the little wretch had run off and gotten himself picked up by some low-life who *would* hurt him? She couldn't stand to think about it.

On the other hand, she couldn't seem to make herself *stop* thinking about it.

Or he could have had an accident in the dark and fallen into a gully, or... Lord, if he didn't turn up soon, she was gonna lose what little was left of her mind.

"Quit that, Jaynes," she grumbled. "Just feed the dogs and get a damn grip."

Determined to do exactly that, she opened the bin and reached for the scoop without really looking at it. When her hand closed around a folded piece of paper instead of the usual metal handle, she gasped, yanked the paper out and opened it with trembling fingers.

She recognized her brother's messy handwriting, and hope sprouted, filling her with anxious anticipation. By the time she finished deciphering his miserable spelling and grammar, her knees felt so weak she had to lean against the shed wall to hold herself up. "Oh, thank God," she murmured, closing her burning eyes for a moment.

This was not the time for tears. She had to go on about her business as if nothing had happened. She hated to let Bud, Peg and Steve worry about Daniel one second longer than necessary, but it couldn't be helped.

Johnny had been crazy enough to shoot at her and Steve yesterday. He was offering to trade Daniel for the little blue bear, but there was no telling what he might do if she didn't follow his instructions. He'd specifically ordered her to come to the meeting alone. Since Steve would never allow her to do that, she couldn't tell him about it.

Straightening back up, she stuffed the note into her hip pocket and hurriedly filled the dogs' dishes with kibble. The first giddy rush of relief at knowing Daniel was with his dad faded while she carried them from the shed to the dog run. Insidious as a noxious weed, worry slid into her mind again, taking her back to the issue of Johnny's mental state.

He wouldn't hurt his own son. Would he?

Probably not. Unless, of course, Daniel seriously provoked him. Given the right circumstances, most kids could be annoying. Unfortunately Daniel could make annoying adults into an art form, and Kelly accepted full responsibility for his talent.

According to the books on parenting she'd read about the time Daniel had started kindergarten, teaching a kid to think for himself was supposed to protect him from peer pressure. That had sounded like a pretty good deal to Kelly. By golly, those lessons had worked great, too, because Daniel certainly had a mind of his own.

The only glitch was, he insisted on thinking for himself all the time—with adults as well as with his peers. He didn't hesitate to question authority, which occasionally tended to tick off his teachers. If an adult told Daniel to do something, they'd better have a darn good reason for it, and he would argue passionately—and loudly—if he felt he was being unfairly treated. Kelly was used to coping with him, but Johnny was hardly the mature sort of adult who would tolerate such behavior from a kid.

What would he do if Daniel openly defied him?

Actually, knowing Daniel, it was more a matter of *when*, not *if*. And, knowing Johnny and the violent world he'd been living in... Well, Jay was probably with them, and while Jay wasn't exactly a mature adult, either, she didn't think he was anywhere near as crazy as Johnny. Surely *he* would look out for Daniel.

Wouldn't he?

The problem with a family like hers was that she honestly didn't have answers for her worrisome questions. She was ashamed to admit it, but she had no idea how Johnny or Jay would react to the little boy they should love and protect. The thought of either of them raising a hand to Daniel enraged her, but she knew it was a distinct possibility.

Which was all the more reason for her to handle this situation herself. Steve just wouldn't understand the complicated dynamics in the James family. Hell, she wasn't even sure she did. But one way or another, she had to find a way to sneak off without Steve before this afternoon. It wouldn't do to upset Johnny when he held Daniel's life in his hands.

* * *

With guilt riding his back and worry clawing at his gut, Steve unsaddled Reload, rubbed him down and turned him into the pasture for a well-deserved rest. After taking one last scan of the countryside, he finally gave in and headed for the house. Where *was* that kid?

He'd thought Kelly was overreacting last night when she hadn't been able to find Daniel in the barn or the other ranch buildings. Growing boys needed privacy when they were as upset as Daniel had been. Steve had assumed the kid would turn up when he was darn good and ready, but even he had started feeling frantic by midnight.

It was going on seven now. Daniel was a pretty responsible kid for his age. He knew they'd all be out looking for him the second anyone figured out he was gone, and he knew better than to worry other people this way.

Damn, where was that boy?

And why the hell had he interfered with Kelly last night? Why hadn't he let her go after Daniel when she'd wanted to? Who had he thought he was, telling her how to handle Daniel, when he obviously didn't know beans about raising children? Sure, he'd helped Anne with Chad, but *she* had made all the tricky decisions.

His head ached. His eyes felt dry and gritty. His stomach roiled with acid. If he felt this awful, Kelly must be a complete wreck by now.

Rounding the corner of the barn, he saw Bud's camper parked by the back door and heaved a small sigh of relief. After Johnny's threat against his aunt and uncle yesterday, Steve had felt there was no choice but to get them out of harm's way. He'd had to threaten Bud with protective custody to get him to leave again so soon, and he was glad to see his uncle wasn't going to use Daniel's disappearance to renege on their agreement.

Thank God, Anne and John Miller were willing to take Bud and Peg in for a few days. Bud and John's dad would enjoy each other's company, and Peg would get a huge kick out of the Miller kids—especially the new baby. Steve had no doubt they would all get along famously, and he realized it was time he went back to Bozeman and renewed his own friendship with the Millers.

Knowing it would hurt too much to see Anne with her husband, he'd avoided the Millers for the past two years. But it was okay now. As soon as this mess was settled, he intended to take Kelly and Daniel with him for a weekend visit.

Yeah, he thought, smiling at the mental images forming in his head of introducing his new family to Anne and John, it really was okay now. They'd all talk and laugh and eat too much. Chad would follow Daniel around like an eager pup, and Daniel would probably develop a crush on Holly.

If they ever found Daniel.

The grim reality of that thought wiped away his smile. Telling himself he would cope better with a couple of cups of coffee and some food in his stomach, he hurried up the steps and entered the kitchen. Bud and Peg were bustling around with sad expressions, getting ready to leave. He'd expected as much. It was Kelly who surprised him.

She should have been pacing by the windows, looking pale, exhausted and gaunt. Maybe drinking coffee, if she could keep even that much down. At the very least, she ought to be wringing her hands and have anxiety stamped all over her face.

Instead, there she sat at the table, finishing a plate of bacon, eggs and hash browns. She looked tired and worried, all right, but he didn't see the bristling tension, the raw nerves, the sick fear for Daniel's safety the situation legitimately called for. He crossed the room to wash his hands at the sink, asking himself, what's wrong with this picture?

Bud looked up from filling a thermos with coffee. "Find anything?"

Steve shook his head. "Not a trace. You?"

"Nope." Bud let out a disgusted laugh. "If I didn't know better, I could almost believe aliens grabbed that boy."

Peg came over and put her arm around Steve's waist. "It doesn't seem right for us to leave with Daniel missin' like this," she said in a low voice.

"Yeah," Bud agreed. "There's one hell of a lot of territory to cover out there."

"Don't start," Steve said. "I'll call in reinforcements in a little while."

"But Kelly might need our support," Peg said.

Steve glanced at the table before turning back to his aunt. "She looks like she's holding up pretty well to me."

"That's Kelly," Bud said. "She always holds up, but the way she loves that boy, she's gotta be dyin' inside."

Steve clapped his uncle on the shoulder. "I'll take care of her, Uncle Bud. You guys get on the road and give me two less things to worry about."

Bud scowled, then gave him a grudging nod. "Okay. Come on, Peg, let's go."

"I left you some food in the oven, Stevie-boy," Peg said, hugging him hard. "You take care of yourself, too."

"I will, Aunt Peg. Call me as soon as you get in, and give my love to Anne and Chad."

The Ryans gathered up their things and said goodbye to Kelly. Steve accompanied them to the back step, waved them off and went back inside, determined to find out what was really going on. Retrieving his breakfast, he carried it to the table and sat across from her. She pushed her empty plate aside, and he pointed his fork at it.

"Glad to see you've still got your appetite," he said. "Some people can't eat when they get under this much stress."

Kelly shot him a startled look, then immediately glanced away. "Yeah, well, a body's gotta have fuel."

Steve peppered his eggs. "Uh-huh. I'm a little surprised you're coping so well. You couldn't eat much at all when you got that letter from your dad. You seemed so upset last night—"

"Hey, I'm *still* upset." She got up, took her dirty dishes over to the sink and banged them down beside it.

Steve studied her, letting silence work on her nerves along with his steady, questioning gaze. Something was going on, all right, and it was making Kelly as jumpy as a frog with a pack of little boys on its trail. "I can see that, Kel."

She came back to the table, grabbed her coffee mug and refilled it. "So, uh, these people Bud and Peg'll be stayin' with are friends of yours?"

"Uh-huh. Anne and John Miller."

"I thought you told Peg to give your love to Anne and Chad."

Steve nodded. "Chad is one of their sons. They just had a new baby boy and they've also got two older girls."

"So, why not send your love to the whole family?"

"I'm closer to Anne and Chad than I am to the others."

"Why is that?"

"With Daniel missing, why would you care, Kelly?"

"I don't, really," she said, frowning at him. "I'm just makin' conversation. Tryin' to take my mind off Daniel for a little while, you know?"

"Sure. No problem."

She waited for him to swallow a bite of hash browns. "So? Why are you closer to Anne and Chad?"

"I spent almost seven years guarding them under the Witness Protection Program."

"Guarding them? From who?"

"Drug dealers. The only reason we all got through it alive was that Anne trusted me completely. She had great instincts, and every time anything made her feel uneasy, she told me about it right away."

Kelly looked at her hands, studying each scratch and callus as if she'd never seen such things before. "So, uh, where was the rest of the family?"

"In Montana. It's a complicated story. Anne and John were divorced, but they were trying to get back together, so he took the girls to stay with his folks in Bozeman. While he was gone, Anne just happened to be in the wrong place at the wrong time, and witnessed a murder. She decided to go into the program by herself rather than risk John and the girls' safety."

"That sounds pretty gutsy," Kelly said.

"It was." Steve pulled his wallet out of his back pocket, dug out his picture of Anne and Chad and slid it across the table. "She's the bravest woman I've ever known. She didn't know she was already pregnant with Chad when she made that decision. I ended up being her labor coach, so I'm kind of an honorary uncle for him."

Kelly looked at the picture. "He's a cute kid."

"Yeah. Daniel reminds me of him sometimes." When Kelly didn't respond, Steve continued. "You know, Anne's not the only one with good instincts. Right now, my instincts are saying you're hiding something, Kelly."

Irritation flashed in Kelly's eyes. "Oh, yeah?" She slid the photo back to Steve, then pointed at it. "Well, my instincts are saying that's the woman who broke your heart, pal. You're in love with her."

"I was," Steve admitted without the least inclination to flinch from her accusing gaze. "But I'm not now, Kelly."

She snorted as if in disbelief. "Oh, right, Anderson. You just happened to get involved with another woman who's raising a boy by herself and just happens to be in trouble? You really expect me to believe you're over her? That I'm not just a substitute?"

"It doesn't matter whether you believe it or not, because that's not the point. Daniel has been missing for almost eleven hours now. Do you know where he is?"

Her gaze veered off to one side of his face. "No."

"Do you know where the blue bear your brother wants is?"
"No."

"I don't believe you, Kelly. I guess Daniel was right. You really don't trust men at all. Not even us good guys."

That brought her gaze back to his in a hurry. "Good guys? I thought Jay and Johnny were good guys once. Seems like I'm not very good at tellin' the good guys from the bad ones."

"You're better at it than you think. You trusted Sheriff Johnson and he came through for you, didn't he? You found Bud, and from what I can see, he's treated you like a daughter."

"There was no way they could advance their careers by helpin' me, Marshal." It felt as if she were staring a hole right through him. "And, they were both happily married men. They didn't want to sleep with me."

Steve stared back at her until he realized he'd been holding his breath. Then he let out a bitter laugh and slowly shook his head in amazement. "Damn, but you're cynical."

She shrugged one shoulder. "I ran into a lot of jerks between Andy Johnson and Bud."

Needing to move, he carried his dishes to the sink. After setting them on the counter, he turned around, braced his butt against the cupboards and crossed his arms over his chest.

"That's not the problem, Kelly. I think you just don't know how lovable you really are."

The same shoulder went up and down, but she didn't speak. He shook his head again, in frustration this time.

"I guess this is what you call irony," he said. "Anne trusted me with her life and Chad's, but she didn't love me. You love me, whether you'll admit it or not, but you don't trust me worth a damn. Do you suppose there's a woman out there somewhere, who can do both?"

"Maybe you should go out and try to find one," Kelly suggested, her tone laced with anger.

"Yeah, maybe I should." He pushed himself away from the cupboards and shoved his hands into his front pockets. "I just hope you come to your senses before it's too late, Kelly."

"What's that supposed to mean?"

"Johnny's not the only one out there, sweetheart. He's got a couple of drug dealers after him, and they're not going to give up until they find him and get their money back. If he's got Daniel, you'd better hope I find him first. The Reyez brothers don't leave witnesses."

He crossed to the doorway leading into the living room, then turned back to her. "Let me know if you suddenly happen to find that blue bear."

"Where are you goin'?" she asked.

"I need to check in with the DEA team. They can bring in more resources to help us find Daniel." She suddenly looked smaller, somehow, and lost and alone. "Why don't you try to grab a couple of hours of sleep? I'll wake you if anything happens."

"All right. Maybe I will."

"Oh, and, uh, Kelly? Don't worry about me hitting on you again. From now on we'll have a professional relationship. You've already got enough to worry about."

Kelly watched Steve walk away with a sinking sensation in the pit of her stomach. She'd never had many friends to start out with, and she hated knowing she'd hurt one of the few really good ones she did have. Dammit, she hadn't meant to make Steve think she didn't trust him. She'd just wanted to make him back off a little so she could sneak out and make the trade for Daniel.

Well, he'd given her the perfect opportunity right now, and she intended to take it while he was on the phone. She'd have to sit him down and sort out this trust thing with him later. If he really thought she was all that lovable, surely he would listen and eventually understand.

She hurried up to her room, climbed onto the wooden straight chair that usually sat by the window and lifted one of the panels in the suspended ceiling. The little stuffed bear toppled out as if he'd been waiting for her to come get him. She caught him in one hand, climbed onto the floor, and examined the hand-sewn stitches again.

Using a pair of nail scissors, she carefully snipped off the knot and removed the threads. White stuffing material popped out of the opened seam. Bit by bit, she pulled the puffy strands of polyester free until her fingertips touched something hard. She turned the bear right side up and shook it over the bed, and a brass key bounced onto her pillow.

Kelly grabbed it and held it up to the light. If she wasn't mistaken, it was a safety-deposit-box key. Now, at least some of her brother's weird behavior was starting to make sense.

Johnny must have a fortune in cash stashed in a bank some-where, and he needed this key to get at it.

In his dreams.

She'd rather die than give it to him, and she thought there was a way she could thwart him without putting Daniel in any more danger. Walking over to the dresser, she picked up her key ring and compared her own safety-deposit-box key to John-ny's. Though they were hardly identical, they were pretty darn close, and Johnny hadn't seen his in at least eight years.

"He'll never know the difference," Kelly muttered, smiling with grim satisfaction.

She tucked Johnny's key into her front pocket, then took hers off the ring and carried it back to the bear. In five min-utes she had him restuffed and resewn. She needed to get go-ing. She still had to sneak her saddle out of the tack room and catch Babe, and it would take the rest of the time she had left to ride up to the meeting site.

Still, she hesitated a moment longer, battling a sudden case of nerves. She might not trust Steve as much as he wanted her to, but she didn't trust Jay or Johnny at all. Maybe going alone wasn't such a good idea. For damn sure, she'd be a fool to go unarmed.

Unfortunately the only handgun she owned was a derringer she wore in her boot when she went out on the highway. It would work in a pinch, but it didn't look very intimidating and it didn't have much firepower if both Johnny and Jay came af-ter her at the same time. Well, she knew where to find a better one.

Grabbing a jacket, she opened the door, listened for a mo-ment, then crept down the hall to Steve's room. He was al-ready wearing his .45, but one night they'd gotten into a discussion about guns and he'd shown her a real nice 9 mm semiautomatic pistol he'd brought along for target practice. She found it way in the back on the top shelf of his closet, took one of the twelve-round magazines as well, and headed for the door.

Almost there, she hesitated again. While she didn't really intend to shoot anyone, she felt better having Steve's pistol tucked into the back of the waistband on her jeans. But what if something went wrong, and she got hurt? Did she want to risk leaving Daniel at the mercy of Jay and Johnny?

No way.

The very least she could do, it seemed, was to leave some kind of a clue behind, so Steve would know where to start looking if she didn't come back. She thought it over for a moment, fished Johnny's note out of her back pocket and dropped it in the middle of Steve's bed. Then she pulled on her jacket and tiptoed out of the house.

Chapter Sixteen

Leaning back in Bud's desk chair, Steve rubbed his tired eyes with a thumb and forefinger. "Say *what?* You've got to be kidding."

"Nope, that's two positive IDs, now, pardner. One from the motel clerk and one from the mountain gear store," Carl Watson said in about the worst excuse for a Western drawl Steve had ever heard. But then, what could you expect from a New Yorker who suddenly found himself stuck in Wisdom, Montana? "The Reyez brothers were in Butte yesterday."

"That's *Butte,* Watson. As in *beau*tiful. Not Butt-eeee. Got that?"

Watson replied with all the fervor of a Marine recruit. "Sir, yes, sir!"

Steve grinned in spite of his new worries. Thank God the DEA had sent Carl Watson out to coordinate the operation. Steve had worked with him before, and while Carl was quite a kidder, he was the best. Whenever he was around, almost any needed resource could be expected to appear, on time and in good working order.

A burst of static came from Carl's end of the phone line. "Hang on a sec, Anderson. That's our boy up on the hill behind your house. Sent him in after you called last night."

Drumming his fingertips on the desk, Steve waited out the moment of silence.

"There's a rider leaving your ranch, ol' buddy. Headin' north. Dark brown horse. Beige cowboy hat. That's the rider, not the horse. Also a turquoise jacket. Again, that's the rider, not the horse. Boy says they're really makin' tracks."

"Kelly," Steve muttered. "Dammit, hold the line, Carl. I've got to check this out."

"I'll be right here, pardner."

Steve set the receiver on the desk, vaguely recognizing the tune Carl had started whistling as "Home on the Range," then bolted for the stairs. An emotion he didn't want to call fear filled his chest when he saw Kelly's empty room, the scissors, pincushion and a spool of blue thread sitting on the bed. The door to his own room stood ajar. He looked inside, saw the open closet door and felt his heart drop like a renegade elevator. Dammit, she'd taken the 9 mm. Something was going down, all right. Right now.

He turned to leave. Saw the paper on his bed from the corner of his eye. Grabbed and read it. Charged back down the stairs. Snatched up the phone.

"I know where she's going, Watson. Call in the chopper and tell the boys to wear their vests. This could get ugly."

By the time Kelly arrived at the meeting site, the clearing where Johnny had taken potshots at her and Steve, she was sweating almost as much as her mare. Even up here in the mountains, summer had arrived in full force. She couldn't take off her jacket without exposing Steve's pistol, but she shoved the sleeves halfway up her forearms and fanned herself with her hat while she walked Babe back and forth to cool her off.

Ten nerve-racking minutes passed before a scrubby stand of willows at the other end of the clearing rustled, and Johnny, Jay and Daniel stepped into view. Daniel's face lit up when he saw her. He took a step toward her, but Johnny grabbed the back of his T-shirt and yanked him back.

Scowling, Daniel raised his chin to its most belligerent angle and opened his mouth. Kelly shot him a warning look. He hesitated, shot her a disgruntled look in return, but closed his mouth without speaking.

"Hello, Kelly," Jay said. His voice sounded loud and a shade too hearty, even for him. His eyes telegraphed a message she wasn't sure how to read, but he was definitely uneasy.

"Hello, Jay," she replied. "Johnny."

Her brother waved her greeting aside with his rifle, carelessly letting the barrel drift in her direction. "Didja bring the bear?"

Confident of Babe's training, Kelly dropped the reins onto the ground and walked four steps closer to Johnny. Then she dug the toy out of her jacket pocket and held it up where he could see it. "It's right here."

"Well, let's have it." Johnny held out his free hand and wiggled his fingers as if he expected her to toss it to him.

"Let Daniel go first," Kelly said.

"What'sa matter, Sis? Don'tcha trust me?"

Kelly calmly returned his challenging stare. " 'Bout as much as I'd trust a rattler."

He brayed a laugh, then raised his hand as if he would cuff Daniel's chin. Daniel jerked away, eyeing his father with undisguised loathing. Johnny tightened his fist in a mute threat.

"Cut it out, Johnny." Kelly struggled to keep all emotion out of her voice. Her brother would love nothing better than to see her lose her cool. "Send him over right now. Then you can have the bear."

"He's *my* kid. You had no right to take him away—"

"Well, I guess I could have let him go into foster care. Then you could fight with the State of Wyoming to see him."

"Well, hell, at least I'd always know where to find the damn State of Wyoming. Wouldn't I?"

"That's enough," Jay said. "We haven't got all day, Johnny. Turn the boy loose."

Johnny glared at Jay for a moment, then reached out, grabbed Daniel's shoulder and gave him a shove. "All right, go on, ya little brat."

Daniel glanced back as if he would speak. Hoping to distract him, Kelly snapped her fingers. "Come on, Daniel. Your grandpa's right. We haven't got all day."

Still scowling, Daniel obeyed. God, but she loved every sullen line of his little face, every freckle, every dirty smudge. Halfway across the clearing, he broke into a run. She went down on one knee and opened her arms to catch him.

The collision when he arrived sent a sweet shaft of joy and relief right through her. She hugged him fiercely, then pulled back, desperate to check him over. "Are you okay, sweetie?" she whispered.

His eyes watery and his chin trembling, he gave her a jerky nod. "Yeah, Aunt Kelly. I'm fine."

"All right, you've got the kid," Johnny shouted. "Give me the damn bear."

Kelly squeezed Daniel's shoulder in reassurance and quietly told him to go climb into Babe's saddle. She watched him until he reached the mare, then rose to her feet, turned back to face Johnny and tossed the stuffed toy to him. He caught it in his right hand. Setting his rifle on the ground, he fished around in his left front jeans pocket and pulled out a knife.

Kelly silently backed up, halting when she felt the mare's warm breath on her neck. Johnny's knife slashed at the toy until bits of white stuffing fell around his feet like a miniature snowstorm. He cursed, poked his fingers around in the bear's body again and finally gave a triumphant shout.

Tossing the empty toy aside, he held up the key. "See this, Kelly? It's our ticket to the good life. Half a million bucks lasts a long time in some places."

"That's real nice, Johnny." Kelly forced a smile. Casually gathering the reins into her hands, she moved around to Babe's left side. "I hope you enjoy it."

"Damn straight, we'll enjoy it. Won't we, Dad?"

Jay nodded. "Yeah. We sure will."

Johnny sneered at Kelly. "If you'd taken your turn like you were supposed to, you could be comin' with us. I don't suppose you'd want to, though. You'd rather freeze your butt off chasin' a bunch of stupid cows than sit on a nice warm beach and drink rum, wouldn't you?"

"Yeah, silly me." Kelly stuck her foot into the stirrup and swung herself up behind Daniel. "I just feel more comfortable livin' on money I've earned myself."

Johnny's face flushed. "Damn you, Kelly. You think you're better than me, but you're not. That marshal you've been shackin' up with only wants to get into your pants. He'll never marry you."

"Now there's a real hoot for you, Johnny," Kelly said. "He already asked me to marry him, but I turned him down because I figured I'm too much like you and Jay."

Daniel whipped around and stared at her, then said fervently, "You're not like them, Aunt Kelly. Not at all!"

Kelly grinned at her nephew. "I'm startin' to see that, Daniel. You're not much like 'em, either." She turned Babe around, pausing to look back at her dad and brother for what she hoped would be the last time. "Well, I guess this is it, huh? You guys have a nice life."

Jay smiled, but his eyes looked sad. "You too, Kelly."

"Yeah, Sis," Johnny said. "While you're shoveling manure for the next fifty years, think about us once in a while. We'll be livin' it up."

A deep and definitely amused, masculine voice came from the willows behind Johnny. "Hey, man, I win the bet. I told you he wouldn't give back our money."

Guns drawn, two swarthy men stepped into the clearing. Johnny gaped at them, then dove for his rifle. The taller man showed no evidence of hurry, but still managed to plant a foot shod in a brand-new, obviously expensive hiking boot on top of Johnny's outstretched hand. Still moving calmly, he picked up Johnny's rifle and heaved it a long way off into the bushes.

The shorter man aimed his gun at Jay's chest in warning. "You didn't tell us your sister was such a beautiful woman, Johnny. I'm disappointed in you."

The taller man put more weight on Johnny's hand, making him cry out. "Yeah, we're both disappointed in you, man. We paid you real good, but you had to go and steal from us anyway. Why did you do that?"

"I didn't," Johnny said between gasping breaths. "Honest, I didn't, Ramon."

"We heard you bragging, man." Ramon stomped on Johnny's hand. "I don't want to hurt you any more than I have to, so just give me the key and tell me where you stashed the money."

"If I do, you'll kill me."

"Johnny, you fool, we're going to kill you, anyway." The shorter man laughed, but the sound held no humor. "You know we can't let you set a bad example for our other business associates. The only question is, will we kill you fast, or really, really slow?"

The man's tone implied he would enjoy taking his time and inflicting as much pain as possible in the process. Lord, Kelly thought with a shudder of revulsion, she'd always considered Johnny and Jay to be slimy characters, but compared to these guys, they were rank amateurs.

Daniel whimpered softly, and Kelly suddenly realized this was real life she was watching, not some bizarre B movie she'd stumbled into. Damn. She should've kicked Babe into a gallop the second these two creeps arrived, but it had all happened so fast, she still could hardly believe her own eyes and ears. She'd take off now, but she was afraid Daniel might get hurt.

"Edward, please," Ramon said, "you're scaring the pretty lady and the boy."

The shorter man, Edward, flashed Kelly a smile she might have found charming under other circumstances. "My apologies, Miss James."

"I ain't scared of you," Daniel grumbled, even while he pressed back against Kelly.

"Hush, Daniel," she murmured. "Don't rile him."

Motioning with his gun for Jay to come with him, Edward slowly approached Babe. "She's right, you know," he said to

Daniel. "We men like to be brave, but there's no reason we have to be stupid about it, eh?"

"Are you gonna kill my grandpa, too?" Daniel demanded.

"I'm afraid so. It was his idea to steal our money, and we can't let him set a bad example for our other partners, either. You understand?"

"Leave the boy alone," Jay said. "Kelly, too. They don't know anything about your business, Edward. If you'll let them go, I'll make Johnny tell you—"

"I ain't tellin' them nothin'," Johnny shouted, earning another stomp on his hand from Ramon.

"It doesn't matter, Jay," Edward replied. "Sooner or later, Ramon will convince Johnny to talk. Unfortunately your daughter and the boy have seen our faces and heard our names. That makes them loose ends."

Jay's voice took on a desperate note. "No, Edward. They won't talk. I promise."

Kelly got the horse to shift a quarter turn sideways by surreptitiously nudging Babe with her left knee. Then she slowly slid her right hand to the back of her waist.

"One more inch, Miss James," Ramon said, his tone as pleasant as if they were having a friendly chat about the weather. "And I'll kill the boy. I'm a very good shot."

Kelly froze, moving only her eyes until she could see him. Still standing on Johnny's hand, he smiled at her and aimed the barrel of his pistol directly at Daniel's head. Time. She had to buy some time, dammit.

Surely Steve had found her out by now. In fact, knowing him, she wouldn't be surprised if he showed up here any minute, ready to save her whether she wanted him to or not. Whether she deserved it or not. Which she probably didn't. But, God, she really hoped he would come after her anyway.

She sure could use a little help. Or at least an idea, some way to distract those jerks long enough to put Steve's 9 mm to good use. Since both Ramon and Edward seemed to be enjoying the drama of the moment, the best she could come up with was an emotional outburst to hold off the inevitable ending they obviously had in mind.

"Who *are* these guys, Daddy?" she demanded in a loud, grating tone, looking hard at Jay. Surprise flicked across his features, undoubtedly because she hadn't called him anything but Jay since she was ten years old. Then he gave her a subtle wink and played along with her.

"You don't want to know, honey. But don't be upset. Everything's going to be fine. Just fine."

Kelly glanced at Ramon, shuddered and turned back to her father. "Fine? How can you say that when they're plannin' to kill all of us? You've just gotta start associatin' with a better class of people, Daddy."

"Miss James?" Edward took his gun off Jay and aimed it at Kelly. "Be quiet."

"Well, now, Edward, I'd like to help you out," Kelly drawled. "But, frankly, I really don't see the point. I mean, if you're gonna kill us no matter what, why should I make it one damn bit easier for ya? And just where are you boys from, anyhow? Mexico?"

Edward flashed his charming smile at her again. Kelly thought it was damn spooky how these guys could smile and act so polite while they were planning to shoot a person.

"Not Mexico, Miss James. A bit farther south."

"I think he means Colombia, Aunt Kelly," Daniel grumbled. "They're drug dealers."

Kelly faked as much surprise as she could. "No kiddin'? Are you sure of that, Daniel?"

Daniel shot a have-you-completely-lost-your-mind? look over his shoulder at her, then heaved a disgruntled sigh. "Yeah, I'm pretty sure, Aunt Kelly."

"How can you tell?"

"Well, they talk like these bad guys I saw on an old TV show one time when I was over at Billy's house. I think it was called Miami . . . something."

Jay stepped closer to Babe and smiled up at Daniel. "You mean *Miami Vice?*"

"Yeah," Daniel said. "That's it. All the drug dealers talked just like these guys. And then the cops blew 'em all away. It was really cool."

"Indeed?" Ramon said, both eyebrows raised with evident interest in the conversation.

"Get off my hand, you son of a bitch," Johnny groaned.

Ramon kicked him in the ribs, then turned back to Daniel. "Unfortunately for you, in real life the cops don't always win. And for your information, we speak better English than you do."

Kelly laughed. "Aw, ya do *not*, Ramon. I coulda picked you out as a foreigner the minute you opened your mouth."

She had both Ramon and Edward's undivided attention now, and from the way Jay was slowly moving in behind Edward, she figured she wasn't the only one who realized it. If Jay would just act in the next few seconds, they might have a hope in Hades of getting out of this mess. Forcing herself to look anywhere but at him, she continued.

"Your English is pretty correct, all right, but this ain't exactly England. Americans are a lot less formal when they talk."

Edward shrugged. "So? What's your point?"

Kelly shrugged back at him. "Don't have one, really. It's just that, if you were Americans, you'd probably call each other Ray and Eddie."

"Ray and Eddie?" Ramon said, his tone and expression doubtful.

"Yeah." Jay sidled closer to Edward, and Kelly struggled to keep the conversation going. "Ramon and Edward are nice names, and all, but they just sound sort of, well...stuffy. Know what I mean?"

Edward laughed. "You know, that's an interesting point. I hadn't thought of that before."

"Always glad to help a friend, Eddie," Kelly said quickly. Jay was almost there, his gaze focused on Edward's gun with obvious intent, his hands starting to rise. "Of course, you're not really much of a friend, are ya?"

Before Edward could respond, Jay latched onto his arm just above the wrist, yanking the gun down and away from Kelly and Daniel. Edward cursed. Ramon cursed. Kelly gave Jay a hand, or, to be more exact, a well-placed kick to Edward's groin area. Turning Babe to put herself between Ramon's gun and Daniel, she reached for Steve's 9 mm.

Ramon screamed that he would blow Johnny's head off. When neither Kelly nor Jay reacted to the threat, Johnny started blubbering that he didn't want to die. Then an explosion ripped through the clearing. Babe shied. Daniel shrieked. Kelly quickly brought the mare back under control.

"Damn." Jay studied the red stain spreading over the front of his shirt with what looked like surprise and consternation. Then he glanced up at Kelly and gave her a lopsided grin. "That one's gonna hurt."

Kelly handed Daniel the reins, slid off Babe's rump and smacked the mare's hind end to get her moving. "Go back to the ranch," she yelled. "Find Steve. He'll take care of you."

While Babe's hoofbeats faded away, Jay's eyes rolled back in his head, his knees buckled and Kelly rushed to him, barely catching him before his head hit the ground. She tore his shirt open, stripped off her jacket and folded it into a square. The bullet had entered the left side of his torso, just below his ribs, and exited through his back, but it looked as if it had missed his vital organs. Kelly figured he'd make it if he didn't bleed to death.

Ramon and Edward yammered at each other in rapid-fire Spanish. Holding the makeshift bandage to Jay's side with her left hand, Kelly raised the 9 mm with her right. Unfortunately, Edward had been paying more attention to her than she'd realized, and she immediately found herself staring into that ugly black hole at the business end of his pistol again.

"Drop it, Miss James," he said.

His face had gone all cold and hard. Every trace of affability had vanished from his voice. The fury in his eyes promised retaliation for the kick she'd delivered, and exposed the killer hiding beneath the slick, surface coating of charm.

Reluctantly obeying his order to drop her gun, Kelly told herself it could have been worse. At least Daniel had gotten away before these jerks murdered the rest of his family. He would be traumatized, but she had not the slightest shred of doubt that Steve *would* take good care of him. She also knew, deep in her heart, that he would have been here to save her if it had been within his power to do so.

If she hadn't been too damned stubborn and independent to accept his help. If she hadn't been so scared to trust him or anyone else. If she hadn't been such an idiot, he would have been here by now.

It was one hell of a way and an absolutely miserable time to figure out exactly how much she actually did trust him, but sometimes life was like that. People didn't always learn the right lessons in time to do them any good. She wished she could have told him she loved him, though, just once before she died.

The word *died* set off a warning bell in her nervous system. Had she already given up, then? To these drug-dealing low-lifes? The idea stiffened her spine. Not hardly. And not without one hell of a fight.

"We're out of time for having fun with you," Edward said.

Kelly grinned at him. "I hate to disappoint ya, Eddie, but this ain't exactly my idea of a good time."

His eyebrows lifted in surprise, whether at her grin or her flippant reply, she wasn't sure. Not that it mattered at this point. The best she could hope for now was to unsettle these guys enough to keep them from pulling any more triggers for a few minutes.

"Oh, and Eddie?" she added. "You might want to tell Ray not to bother with torturin' Johnny. Even if he tells ya where he stashed the money, that key he's got won't do ya any good."

"Why is that, Miss James?"

"Because," Kelly drawled, "it belongs to my safety-deposit box in Hamilton, and believe you me, there's no half a million dollars in it."

"What the hell are you talkin' about, Kelly?" Johnny shouted.

"I switched keys, Johnny. That one you've got there isn't the one they want."

Ramon finally let Johnny up, then motioned with his gun for him to join Jay and Kelly. Holding his wounded hand in front of his waist, Johnny trudged across the clearing and carefully lowered himself to the ground beside Jay. Ramon followed. Standing next to Edward, he frowned down at the prisoners.

"And where *is* the key we want, Miss James?" Edward asked.

Kelly grinned at him again, then winked at him for the sheer hell of it. "I'm afraid we've got us a little problem with that, Eddie. I haven't always seen eye to eye with Jay and Johnny about a lot things, so I don't exactly trust 'em too much. Know what I mean?"

Ramon snorted and muttered something in Spanish. "Miss James, we don't care about your family problems. Where is the damned key?"

"Don't get your drawers in a twist, now, Ray. I'm gettin' to that. Since I didn't really trust Jay and Johnny, see, I, uh, well, I really hate to tell ya this, but I left the real key back at the ranch."

Jay's chest vibrated and more blood darkened the bandage. Kelly looked down, saw a big smile on her dad's mouth and realized he was laughing. "Daddy," she scolded, putting more pressure on his wound. "You'll bleed like a stuck pig if you don't cut that out."

He studied her face as if he'd never seen it before. "Lord, Kelly, you're so much like your mother sometimes, it's scary."

A lump formed in her throat, forcing her to clear it before she could answer. "Thanks. I'll take that as a compliment."

"Good. I meant it that way."

"Very sweet." With a force belying his words, Edward grabbed Kelly's forearm and yanked her to her feet. "But now, you're going to take me to your ranch and give me the real key."

"No, I don't think you want to go anywhere near the ranch."

Without changing his facial expression, Edward gave her arm a vicious twist. "I'm running out of patience, Miss James. No more games."

Kelly refused to give him the satisfaction of showing any pain. "I wouldn't dream of it, Eddie. The ranch is probably swarming with DEA guys by now, but hey, if you want to go down there, I'll be glad to take ya."

"DEA guys?"

"Yeah. You probably heard Johnny mention my boy-friend? The U.S. marshal? He's technically on vacation now, but you know what cops are like. They're never really off duty. Anyway, to make a long story short, when I told him about my, uh, illustrious family connections, he called his boss and found out the Drug Enforcement Administration was real interested in findin' my big brother."

Ramon said something in Spanish that sounded an awful lot like a whole string of cuss words to Kelly. It just had that kind of emphasis and intonation about it. When he'd finished, she continued.

"They were lookin' for a couple of drug dealers who were supposed to be after Johnny, too. I think their name was Reyez, or something like that. I figure that'd be you boys, right?"

Now it was Edward's turn to blow off some steam. Know-ing from personal experience that he'd feel a lot better for it, Kelly patiently waited him out.

"Anyhow, when I left to come up here," she said, "my boyfriend was on the phone with those DEA guys. I, uh, kind of left him a note about where I was goin', just in case any-thing went wrong. My guess is, they'll all be here any second."

His face contorted with fear, Ramon looked left and right, then raised his gun hand over Kelly's head as if he intended to hit her with it. "You stupid b—"

"Freeze, Reyez," a hard, but wonderfully familiar voice said from somewhere behind Kelly. "Don't touch her."

Confident that anyone with half a brain would obey that command, Kelly looked over her shoulder. Her heart con-tracted at the sight of Steve striding out of the brush with a shotgun in his hands. Two men flanked him, both wearing dark jackets with DEA stamped in big white letters on them. They also carried shotguns, and when four more officers came in past the willows, Ramon and Edward surrendered without firing a shot.

Relief hit Kelly. Her pulse raced, slowed, then raced again, as if it couldn't find a steady rhythm. Her breathing hitched and her vision blurred. Her knees buckled like a sawhorse snapping under too much weight, making her butt hit the ground with a bone-jarring thump.

"Kelly?" Clutching the bandage against his side, Jay struggled into a sitting position. "Kelly, are you okay?"

Finally catching her breath, she nodded. "Yeah, Jay, I'll live. How about you?"

"It hurts, but I'll live."

One of the DEA officers approached, checked out Jay's wounds, radioed for a helicopter to take him to the hospital and gave Kelly a first-aid kit. She asked if anyone had seen a little boy on a horse. The officer assured her both Daniel and Babe were fine, then moved on to Johnny.

Within seconds, a spine-chilling shriek startled Kelly half out of her wits. Cradling his mangled hand in front of him, Johnny scooted backward on his rump, sobbing like a terrified child and begging the DEA man to stay away from him. The officer held up his hands in a calm-down gesture, and looked to Jay and Kelly, as if asking for advice.

"Johnny," Jay called. "Johnny, stop it. Nobody's going to hurt you now, son."

"Yes, they w-w-will, Daddy," Johnny wailed. He shook his head violently, then pulled his arms and legs in close to his trunk and started rocking in quick, jerky movements. "Th-they're g-g-gonna make me go b-b-back to p-prison. There's m-m-mean guys there an' they always b-b-beat me up an' h-hurt me real b-b-bad. Please, don't m-make m-me go b-b-back there, Daddy."

"Good Lord, Jay," Kelly murmured, sadly shaking her head. "His mind has snapped."

Johnny rocked faster. "The m-money k-kept me alive last time. Now, they'll k-kill me for sure. Yeah, they w-will. They'll k-k-kill me f-for s-sure. Kelly's turn. It's s'posed to b-be K-Kelly's turn. Make *her* go this time, D-Daddy. Please, make K-Kelly g-g-go."

Jay sighed, then called, "Johnny, shut up. It'll be all right."

Johnny continued to rock, mutter and sob. Kelly tried to tell herself her brother deserved whatever happened to him. After all, he'd terrorized her, poisoned Wild Bill, shot at the man she

loved and kidnapped Daniel. But there was something so piti-
ful and . . . wounded about him, she couldn't maintain any real
anger at him.

There were family ties that were too strong to cut completely. Somewhere deep inside, this broken wreck of a man
would always be her big brother. And somewhere deep inside
herself, she would always love him.

Two members of the DEA team handcuffed the Reyez
brothers and, with a third officer reading them their rights, es-
corted them out of the clearing. Ramon gave Jay a chilling look
as he passed by. Edward told him he shouldn't plan to live long
enough to testify at any trials. Kelly told him, clearly and suc-
cinctly, what he could do with his damned threats.

When the officers hauled the brothers away, she used the
contents of the first-aid kit to put a better bandage on Jay's
wounds, then went to see what she could do for Johnny. Steve
was already kneeling beside her brother, talking to him in a low,
soothing voice. Kelly crouched down on Johnny's other side
and smiled at Steve.

"I don't know how to thank you," she said.

Steve flicked her an assessing glance. "Just doing my job,
Ms. Jaynes." Then he patted Johnny's shoulder as if he were
Daniel's age instead of a grown man, stood and walked away.

Feeling as hurt as if he'd slapped her, Kelly watched him walk
over to Jay. Considering her actions, she'd expected Steve to be
furious with her. She wouldn't have blamed him if he'd yelled
his head off at her. She would have preferred it, in fact, to this
cool sort of . . . well, it felt like a dismissal.

A lump grew in her throat. She gulped at it, but it didn't go
away. Every time she looked at Steve and saw that distant,
emotionless expression on his face, the lump felt bigger, harder,
sharper.

She would apologize to him if she thought it would do any
good. But it wouldn't. It was as plain as the ice in his eyes, the
clipped, professional tone of his voice, his careful avoidance of
touching her. Yeah, she'd really gone and done it this time.

And for what? A bunch of irrational fears about her genetic
heritage? A misplaced sense of responsibility for Jay and

Johnny's criminal behavior? Her battered self-esteem? Funny how she'd always worked to make sure Daniel felt good about himself, but she'd never bothered to shore up her own self-image.

Everything Steve had tried to tell her suddenly made sense, but would he believe her if she told him that? She glanced at him again and felt her heart sink. She'd been so intent on doing things her own way, she hadn't stopped to think about how much her actions might hurt him.

And it didn't look like there was any way to make amends.

Chapter Seventeen

"Nice to see you again, Marshal," Jay James said.

Grunting an acknowledgment, Steve knelt beside Kelly's father and checked his bandage. He was too professional to take a chance on letting a prisoner bleed to death, but he didn't have to like Jay or talk to him beyond the call of duty. If he had his way, he wouldn't speak a word to this jerk.

Unfortunately, Steve wasn't going to get his way. This was an excellent opportunity to help the government win a battle in the war on drugs. Duty demanded that he pursue it. Sitting back on one heel, he silently studied Jay until he squirmed.

"How much do you know about the Reyez brothers' operation?" Steve asked.

"A lot. I can tell you who they report to, anyway." Jay's eyes narrowed with calculation. "Why? Can you do something for Johnny and me?"

"Maybe," Steve said. "I can't promise anything but a shot with the U.S. attorney who'll be prosecuting this case. If you can convince him you've got enough information to be worth the trouble, you might qualify for the Witness Protection Program."

"Really?" A sly smile curved Jay's mouth. "Besides testifying in court, what would we have to do?"

"Come on, James, you know the drill. You'd both get a new identity, but you'd have to keep your noses clean for a change. You'd have to get a job. A *real* one. The government won't support you forever, you know."

"Yeah, yeah," Jay grumbled. "What else?"

"If you want to stay alive, you can't break your cover. You have to leave everyone and everything from your past behind."

"Including Kelly and Daniel?"

"Especially Kelly and Daniel," Steve said. "You've already endangered them enough, don't you think?"

"I suppose I have." Jay cleared his throat. "We could come to the wedding, though, couldn't we?"

"What wedding?"

"Yours, of course." Jay grinned. "Yours and Kelly's. She told us you asked her to marry you."

"She turned me down."

Jay laughed. "Now, really, Marshal, you're not going to give up so easily, are you? I'm sure Kelly didn't mean—"

Steve cut him off with a glare. "Yeah, she did. There won't be any wedding, James. Thanks to you, I doubt Kelly will ever get married."

"Now, wait a minute. I'll admit I've made some mistakes, but I fail to see how you can blame that on me."

Steve wanted to hit the man. Wounded or not, he wanted to smack Jay James upside the head hard enough to give him whiplash. Too bad all he could do was give him a tongue-lashing.

"Well, try this one on for size, *Daddy.* She loved and trusted you to take of her like any little girl would, but all you've ever done is cause her a lot of hurt and humiliation, deprive her of a chance to get an education, and cheat her out of the only home and livelihood she ever knew."

Jay sputtered and shook his head in denial, but Steve wasn't about to put up with it. Without hesitation, he got right down in Jay's face. "Because you refused to act like a man and support your family with honest work, you've taken away Kelly's ability to trust me or any other man. Hell, she doesn't even know what love really is. How could she, with a miserable excuse like you for a father?"

Jay looked away, and to Steve's surprise, an emotion that might actually have been regret flitted across his face. Following the direction of the other man's gaze, Steve saw Kelly on her knees, holding her brother and rocking with him like a mother comforting a hurt child. The tragic picture they made gave his heart a fierce wrench.

"And as for Johnny..." Steve paused and shook his head in disgust. "From what I can see, your son belongs in a psychiatric hospital, not a prison. I don't suppose you feel any responsibility for him, either, just because he took a few *turns* for you?"

Jay's eyes came back to Steve. "If we go into this program, will it be possible to get Johnny some professional help?"

"Maybe. I've seen it happen, but, again, I can't promise anything until you tell the U.S. attorney what you know. If you're accepted into the program, you should try to negotiate that before you sign any agreements."

"All right," Jay said. "I'll spill my guts to the prosecutor, Marshal."

"Neither you or Johnny will ever be able to contact Kelly or Daniel again. I don't care if the Devil himself is on your tail, James, you have to leave them alone. Agreed?"

"Agreed. May I say goodbye to Kelly first?"

Steve nodded, then rose to his feet and went to get Kelly.

Reluctantly leaving Johnny to a grim-faced Steve's care, Kelly hurried back to her father. "What's wrong, Jay? Are you in pain?"

"It's not too bad. Sit down a minute, Kelly."

She obeyed his request, then tipped her head to one side and studied him, trying to figure out why he seemed different.

When she realized he was absolutely serious for a change, she felt a cold, empty spot opening up under her rib cage. "What is it?"

He told her about Steve's offer to help him and Johnny enter the Witness Protection Program, his decision to do so and what that decision would mean for all of them. She had to admit the idea had merit, especially if Johnny could get some help. At the same time, however, she felt strangely ambivalent about the prospect of never seeing her dad or her brother again.

Neither of them intimidated her now as they once could, and Johnny and Jay were the only blood relatives she and Daniel had. Despite her attempts to deny it, they were, after all, family. When she said as much, Jay gave her a sad smile and slowly shook his head.

"The Reyez cartel won't give us a choice, Kelly. Johnny and I need the protection, and we haven't been a real family since your mother died. You and Daniel need to start your own family." Jay paused and inclined his head toward Steve. "You love that marshal, Kelly."

She nodded, then lifted one shoulder in a helpless sort of shrug. "I've fouled that up, Jay."

"Perhaps you could fix it."

Kelly glanced at Steve, saw the hard set to his jaw and sighed in defeat. "Nope. Don't think so. It's just as well, though." She sniffed a little, forced a smile and trotted out the old, comfortable excuses. "Shoot, with this James blood, all my kids would probably turn out to be hellions, anyhow."

"That is such bull, it's not even funny."

She frowned at him. "Excuse me, pops, but you're the one who always said—"

"That's why I *know* it's such bull, Kelly. In the first place, I lied about our connection to Frank and Jesse James. They're a completely different family." He reached over, took one of her hands and squeezed it. "And in the second place, darling girl, our blood had nothing to do with this mess in which Johnny and I now find ourselves."

"What do you mean, Jay?"

"That was nothing more than a weak excuse for a weak and lazy man. Every time I committed a crime, I always had a choice, and I always chose the easy way out." He squeezed her hand again, then released it. "I taught your brother to do the same thing, and look what's happened to him."

"So, uh, what's your point?" Kelly asked.

"My point is," he said, "that you and Daniel aren't like me and Johnny. You've always had your mother's sass and spunk, and you've never been afraid to work hard. You can hold your head up with anyone, Kelly. Even a marshal." A smile tugged at the corners of his mouth. "Who is not nearly as indifferent to you as he's trying to pretend."

"Oh, yeah?" Kelly glanced over at Steve again, winced and looked back at her father. "I don't know, Jay—"

Jay chuckled. "Trust me on this one. He loves you, and I believe he's a very good man."

"I never doubted that. But I'm not so sure he loves me anymore. I hurt his feelings pretty bad."

"He'd make a wonderful father for Daniel. Daniel talked about him the whole time he was with us, by the way."

"He did?"

"Oh, yes. Made your poor brother terribly jealous, especially since he was a lawman. Daniel picked right up on that, of course."

"Of course," Kelly agreed, having no trouble imagining Daniel giving Johnny a hard time. "You're really sure we're not related to Frank and Jesse?"

"Positive."

They enjoyed a companionable silence for a moment. Then a helicopter with a red cross on its side flew into view. Moving slowly and carefully, Jay sat up straighter and smiled at Kelly.

"That's our ride. I'm sorry for all the grief I've caused you. We won't see each other again, but we won't forget you."

This time, it was Kelly who reached over and squeezed her father's hand. "All right, Jay. Take care of yourself and Johnny."

"I will. You take care of yourself and Daniel. And that marshal. Don't be afraid to love him."

The helicopter landed. Two paramedics jumped out and loaded Jay, Johnny and Steve. Whether Steve was going along to guard the others, protect them or just get the hell away from her, Kelly couldn't say. The answer really didn't matter much in the greater scheme of things.

The only thing that mattered to her now was discovering how empty she felt when she realized he was leaving, and she wasn't all that sure he intended to return. She'd thought a person couldn't feel any more lost and alone than she had the day Jay and Johnny had been sentenced to prison, leaving her to care for Daniel when she hadn't even been sure she could take care of herself.

But seeing Steve climb aboard the helicopter with no smile for her, no promise to talk when he got back, no... nothing, well, it was at least a hundred times worse.

More like a thousand times worse.

As long as she could draw a breath, she would never forget standing beside the last DEA officer on the scene, watching the helicopter lift off and float away with that weird thumping sound from the rotary blades beating against her ears. God, but it hurt. It was like losing her mother and the ranch, her dad and her brother all over again. And then some.

When that helicopter carried Steve Anderson around the side of the mountain, it carried off her best friend, her lover, the only man who had ever taken the trouble to get to know her—crazy family and all—and had still loved her. She'd been such a fool.

It wasn't going to be easy to convince him to give her another chance; he had a stubborn streak in him the size of Colorado and Utah combined. So who wanted easy, when she could have Steve? Smiling to herself, Kelly took one last look at the spot where she'd last seen the helicopter, then accompanied the DEA officer back to his Jeep.

She'd never known Jay's advice to be worth a whole lot, but this time, she intended to take it. Just as soon as she could get her hands on Steve Anderson again, she'd have to convince him that, lawman or not, he belonged with her and Daniel. And that herd of kids he wanted so much.

* * *

It was almost dark by the time Steve returned to the ranch, driving the car he'd rented at the Butte airport. After taking Johnny and Jay to the hospital and dealing with the negotiations and paperwork involved in getting them into the Witness Protection Program, he was tired, hungry and edgy. He'd had enough of the James family for one day, thank you very much. The last thing he wanted to do was rehash this whole mess with Kelly.

Well, he wouldn't mind giving her an earful for ditching him, he thought, climbing out of the car. He wouldn't mind ripping a few pieces of hide off her for playing games with the Reyez brothers. He wouldn't mind telling her to find another sap to bail her out the next time she took off by herself and got herself in trouble, either.

But what would be the point? Kelly couldn't help being who she was. Yelling at her might help him feel better temporarily, but it wouldn't make her love him. Or need him. Or trust him.

If she didn't feel those things for him by now—and she obviously didn't—it was highly unlikely she ever would. So why beat his head against the proverbial brick wall? Wouldn't it be easier for everyone involved if he simply accepted reality and left her alone? Of course, it would.

If and when Kelly chose to leave the Haystack for another job, he could always come back and take over for Uncle Bud. In the meantime . . . well, at least working as a U.S. marshal wasn't boring. And, hey, so what if he'd fallen in the love with the wrong woman again? He'd only done it twice so far. Maybe it just took practice to fall in love with the right woman.

"If you believe that stinking pile of rationalization, Anderson, there's this pretty little piece of swamp land in Arizona . . ." he muttered.

Then he sighed, shook his head in disgust and entered the house through the back porch. The hearty aroma of a beef stew simmering on the stove greeted him at the door. His stomach growled in response, and Kelly turned away from the oven, plunked a pan of oddly shaped rolls, or maybe they were biscuits—sometimes it was a little hard to tell for sure when she was involved—onto a trivet.

"Hi, Steve."

She flashed him a warm, welcoming smile. Her face was flushed from the oven's heat, wisps of hair escaped from her ponytail and there was a big smudge of flour on her nose. He'd never wanted her more. Knowing he couldn't have her made his reply sound brusque, even in his own ears.

"Hi."

"I hope you're hungry," she said. "I don't know what came over me, but I got this insane urge to cook after Daniel went to bed."

"Is he all right?"

"Yeah, I think so. He didn't get much sleep when he was with Jay and Johnny, and today was real stressful, of course. We had a good talk after I got home, though. Jay and Johnny okay?"

Steve nodded and walked farther into the kitchen. Was he crazy, or was there something different about Kelly tonight? She seemed calmer than usual, more sure of herself. Maybe even happier. But then, why wouldn't she be happier? She'd just gotten rid of a father and brother from hell.

"They're fine," he told her. "We stopped at the hospital in Butte, the U.S. attorney met us, and they're now en route to an unknown destination, compliments of the Witness Protection Program. Jay had enough dirt on the Reyez operation to get a good deal for both of them, so you don't have to worry about them anymore."

She crossed the room, stopped directly in front of him and gazed up into his face with a sweet, serious expression that left no doubt in her sincerity. "Thank you. They didn't deserve your help and understanding, but I'll always be grateful you had it in you to give."

He turned aside, leaned back against the refrigerator and shoved his hands into the front pockets of his jeans. "I was just doing my job. I don't want your gratitude."

She came right back and faced him again. "How about an apology, then? I know I did a really stupid thing this morning when I left that way, but—"

"It doesn't matter, Kelly."

"It doesn't?"

"The crisis is over. Everybody lived through it. Case closed."

She raised an eyebrow at him. Shifted her weight to one foot, making the curve of her hip jut out. Crossed her arms over her midriff. "Just like that?"

"Just like that."

"Well, that's funny, Marshal," she drawled. "If I was you, I think I'd really want to do some major yelling at this point. I'd probably cut loose with a few choice goodies like 'dangerous, irresponsible, damn fool thing to do.' You know what I mean."

"Since you already know what I think, there's no need for me to say it, is there?"

She grinned. Leaned a little closer. Lowered her voice to a husky whisper. "Aw, Anderson, you're awful cute when you're madder than hell."

Despite his best efforts to hold it in, a laugh sputtered out of him. Dammit, he'd made up his mind, and she wasn't going to get to him again. He straightened to his full height, took his right hand out of his pocket and gestured toward the table and chairs. "Sit down, Kelly. We need to talk."

She studied him for a moment, a thoughtful frown creasing her forehead. Then she ambled across the room, pulled out the chair at the near end of the table, sat on it and crossed one leg over the other. Folding her hands on the table in front of her, she watched him get settled in the adjacent chair. Her expectant expression made him feel ridiculously nervous.

While he searched for the appropriate words to end their...affair, silence pressed in on him, thick and muggy as July in the midwest. Finally, in desperation, he simply said, "I'm going back to Chicago in the morning."

Her face lost all expression. "No."

One soft, implacable little word could be disconcerting. She ought to know, because he'd used the same technique on her not long ago. "I beg your pardon?"

"You can beg all you want, Steve, but you're not goin' anywhere."

"Look, Kelly, I decided you were right about us, so—"

"Well, I changed my mind. I accept your proposal of marriage."

"The proposal has been withdrawn."

"Tough, Anderson. You're stuck with me." She grinned. "I already told Bud and Peg we're gettin' married."

He planted his palms on the table and came half out of his chair. "You did *what?*"

"You heard me. I called 'em in Bozeman, and I told 'em we're gettin' married. Peg's already plannin' the reception."

He collapsed back into his chair and studied her for a moment. Damn, she really could fight dirty when she put her mind to it. "Are you pregnant?"

"Not that I know of." She lowered her voice to a sexy purr and batted her lashes at him. "But I'd be glad to work on it anytime you want, honey."

"Dammit, Kelly, stop it."

"Stop what, sweetheart?"

"Stop the wide-eyed innocent act." He got up, walked around behind his chair and braced his hands on the back. "Stop the flirting. And for God's sake, stop all this nonsense about getting married. It's not going to happen."

"You still love me, Anderson."

"It doesn't matter whether I do or not."

"It matters to me."

"Why?"

"Because you were right. I love you. I want to spend the rest of my life with you, and have babies with you. You promised me a whole herd of 'em."

She said it with such quiet conviction, he believed she meant it. Dammit, he *wanted* to believe she meant it.

"You don't need me for that, Kelly. There must be plenty of guys out there who'd be happy to give you babies."

"Sweetheart," she drawled, rolling her eyes in exasperation, "it took me darn near thirty years to find one man I'd sleep with. By the time I find another one, I'll be too old to get pregnant. Besides, I don't want just any old babies. I want yours."

His chest filled with emotion, and he knew his resolve was weakening by the second. His feelings were too bruised and tender to give in just yet, however. She started to stand, but sat down again when he scowled at her.

"Whaddaya want me to do here, Anderson?" she demanded, scowling right back at him. "I tried to apologize for actin' like an idiot this mornin', but you didn't want to hear that. I told you I love you. What else is left?"

"Why me, Kelly? Besides the babies, what do you need *me* for?"

"Is that what this is about?" she asked. "Whether or not I need you?"

"That's part of it. It'd be nice if you trusted me, too."

"When I sent Daniel out of the clearing today, I told him to find you, because I trusted you to take care of him. I trusted you to find that note I left. I trusted you to come after me just as soon as you could. I trusted you to come bustin' through that brush if I just held on a little longer."

"Why didn't you let me come with you from the beginning?"

"It wasn't that I didn't trust you personally, Steve."

She stopped, looked up at the ceiling and squeezed her lips together, obviously fighting for control of her emotions. He ached to go to her, but he had to hear the rest. Finally she gulped and went on.

"It's just that I've been alone so long, you know? And so responsible for taking care of Daniel, and there's never been anyone I could count on since my mom died. I knew you'd help me, but the truth is, I was afraid to rely on anyone else. I didn't know how. Daniel could've died today because of that."

"You could have, too."

She nodded. "I know. And you'll never know how much I wished I'd told you how I really felt about you."

If eyes were the windows to the soul, what he saw in Kelly's started to unravel the cold, hard knot that had lodged deep in his gut the moment he'd realized she had gone to meet Johnny without him. A tear rolled down her cheek and clung to the side of her jaw. Continuing to meet his gaze with her heart laid wide open, she wiped the tear away with the back of her hand.

"Tell me now, Kelly."

"You brought the colors back."

"The colors?"

"Yeah. I learned how to survive. How to take care of Daniel. How to be...content. Sort of. But my life was all work and not much fun. There just weren't any colors. And then you came along."

"And . . ." he prompted.

"And you made me laugh with your terrible singing and your obnoxious personality." Her watery smile washed away any sting her words might have held. "You eased my work load and taught me to enjoy a man's company. You were even nice to my nephew and my dopey dogs."

She sniffled. Wiped away another tear. Shrugged. "I was scared to death to let anyone get close, but you ignored my kickin' and cussin' and just pulled me out of this...shell I'd built around myself. And you know what, Anderson?"

"What, Kelly?"

"I don't wanta go back in that damn shell. I like all the colors and the commotion and the fun I have with you."

She stood and slowly walked toward him, her voice getting louder and firmer with every step. "And if you think I'm gonna let you give up on me now, when I've finally got my feelings all figured out, well, you'd better just sit your butt back down on that chair and have yourself another think."

He wasn't sure who kicked the chair out of the way, but he opened his arms and she flung herself into them and hugged him until he could barely breathe. Nothing in his life had ever felt more precious or wonderful to him. But he had one more thing he had to know.

"What if I decide I still want to be a cop?"

She clasped her hands on either side of his face and looked him straight in the eye. "I don't care if you're a cop, an undertaker or the president of the whole United States, Anderson. I trust you, I need you and I love you. And you are *not* leavin' me. Is that clear?"

Delight mixed with laughter and bubbled up inside him until he couldn't contain it. He hugged her. Kissed her. Told her he'd much rather raise cows and babies than hunt down criminals. Then he rested his forehead against hers and said, "Aw, Kelly, I love you so damn much. Will you please marry me?"

"Yeah, I will. On one condition."

He put one arm around her back, slid the other one under her knees and scooped her up against his chest. After a long, mutually satisfying kiss, he carried her out of the kitchen and headed for the stairs. Once in his bedroom, he dumped her in the middle of his bed, followed her down and kissed her again. Holding her close, he tucked his chin over the top of her head.

"What's the condition?"

Kelly raised up on one elbow and said with a perfectly earnest expression, "You've really gotta stop that cussin' before the babies get here, Steve. We need to set a good example for 'em."

The idea of her telling him to stop cussing tickled Steve so much, he laughed until Kelly hit him over the head with a pillow. Twice. He grabbed the pillow, tossed it on the floor and rolled her onto her back.

And then, they didn't need any more words for a long, long time. Sighs of pleasure, loving caresses and deep, passionate kisses pretty much said it all. Making love would never solve all of their problems, but Steve figured it was one he—ck of a good place to start.

* * * * *

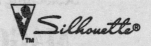

Bestselling Author

MAGGIE SHAYNE

Continues the twelve-book series—FORTUNE'S CHILDREN—
in January 1997 with Book Seven

A HUSBAND IN TIME

Jane Fortune was wary of the stranger with amnesia who
came to her—seemingly out of nowhere. She couldn't deny
the passion between them, but there was something
mysterious—almost dangerous—about this compelling
man...and Jane knew she'd better watch her step....

MEET THE FORTUNES—a family whose legacy is greater than
riches. Because where there's a will...there's a *wedding!*

Silhouette®

SPECIAL EDITION™

COMING NEXT MONTH

#1081 NOBODY'S BABY—Jane Toombs
That's My Baby!
When Karen Henderson claimed Zed Adams fathered the infant nestled in her arms, the disbelieving rancher was caught off guard! Could these two come together for the sake of a child?

#1082 THE FATHER NEXT DOOR—Gina Wilkins
Margaret McAlister's perfectly predictable world was turned upside down the minute Tucker Hollis and his two rambunctious children moved in. She and Tucker were exact opposites, but you know what they say about opposites attracting....

#1083 A RANCH FOR SARA—Sherryl Woods
The Bridal Path
To save her father's ranch, spirited Sara Wilde challenged ex-rodeo champ Jake Dawson to a bull ride. But when the smitten cowboy upped the stakes to marriage, Sara faced the gamble of a lifetime!

#1084 RUGRATS AND RAWHIDE—Peggy Moreland
Retired bronc rider JD Cawthon dreamed of building a successful horse farm, but everything changed after he succumbed to an old desire...and Janie Summers became pregnant. So what was a respectable cowboy to do?

#1085 A FAMILY WEDDING—Angela Benson
To give his young daughter a mother, widower Kenny Sanders wed longtime friend Patsy Morgan. It was a marriage in name only—but how long could they deny their feelings had blossomed into love?

#1086 VALENTINE'S CHILD—Natalie Bishop
Sherry Sterling returned to her hometown to confront J. J. Beckett with the secret that had driven her from his arms years ago—their child. But could she walk away from the only man she'd ever loved?

Harlequin and Silhouette celebrate
Black History Month with seven terrific titles,
featuring the all-new *Fever Rising*
by Maggie Ferguson
(Harlequin Intrigue #408) and
A Family Wedding by Angela Benson
(Silhouette Special Edition #1085)!

Also available are:
Looks Are Deceiving by Maggie Ferguson
Crime of Passion by Maggie Ferguson
Adam and Eva by Sandra Kitt
Unforgivable by Joyce McGill
Blood Sympathy by Reginald Hill

On sale in January at your favorite
Harlequin and Silhouette retail outlet.

Look us up on-line at: http://www.romance.net   BHM297

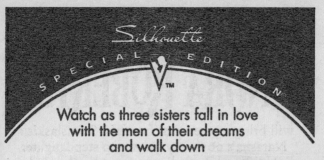

Silhouette
SPECIAL EDITION ™

Watch as three sisters fall in love
with the men of their dreams
and walk down

The Bridal Path

A delightful new Special Edition trilogy
by **Sherryl Woods**

Sara, Ashley and Danielle. Three spirited sisters raised on a
Wyoming ranch by their strong-willed widower father—and
each one nothing alike. Feisty Sara is a rancher through and
through who wants to follow in her father's footsteps.
Beautiful Ashley is a rebel model who doesn't want to settle
down. Warmhearted Danielle is a homemaker who only
wants to find a husband and raise some children.

A RANCH FOR SARA
(Special Edition #1083, February 1997)—
Sara fights for her ranch and her man.

ASHLEY'S REBEL
(Special Edition #1087, March 1997)—
Ashley discovers love with an old flame.

DANIELLE'S DADDY FACTOR
(Special Edition #1094, April 1997)—
Danielle gets a family of her own.

Don't miss a single one of these wonderful stories!

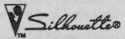